CRUEL MASTER
A DARK MAFIA ARRANGED MARRIAGE
AGE GAP ROMANCE

SINISTER ARRANGEMENT
BOOK TWO

LUCY SMOKE

A.J. MACEY

Developmental Edits and Proofreading by Lunar Rose Services

Line Edits by Your Editing Lounge

Original Cover by Quirah Casey

For the spicy girls and guys.
Life is short. Eat Carbs. Read Smut.

TRIGGER WARNING & NOTICE

This book contains very dark content that may be triggering for some readers.

Some of these themes include, but are not limited to, graphic violence, kidnapping, unlawful imprisonment, explicit sexual situations, masochism, sadism, degradation, humiliation, sexual bondage, dubious consent, sexual violence, murder, loss, and other themes that are common in dark romance.

All of the events and people contained within this book are works of fiction. Any similarities to persons living or dead are purely coincidence.

If you do not enjoy these themes listed above, or have specific triggers that are harmful to your mental health, please do not read.

Final note, though this book may contain BDSM elements, this is not an accurate representation of safe and correct BDSM commitment and play. Please do not use this book as an educational tool for understanding and learning about the BDSM community.

This book is recommended for 18+ due to sexual content and adult situations. ***Please read responsibly.***

PROLOGUE
GAVEN

18 years old...

S now sounded like fire embers when it was falling. Few people realized that. No, they wouldn't ever realize that unless they shut the fuck up long enough and just listened to the sound of it. I supposed that, were I in different circumstances, I wouldn't know something so trivial either. Still, it didn't make the idiots of this world easier to deal with.

While everyone else was shopping for Christmas presents on this frost-covered December night, I was here—several miles outside of the city with little more than a thrifted, hole-infested winter coat that might have been quite nice several decades ago to keep the chill at bay. As if to punctuate my own inferiority to the rest of the world, my stomach rumbled with hunger.

"Fuck." I rolled onto my back and closed my

eyes, shutting out the dark covering of trees over my head. I shivered as the layer of snow beneath me soaked into my back.

I'd been out here for hours—dropped off long ago by the man I was currently working for. Or rather, I'd been dropped off by one of his hench-men. There was no way, after all, that a man as powerful as Jason Perelli was going to be seen with a wannabe hitman when I hadn't even proven myself. For all he knew, I'd get caught after my first kill. To him, I was little more than a greedy cleaner wanting a better life, and he needed plausible deniability.

My stomach rumbled again and I settled a hand over my lower abdomen.

When was the last time I'd actually had something to eat and it hadn't left me craving more?

Unlike most of the guys I worked around—I didn't work out to stay in shape. I didn't have to. Instead, I hauled boxes down by the bay during the day, and during the night, I was shipped around to various places in the city as a glorified janitor to clean up messy kills for the crime families in the area.

I wondered how many people in the city tonight went to bed with the comforting unknowing of all the evil and wicked things that lingered in this shit world. How many of them hadn't seen the brain matter of a half-naked woman sprawled across an expensive ivory-marbled floor or had to get on their hands and knees and scrub out blood from the grit of the tile in some millionaire's bathroom?

Most of them, I figured silently. Lucky fucking bastards.

Then again, if it hadn't been for my one foster brother some years back, I likely never would've known myself. Too bad for Antonio, though. He'd died only a few months into what would also be my last foster home—gunned down outside of the theater because the stupid fucker had run his mouth about the great new job he'd gotten working for the Perelli man.

His loss though had been my gain and when Jason Perelli's men had come around the next time, I'd lined up for the empty position. The money, however, was never enough. It never went far—clothes, food, rent. New York was a massive pile of leeches, sucking the life out of any man or woman that was miserable enough to get stuck here without a way out.

I opened my eyes at that thought and rolled back over, my thinly gloved finger finding the trigger as I settled back into my earlier position. This would be my out, I swore.

Blood. Murder. Havoc. War. It didn't matter what I had to do. Someday, I would be one of those rich fuckers who called little shits like me to come and clean their messes. I didn't care how many lives I had to take to feel some of that warmth. A fire on cold, dark nights like this.

Ultimately, this world was all about survival of the fittest, and I was going to be one of them.

As if thinking that conjured my target from the

depths of the shadows, a car finally appeared along the edge of the property I'd been hunkered down in for the last half a day. Hours and hours, I'd fucking waited for this motherfucker, and now he was about to be mine.

The town car moved slowly up the snow-lined pathway towards the manor house at the end. I didn't know who this guy was—that wasn't part of my job. All I knew was that if I did this right, then Perelli wasn't the only one who'd want my skills. Someone bigger and far scarier than him would. Raffaello Price. The head of the Price Family Syndicate. He'd already said as much during our single interaction.

My finger moved calmly over the trigger of the Remington 700 Sniper Chassis. A gift. A game changer. I don't know what the man had seen in me the day he'd caught sight of me outside of Jason Perelli's mansion. I'd only been there out of curiosity —hoping that maybe Perelli had an opening as a guard. More solid work. Even if I was just cannon fodder, I couldn't take much more of living in a rat and roach-infested studio. I wasn't just hungry—I was mad with starvation.

I wanted more. More money. More chances. More of a better fucking life than the one I'd been dealt. Maybe something in my expression had tipped him off, but as it stood, he'd made a deal with Perelli to give me an opportunity to take out a target that both of them wanted rid of. Then again, maybe for a change, I'd actually gotten lucky because it seemed to me that with the impending second child from his very pregnant wife, Raffaello had been kinder than any mafia man I'd met before him.

He'd given me this gun, silencer and all, and promised me that if I managed to pull this off, there would be more work for me in the future. Work that would take me out of the dark and push me into the blood-soaked light.

The car continued around the path, stopping as it neared the front of the building. My breath was harsh in my lungs, burning a path up my windpipe as the cold air seared the insides of my throat.

Inhale.

Exhale.

So close. Almost there.

My eyes landed on the back door as the driver stopped the car and got out, circling the vehicle until he got to the backside. A dark head of hair appeared, and then the man's face was turned upward as he took a look at the darkened hull of the countryside mansion.

A supposed safe house that he had no clue was already compromised. It struck a desolate figure against the backdrop of black woods and white snow. I closed one eye and captured the man in my sight.

He didn't know it yet, but he was the key to a better future for myself. One little bullet hole in his head would cost me nothing and him everything.

Everyone takes from someone else to give themselves more,

Raffaello had said to me. *Don't think that we are any different. If you want something, take it. Fuck the rest.*

I wanted it, alright. I wanted it so fucking bad that I was sleepless with the desire. More than sex. More than pain. I wanted power—control. All of it I'd never had before.

The man moved away from the car as the back-door was closed.

One. He glided away from his man and towards the steps leading to the mansion's entrance.

Two. He didn't look around, likely secure in his knowledge that he'd made it. That he was safe.

Three. He was wrong.

I pulled the trigger, and the rifle jerked, a pop going off next to my ear—much quieter than it would've been without the silencer, sounding more like a *thud* than the *pow* it should have been.

Several yards in the distance, the man's head jerked down and for a moment, his body suspended in the air. It was as if he was still alive for the briefest of seconds and he couldn't quite believe what had happened. Then, ultimately, the target's body crum-pled to the ground. His knees hit first then his chest, and finally, the crack of his skull as it bounced off the step.

I did it, I realized. I pulled the trigger. I killed my first target.

Heat spread through my limbs and my hand slapped over my mouth as a bubble of laughter echoed out. Holy fucking shit. I actually did it.

I roll away from the Remington 700, and this time, I don't close my eyes.

That man had been alive when he'd arrived, and now he was dead. Not even inches from his supposed safe house. I'd done that. I'd taken his life from him and, in essence, mine was about to be renewed.

Pulling away from my face, I hold my hands out in front of me and stare at them. These hands took a life. They held someone else in their grip and decided that man's fate. A rush of euphoria swept through me. I'd never felt this kind of power before.

Finally, I was the one in control.

I closed my eyes and laughed, muffling the sound as I turned my face into the snow. The iciness of it faded in light of my new circumstances. Never again would I fear the world. Never again would I want or crave what someone else had.

If I wanted it—I could take it. All the power was right there … and a bullet and a gun were my weapon and payment.

1

ANGEL

Sydney, Australia
21 years later...

I eyed the chocolate martini that a big-chested blonde held against her boobs as she fake-giggled at something the balding man at her side said. I loved chocolate, but instead, I held in my own hand a Negroni Sbagliato topped with a bit of Prosecco. It was a pretty reddish color, and bubbles danced within the clear glass, spreading around the orange peel that had been expertly added as a garnish.

Why was I drinking this and not the chocolate martini? Easy, because I saw some stupid video on the internet and it made it sound so cool and mature. That was the air I was going for, too. Cool and mature. Nothing like the fresh twenty-one-year-old I actually was. My ID said I was twenty-five. Not that I really needed it here. In the last few years, I'd learned that practically every other country on Earth could give a shit less about the drinking age so long as you weren't completely smashed and causing a scene.

Still, it felt like I'd really come full circle now, three years after my wedding, sitting in some random fancy bar with my first 'legal' drink. Sure, it'd been legal in all the other countries, but sometimes, I still liked to pretend I was back in America. It was home, after all, and even if it wasn't my father's homeland—it was my mother's. Australia didn't have the same drinking laws as the United States, but still—at least to me—today was supposed to be special.

My stomach rumbled with hunger, but I hadn't been able to bring myself to eat today. Not when I was very much expecting to get drunk off my ass and wobble my way back to the apartment I had rented in the heart of Sydney, so close to Barangaroo that I woke up with a view of the bay every morning. It was an impossibly expensive apartment, but I had to keep up appearances. My clients wouldn't trust someone who lived in the gutter. I was supposed to make them disappear, after all, in style.

Criminals—even criminals on the run—could rarely ever let go of the millions they'd gained. Not that all of my clients were criminals, but many of them were. Some, however, were just unfortunate enough to need my help.

A sigh escaped me as I noticed a trio of young

women, one with a sash across her chest downing shots in the corner near the band playing the cover of some famous Australian singer that I'd heard on the radio here. Though the sash read Bride-To-Be, the glimmer of glitter and jewels that decorated it made me think of other things—specifically what I was supposed to be celebrating. My fingers grazed my neck where the choker Gaven had given me—or rather his collar of ownership—had once rested. I felt strangely naked there now.

It had been the first thing to go when I'd run away. Not necessarily because I'd hated it, but because selling off the diamonds inside had been a necessity. It had funded my new start and given me an actual chance. I'd known I had to be smarter the second time I'd escaped. Gaven had proven himself to be resourceful and domineering. My nail scraped the skin of my throat. Still … it hadn't been easy to let go of.

As I stared at the bride and her posse celebrating her bachelorette party—or hen party as they called it here in Australia—I felt a twinge of remorse and envy. I withdrew my hand from my neck and sipped my drink while watching their little group.

I'd always imagined commemorating my twenty-first birthday would happen with girlfriends. All of us dressed in much the same way I am now—slutty cocktail attire—as we laughed and giggled our way from club to club, drowning ourselves in the bliss of youth and shots of vodka or tequila. In some scenarios of what I imagined today would be, I would've been home, sitting in my father's study as we shared my very first legal drink together.

Grimacing at that last image in my head, I tipped the glass back and sucked down a mouthful of alcohol. It was sweeter than I anticipated, a little tart and sharp, but not bad at all. All around me in the darkened, shadowy lounge bar, conversations poured into my ears.

Three incredibly long years, I'd been away from home, and this was as close as I'd dared to get. A fifteen-hour flight to the nearest mainland of the United States. My computer skills had certainly come in handy that fateful night—my fucking wedding night.

My fingers gripped the glass in my hand tighter as I recalled the betrayal of my sister and my current predicament. She was the reason I wasn't able to enjoy being home or even attend college. Even if I could have tried to do something online once I was away from her and the Price Empire, it wasn't like I could keep up with a curriculum when I was too damn busy running from her and building a business to keep myself safe. It had nothing to do with my forced marriage but everything to do with her jealous, vile act of cruelty.

Without a second thought, I put the glass back to my lips and downed the rest of the liquid in one gulp. Just like that, too, the sweet-ish taste turned bitter and the alcohol burned a path into my stomach. I had been a mess the night I'd run away, but I'd done better the second time than the first. I'd learned a valuable lesson. Sometimes, you had to accept the reality and lean into what you were capable of or risk everything.

I was an ex-Mafia Princess and now a criminal. I no longer had the choice of normalcy. If I wanted to survive my sister's wrath, then I'd had to accept that part of myself. In the last three years, I'd donned several masks—different identities—and even taken on this new business of mine. The kind of business that allowed others to disappear somewhere else in the world, starting new lives as their old ones were irrevocably ended.

Carefully, I set the empty glass down on the bar top and sighed as I turned towards the rest of the lounge area. I'd learned, too, how to read people. Who would be dangerous to involve myself with, and who would be beneficial. If I hadn't learned and learned fast, then I'd be as good as dead. As it stood, *someone* was getting far too close.

My husband.

"Nice night, isn't it?" A smooth baritone sounded at my side, but I didn't jump. I'd noticed a man in a tight black suit, tall and broad, with a no-nonsense expression plastered on his face approaching a few minutes ago. At first, he'd sidled up to the end of the bar, and then with each passing second, he'd edged closer and closer as he worked up the courage to talk to me.

Casting a look at the man, I took him in. He was young—at least in his mid-twenties with thick dark hair gelled away from his face. Perhaps it was the cut of his jawline or his height, but somehow, he made me think of Gaven. Despite the sharp, handsome contrast of his skin tone, though, he looked nothing like the man I remembered in my bed, between my legs.

It had been three years since I'd seen Gaven, and three years since I'd even contemplated sex. We hadn't really known each other, he and I, but he'd left his mark on me, burned deep enough past my skin and into my soul that I couldn't forget what he'd done to me. The way he'd made me feel and the desire my body felt towards him. In reality, the two of us had been thrown together to continue the lineage of the Price Empire. It was a marriage in name only; it was about bearing an heir, not dedicating my life to him. Not really. Somehow, though, I'd never, in the last few years, been able to erase the oath I'd taken when I'd said 'I do.'

Now, it felt wrong to be staring at this man and contemplate … well, what exactly was I contemplating?

Not sex with him, that was for sure. If anything, the nearest thing to sex I was going to have tonight would be back in my apartment with the vibrator I'd bought online two weeks ago. It was the sole source of comfort I'd had—toys that were sometimes too hard and had none of the heat and vile, wicked words that my husband had.

My insides squirmed with memories. Between my thighs, I felt a wetness beginning to build. I couldn't deny that ever since Gaven had fucked me

—ever since he'd introduced me into the world of sexual deviancy, it had somehow made me want more. More seemed impossible, though, *without him*.

It didn't make any sense. We didn't love each other. Still, I felt bound to him. As if he were this great and powerful being and the only thing that could bring me back to that otherworldly pleasure.

"—buy you a drink?"

I blinked my eyes open, realizing belatedly that I'd closed them as the thoughts and memories swarmed me. "What?" I looked back at the man.

"Would you let me buy you a drink?" he asked again.

I was already shaking my head before he finished. "Thank you," I said, "but no."

His face fell. "Oh, well, if not a drink, maybe I could—"

"I'm married," I told him. "But thank you for the offer."

Disappointment etched into his face. I didn't normally pull the married card, but it wasn't a lie and that was something I was used to doing now that I was a fugitive on the run. Behind the puppy-dog-like man sitting next to me, I spotted a tall shadow moving along the back of the room. I sat up straighter.

No, I thought to myself. It wasn't possible. He couldn't be there. I'd been careful with this location. I'd wanted to stay for a while. But there was no denying the race of my heartbeat now galloping in my chest. I knew that shadow. I knew it well—all too well.

Whipping around, I slapped a fifty dollar bill—the shimmering Australian money's color catching in the low lighting as I do—on the bar top and snatched up my purse.

"Wait!" the man cried out, but I ignored him as I made a beeline for the exit.

Stupid. Stupid. Stupid.

Though the man hadn't been Gaven, he worked for him. I'd seen him far too many times in the last three years. Always too close. Just like now.

Outside, I hailed a cab. "Where to?" the cabbie asked as I snapped the backdoor closed behind me.

"Mascot," I said. "Holiday Inn." There were no more flights out today. It was far too late for that, but I couldn't risk returning to my apartment.

The cab driver twisted back to his wheel and steered us into traffic, the car picking up speed as he cut through the lanes toward the highway. Heart racing in my chest, I quickly glanced back to see if the man had followed me outside. It was too dark, though, even with the city lights to see more than figures on the street. I turned back around and forced myself to relax into the seat before closing my eyes and sending a prayer up to the sky.

I knew it was pointless. I wasn't much of a believer in God. Certainly not anymore. I knew, though, how other members of the mafia could be —how the great Prezzo Italian family that the Prices once were—had been. With so much death around them, so much betrayal and loss. It made sense that they would seek out a power higher than themselves.

For me, that power is none other than Gaven Belmonte.

My hunter. My husband.

Reaching up, I dragged my finger over the fogged-over windows inside the cab. It would be dangerous to let him catch me, but still, a small part of me hoped he would. A small part of me enjoyed this game of cat and mouse we were playing—even if it was a constant reminder that there was no returning to the past.

Once, I'd been an innocent girl, frightened of what he could do. Frightened of what the future held. Now, I knew the truth. The future didn't wait for you to get comfortable. It came whether you wanted it to or not. Those who survived it were the ones who had to adapt.

And so … I'd adapted.

I'd run.

I'd survived.

I'd created something of myself.

Now, there was no stopping. So if Gaven wanted to find out the truth, he had a long wait ahead of him because there was no way I'd make capturing me easy.

Catch me, if you can. My deviant husband.

2

ANGEL

Queens, New York
Two years later…

Dreams were like the wind. They were untouchable, but you could still feel them brush against your skin or even invade your presence, hampering you with hopes and failures. All the same, though, you could never hold on to them. Attempting to do so was like trying to capture a human soul—not that I believed those existed anymore, and if they did, my sister certainly had a rotten one. She was rancid and corrupt down to her very core. Only now that I'd experienced the depths of her betrayal—killing our father and framing me for her own sin—and delivered my own betrayal to Gaven by breaking our promise and running after I'd accepted him did I understand what a life of crime truly did to someone.

What it has done to *me*.

As I sat in the Rosemary café on the main street

of Queens, New York City, waiting for my client to make an appearance, I absently reached up and touched the empty place on my throat again above the collar of my silk shirt. Every morning, no matter where I was—Boston, Paris, Vancouver—I woke up and felt the missing jewelry there. I'd thought doing so would reassure myself that what I was doing—the person that I'd become—had not been all for nothing.

It was all for *him*. Even if I wasn't sure if it was love … how could I love a man I hardly knew? I did accept him as my husband before and that meant I had a duty to him, an oath to protect him even if he hated me for it.

Some days, the beautiful metal ring felt like it would burn a patch in my skin and other days it felt like the only thing keeping my feet firmly planted on the ground. Today, it was a mixture of both. Because today was my wedding anniversary. Though I didn't celebrate it, I still always remembered which day it was. It was such a bittersweet day. A bittersweet memory. It made my chest ache with yearning.

I closed my eyes and breathed through my nose as the noise of the café lingered in my ears. The room was small—there weren't too many places on the main strip in Queens with a big enough space to house so many—so the noise was that much louder. I concentrated on it to pull myself back to the present.

I listened to the people chatting around me. The

sounds of a couple arguing quietly over rent and bills in the back corner. The register clicking as the drawer opened when another customer paid for their coffee. The hiss of the steamer behind the counter.

The bell to the café door chimed and my eyes opened as a tall, slender man dressed in an impeccable suit bypassed the short line of men and women waiting to be served at the counter and made his way toward me. His lean face was rather sweaty, not that I could blame him. As one of the youngest and most brilliant of scientists in America, if any of Ronald Wiser's bosses even caught a whiff of what he was doing with his recent invention, he'd find himself on the wrong side of an assassin's scope.

Despite his youth, Ron was a genius. Somehow, he'd managed to develop a way to grow organs that would be compatible with anyone. Organs that were quickly grown that would never be rejected by a host's body. With the long waiting lists for organ transplants across the world, it was a discovery and invention that would rock not just the medical field but the whole world. With that, though, came the unerring dark side of capitalism. Ron's bosses wanted to patent his invention and keep it for themselves. Jacking up the medical costs of such a thing that would leave dying people either destitute or dead. Ron, himself, was not a capitalist, but a humanitarian with a moral compass, which was exactly why he'd found me. To keep him and that genius brain of his safe now that he'd taken all of his notes and findings away from his old company.

"Thank God you're here," he said as he took a seat across from me. Despite his slender build, he still dwarfed the undersized metal chair. "I think I'm being followed."

My back straightened at those words. My eyes cut past him and out into the busy street. Busy was good, it was easy to use to either disappear or cause a distraction if needed. I scanned through the wide, unobstructed windows. Nothing immediately jumped out at me, but that didn't mean anything. I'd learned over the last several years that it was what you didn't see that was more dangerous to you than what you did.

"Was it a car or a person?" I clarified, moving my gaze to the inside of the café. Could they already be here? Did they know where he was going before he arrived?

"Dark blue sedan," he answered. "I think I lost it a few blocks back, but I can't be sure."

I scowled as I watched a dark blue sedan drive past the windows. *Damn.* He had definitely *not* lost it. Ronald was not a spy by any means, or even a criminal on the run—and this only proved to me that he needed my protection, my expertise. Sweat collected at the top of my spine as I tried to think over who would have slipped the information out. The list of people who knew what he was doing was small, but I didn't know them all well enough yet to know who'd sell him out this early.

If it were up to me, no one would know what he was trying to do. Ronald, on the other hand, was far too trusting for his own good. My hands clenched into fists. There was no point in scolding him now. What was done was done.

I sucked in a breath and slowly let it out. It wouldn't help to panic now, either. If I'd learned nothing over the past five years, it was that panicking merely slowed down my thinking process. If Ronald was being followed, someone must have tipped off his competitors. If his competitors knew about the synthetic organ growth project he'd been working on for the last several months, then he was in deep shit. My eyes moved from the street where the blue sedan edged out of view and back to him. It would be back.

Ron was red-faced, his eyes jumping around the room as if any one of the people inside the café would, at any moment, stand up and shoot him. I leaned over and touched his hand, wrapping my fingers around them, and squeezing. His head turned back to me. I offered him a small smile as if we were two friends out for a friendly chat, when inside I felt the sharp tension of immediacy filling me.

"Calm down," I warned him quietly under my breath. "Don't make a scene."

"They're going to kill me, E," he hissed. "I know they are. I've done everything you said. I copied all of the files, all of the information and erased it from their servers. I've sent flash drives of it all out to different media stations, but what if it's not enough? They will want to destroy this information—or worse, take it and use it for themselves. They'll create my organs and then jack up the prices until no one but the rich can afford it. This could save millions of lives and they're going to use this for their own profit."

By the end of his monologue, his voice had turned slightly shrill. More sweat beaded on his brow. I wrinkled my nose as the distinct smell of male body odor reached my nostrils, and I automatically leaned away as I drew my hand from his.

Discreetly, I reached into my purse and removed several tissues to hand to him. He took them and began blotting the sweat on his forehead.

"We don't need to worry about the research," I told him. "Right now, all we need to worry about is how to get you out of here and in a safe place before whoever is trailing you finds a way to get you alone."

"Do you have a safe house set up?" he asked almost pleadingly.

My smile turned pained. If I'd had time, I might have been able to find something suitable. As a one-woman show, however, everything from being his contact and advisor to his personal protection unit fell on me. A safe house for him now would require assistance. I no longer had those kinds of connections. Had things not gone terribly awry five years ago, I might have been able to give him a better answer. I'd once thought that being the wife of a mob boss was the worst thing that could ever happen to me, but now as time had passed and I'd been on the run, I knew that having contacts in the criminal underworld was what kept people alive. That as well as fear and power.

Instead of answering him, I lifted my purse over my shoulder and rose from my seat. "Come on," I said as the same dark blue sedan from before crossed the street once again, this time on the other side of the traffic. "We're going out the back."

Ron's chair scraped back against the café floor as he hurried to follow me. I walked slowly though, and soon he had to slow the quickness of his gait to match mine, though it was clear he didn't want to. I forced myself—and in turn, *him*—to walk at a leisurely pace. If we were going to get him out of here safely, then we had to be smart about it. We couldn't seem afraid or even aware of the danger waiting for either of us.

I lifted my head and turned past the bathrooms and headed for the cafés small kitchen. I'd been here many times—it was why I'd felt so comfortable to meet him in this location. I never went anywhere without several escape routes and this café was one of the many different meeting locations I had on rotation in an effort to stay vigilant of eyes that could always be watching. A few of the younger employees paused and frowned as we passed, but it wasn't my presence that made them question us back here. It was Ron's. He was sweating like crazy and it seemed that his body odor only grew more and more intense with each second.

People believed in confidence, no matter what it sold them. So confident, I became. I'd run into an ex-thief a year or two ago that had taught me that motto. She'd seen me in the bar I was working undercover at and knew immediately that I was running from something. Somehow, the two of us had managed to find ourselves alone at closing and she'd offered her own certain brand of wisdom. Wisdom that I hadn't realized how desperately I'd needed. I missed her right now, but her words still lingered in the back of my mind—a helpful voice to my overcrowded mind.

Look like you belong, I reminded myself. *And they'll believe it.*

Even with Ron's sweating and shaking and his darting gaze, we made it all the way through the kitchen to the back door without anyone stopping us. I popped it open and glanced out into the alley. One side was completely open, while the other was blocked off by a set of dumpsters and a large brick wall. My heels clicked against the pavement as I led him outside. I paused, dug my hand into my purse, and pulled out a rolled-up pair of ballet slippers.

Sliding out of my heels, I kicked them behind the nearby dumpster and put on the more practical shoes. A pity about the heels, but they'd just been for show anyway. Sliding back into my purse, I pulled out a burner phone, a wad of cash that I always kept on hand for emergencies, a non-traceable credit card, as well as a set of keys.

I was afraid this would happen. Thankfully,

though, I'd already planned for it—or rather, I was still in the process of arranging things. This was my option B.

Five years of learning this life.

Sink or swim.

Life or death.

Both good were motivators and made me quickly realize I was truly a Price heir, after all. Even if I never wanted to be a criminal, I had to admit, I was damn good at using the same skillset as the people various mafia families employed. The most important thing the trial and error taught me was to always be prepared for any contingency.

"Here," I said, shoving the card, cash, phone, and keys into Ron's hands.

He gaped at the money and phone and then at me as we came to a stop at the mouth of the alley. "What the hell am I supposed to do with this?"

I watched the sedan cross the street, and before the driver could spot us, I grabbed Ron and ducked behind a low-hanging sign on the side of the building. "Listen to me very carefully," I said, keeping my eyes trained on the sedan. There had to be more, possibly an assassin already after him, but I didn't want to alert him and send Ron into a spiral of panic. He was the type that would definitely make things worse when he panicked. We'd only been working together for a little under a month, and while I wish he would've contacted me sooner … hindsight was twenty-twenty and we were past that. I shifted my gaze back to his face.

"I want you to take that money and card and grab a taxi out of the city. Use the phone I gave you. Here—give me yours—I don't want you using it for the foreseeable future." When all he did was just blink at me, I huffed and began digging through his pockets until I found the phone I was searching for. I shoved it into my purse. "Now, as I was saying…" Ron still hadn't moved or said anything. Instead, his eyes were centered on something over my shoulder. I glanced back but saw nothing. I knew he wasn't used to this kind of life, but still, if he didn't catch up, then he would get himself killed. There was only so much I could do for him if he didn't listen.

With another irritated huff, I snapped my fingers in front of his face and brought his attention back. "Focus," I said. "Take a taxi. Keep that phone but do not use it. I'll contact you when I can and you'll have to stay in a safe place for now—"

"Safe place?" he repeated, his face growing flushed once more. "Where is that? Do you have a—"

"No," I interrupted him. "I don't have a specific place. You'll need to find a motel or somewhere else to hole up in and hide. Grab some food with the money I gave you and stay put until I can come for you. There's enough money there in cash and on the card to last you for several weeks as long as you don't stay somewhere too expensive. Motels—Ron. Stay where they have as little security as you can manage. Don't go out, but if you must, keep your head down, wear a hat, and be wary of CCTVs."

In this age of technology, one could never be too careful. Even if I'd changed a lot in the last five years, I, too, had to be safe. Which was why I'd contracted a few friends I'd made from the dark web to erase any footage I had out there regularly. "Somewhere rural. Out of the city and out of sight."

Ron's face paled, and he swallowed as if fighting back the urge to puke. I had to move this along. My eyes darted back to the street. That fucking sedan had turned back around. This time, it was slowing at a nearby light. The backdoor opened. "It won't be forever," I said quickly. "The phone I gave you is secure. Call me if there's an emergency, otherwise, I want you to wait for me to call."

"W-what are you going to do?"

Hope like hell that one of my contacts would come through in time for me to get him. I stepped out from behind the sign and waved my hand for a taxi. A yellow cabby caught my eye and pulled up to the curb. I stepped back to where Ron stood. Two men were coming down the street. At first glance, they looked like anyone else on the sidewalk— sunglasses and jeans to complement their black t-shirts. The only difference is how they were moving —like eels cutting through the water, dead set on their target.

"Switch cabs often," I pushed the words out in a rush as I latched onto his arm and practically dragged him towards the taxi. "Use the cash," I snapped.

"But—what—!" Ron didn't get to finish his sentence as I slammed the door closed on him.

"JFK airport, please," I told the man in front before casting a look back to Ron as he cursed and rolled the window down. The men were getting closer. "Use the chaos at the airport to switch cabs," I said, lowering my voice and leaning halfway into the cab as I tried to keep an eye on the men coming. I turned to the cabby. "There's a two hundred dollar tip in it for you if you can get him there as fast as possible, sir. He's late for a flight."

The cabby's eyes widened. "Yes, ma'am!" He nodded excitedly, and then—just as every other cabby in New York when there was a hefty tip involved would do—he threw caution to the wind and sped out into traffic. My lips twitched as I heard Ronald shriek just before the taxi was out of range.

Now, time to figure a way out of—I turned the opposite way the men were approaching and ran head-first into a massive chest. I stumbled, nearly going down on my ass, before the man's hands gripped my elbows and steadied me.

Startled, I adjusted myself. Having been to New York several times on and off, it was a rare occasion when someone was kind enough to catch a person when they ran into them, much less if they fell.

Chivalry wasn't dead, after all.

My eyes lifted. My lips parted. A thank you and apology were on the tip of my tongue, but as soon as I met the man's eyes, every word in my vocabulary dried up and withered into dust. Every word except one.

I gaped up at the man and let that word spill from my lips as shock overtook me. "Gaven…"

Gaven's face was hard. Lethal. His eyes were like twin chips of ice as he glared down at me. "Hello again, Angel," he said. "Or should I say, hello, *wife?*"

I was so fucked, and not in a good way.

3
GAVEN

Five years had done nothing to dampen the taste of Evangeline Price on my tongue. Each day had only made the cravings harder. Now, standing before me was the woman I'd been searching for, the woman I'd been hunting. A burst of adrenaline poured into me. I bit down on my tongue, tasting blood. The primal urge to set my teeth to her flesh and rip her open rode me hard. *Animalistic.* That was what this woman made me. Luminous blue eyes turned up to me and widened in a mixture of shock and horror.

She hadn't changed much in the last five years. She was just as beautiful as ever, only older, more mature. She'd cut her hair. Her face was leaner, body more toned as if she'd started going to the gym regularly. She'd changed her style of clothing. I wasn't surprised. She was on the run, after all. Even she would be smart enough to alter her appearance. A part of me, I admitted, was proud of her.

I found myself smiling in the face of her surprise and especially her dread. My dark need for her was going to fuel me over the next several weeks. We'd never gotten that honeymoon of ours. I'd never gotten the chance to introduce her to the darker side of my desires. I'd treated her as a fragile creature, and now she was about to find that I was far crueler than she could have ever feared.

Perhaps she didn't honor the vows we'd made five years ago, but I was nothing if not a man of my word. Those vows had meant something to me. Killer though I was, I'd meant every fucking word I'd said to her. I would honor her. Cherish her. Keep her.

And she would obey me now. Whether she wanted to or not.

"W-what are you—"

"Get in the car, Angel," I ordered, cutting her off. She blinked up at me and then managed to collect herself, her back straightening as she tried to step away, trying to create distance between us. That, I would not allow.

Without a second thought, I brought my hand up to her neck and relished in her gasp as I tightened my hold—not quite cutting off her airway, but certainly keeping my fingers pinned over the blood rushing beneath her skin. "W-wait—" she wheezed.

I leaned down and hovered over her face. Her lips were right there. The very same lips I'd dreamed of for the last five years. The same lips I wanted to be wrapped around my cock as I pressed in deep to the back of her throat. It would be one of the many ways she would show her regret over leaving me. It would be one of the many ways I would punish her in the coming days. Perhaps she thought I'd forgotten my anger. Perhaps she thought she could still find a way out of this. She was so very fucking wrong.

"You should have kept running, Angel," I whispered as I pressed down on her carotid artery. Her lashes fluttered and her hands came up, nails sinking into my forearm as I turned and pressed her against the nearest surface—the black SUV I'd ordered one of my men to bring around. It had neatly slid into place as soon as the cabbie Angel had been speaking to had sped off.

"Gaven…" She gasped and I could see it in her eyes when she realized there was no getting away. The darkness was encroaching on her now, swallowing her whole. I could feel the sting of her little nails biting into my flesh, but nothing could hurt me now with her in my arms. My lying, betraying little wife. "I c-can't … you don't understand … I h-have to…"

I understood perfectly well. I understood that the night we had wed, her father, Raphael Price, had been murdered. And Raphael's youngest, his favorite—my Evangeline—had gone on the run, drawing all manner of speculation. Many believed that she was responsible, but I knew differently. I wasn't a stupid man, but I had been too kind once. Too kind to her. Young and naive as eighteen-year-old Angel had been, seeing her now—five years later —all filled out, further along the cusp of her womanhood and definitely more ballsy and intelligent than even her father had ever thought her capable of being was a fucking masterpiece. She was a piece of art painted in blood, daring anyone who looked at her to delve beneath her layers and discover her secrets.

And discover her secrets, I would. If it took a day, a week, a month, or even a year—Angel Price … no, Angel *Belmonte* … wouldn't be seeing her freedom anytime soon. Not until I heard the truth straight from her lips about what happened on our wedding night and until she paid for her deepest betrayal of all—thinking she could escape me.

"I promised I would come for you, Angel," I said quietly into her ear as she slumped against the SUV's door. I wrapped my arms around her and lifted her up. To any passersby, we'd look like an absorbed couple as I gently maneuvered her into the backseat of the vehicle. "I always keep my promises."

Once the two of us were secured in the car, I lifted my head and gave the driver a nod and he steered out into slow crawling traffic. My attention fell back to the woman in my arms.

She had no idea how long I'd been watching her. Searching for just the right time to drop in and take her. I recalled what she'd mentioned about wanting to go to college before. She hadn't gotten the chance, but then—on the run—she'd proven that she hadn't needed it. She was innovative and far better at keeping a low profile than I'd expected.

It'd just taken the better part of five years to track her down. I'd almost had her two years ago. I didn't know how she'd caught on, but she had. This time, I knew I couldn't fail. So, it'd taken a few months more after finding her for the right opportunity. My hand slid up her face. I touched her cheek and smoothed her hair back. She looked just as beautiful as she had the night we'd said our vows. Only this time I knew the truth. She was a filthy little liar, and I was a fool for wanting her the way that I did.

Soft caramel curls sifted through my fingertips like silk. I leaned down and inhaled her scent. No other woman smelled as she did. No other woman satisfied me the way she did. I had her now and whether she knew it or not, there was no escaping from me this time.

I had been planning for this since the night she had left.

For the next several weeks, Angel Price would cease to exist. She would become nothing but my toy, my plaything, and my little fuck doll. She would do what I wanted, when I wanted, and how I wanted. And if she ever wanted even an inch of freedom left, she would do it all with a smile on her face, a collar around her neck, and the sweet words 'yes, Master' on her beautiful lips.

I looked forward to breaking her down and seeing how the newer, stronger Angel could take my

training. I'd been too easy on her before, too understanding, too afraid of scaring her off. Now that
she'd made my worst fears realized—her inconsider-
ation and abandonment—there was nothing I
feared. She would bow to me, she would kneel for
me, and she would let me back inside of her once
more, and once it was all over ... I'd bind her to me
in the deepest of ways.

My hands settled lower on her body, my fingers
pressing against her stomach. Raphael had wanted
an heir, and whether his little princess liked it or not,
she would provide one to me.

4

GAVEN

Angel's soft features tightened in slumber as I carried her from the car and into the house that I'd had specially arranged for her. Already, the doctor awaited us at the entrance. The second he saw me, the slim man jumped to the door and held it open for me as I entered, only to follow closely behind a moment later.

I strode through the house and into the bedroom where my sweet, betraying wife would spend all of her time until I'd fully trained her in the ways of domestic obedience. I laid her gently upon the surface of the bed as her lashes fluttered.

"Give her something to keep her asleep," I commanded.

The doctor jumped forward as I stepped back. His bag settled onto the floor as he bent over and withdrew a small vial of clear liquid and a pre-packaged needle. I watched him like a hawk, well aware that my men were hovering at the door with only one stepping forward to risk entering the room.

As the doctor prepared the drugs, I strode back to my right-hand man. As tall as he was stone-faced, Matteo Vanini, despite his Italian roots, didn't care that I was an American in their world. He'd been with me for the better part of the last four and a half years—having left Raffaello's house not long after the man's passing.

"I want the men out," I commanded. "I don't want her to see them when she wakes."

Matteo's eyes shifted from the bed to me. "Do you think she would be frightened?"

No. She would likely recognize a few of them— the majority had followed Matteo from Raffaello's reign. I wanted them gone for a different reason, and they didn't need to know why. All they needed to do was obey.

"Just get them out," I snapped before turning back just as the doctor slid a needle into her arm, earning a flinch from her sleeping form. Her lashes fluttered open, but as the doctor compressed the syringe and the sedative entered her bloodstream, the combination of it and the groggy confusion she was likely feeling had her quickly slipping back under.

I watched as her brows pinched together and then eventually relaxed once more. She seemed to sink further into the bed as her whole body loosened, and she fell into a deeper sleep. Behind me,

Matteo barked orders as he stepped to the door and gestured orders at the others.

Once the doctor was finished administering the sedative that would keep her unconscious for a while longer, he began his physical examination. I could practically smell the body odor wafting from the man as he sweated. No doubt it was caused, in part, by the fact that I was now hovering over him, watching his every movement. I couldn't seem to help myself. It'd been five years since I'd been this close to my own fucking wife. I was curious to know what she'd done with the body that was to carry my children in all that time.

After taking her temperature, blood pressure, and heart rate, the doctor glanced back nervously. "Um … sir? I-I need to perform a more invasive examination. Perhaps you could step out of the room while I—"

"No." The word ripped from me as I flashed him a dark glare. "I will assist. What do you need?"

The doctor visibly gulped and turned back to Angel's sleeping form with trepidation. "A-as per your request," he said. "I-I need to undress her and … erm … check for signs of sexual intercourse."

"Understood." Slipping out of my jacket, I tossed it onto a nearby chair before striding around the bed and crawling onto it. Ignoring the doctor's wide-eyed and curious stare, I leveraged Angel's limp body up and began unbuttoning her blouse, slipping it off of her form as I moved down to the rest of her clothes.

Once I was done and she was laid naked before my gaze, I snapped a look back to the doctor. "You will only look at what you need to in order to finish your examination," I growled. "You will only touch what you need to. Is that clear?"

He nodded sharply. "Yes, sir. Of course, sir. I-I would never—"

"A simple *yes* will suffice," I said, cutting him off.

He nodded and jerked his gaze down to Angel. I reclined against the side of the bed that wasn't taken up by the woman lying there and stared down at her upturned face. My gaze fell lower as the doctor's fingers prodded at her stomach and then he lifted her arm, turning it one way and then the other before setting it down and withdrawing a notepad to scribble something down.

She was thinner than I remembered. Too thin. The softness of her cheeks had evened out. The child she might have once been was long gone and in its place was a woman—a conniving, fleeing runaway.

She had scars that weren't there before. Shallow lines across one wrist and another on her stomach. Blade marks? Who would dare have hurt her? A man? An enemy? Was there more I needed to be aware of? Whatever the case, I would soon find out. Everything I wanted to know, I would pull from her very lips even if it meant I had to torture it out of her. So help her, if she'd given herself to another … I'd find them all and slaughter them right in front of her.

"I-I'm going to start the lower examination," the doctor stuttered as he moved to the end of the bed.

With gritted teeth, I offered a singular nod. One wrong move and the Glock sitting in the holster on my chest would get its first workout in a while. I dared him with my eyes to make one wrong move, but he never did. Once the man had been given the go-ahead, he was all professional.

With careful yet gentle hands, he pressed Angel's legs apart and then pulled on a pair of gloves. "This would be easier in stirrups, sir," he said.

"She's not going to an office," I said.

He nodded. "I understand. I'm just saying, though, that in the event you need a second examination—this should be done with the woman awake and in an appropriate and sanitized setting."

"This room is clean," I snapped.

The doctor didn't respond as he moved forward and, with a gloved finger, moved to her pussy. Rage poured through me at the vision of another man touching her in a place that belonged only to me. Even though this was my choice, even though I'd ordered him here, I should have invited a female doctor. Then, at least, I wouldn't have this incessant voice in my head ordering me to slaughter the man at the end of the bed.

I held my breath and briefly closed my eyes, pinching the bridge of my nose as I waited for it to be over. Thankfully, the doctor was speedy. Barely a few minutes had passed when I heard the telltale sound of his gloves being snapped off. My eyes shot open, and I sat up as the doctor reached for a throw blanket hanging over the edge of the bed. He drew it over Angel's form before returning to his bag.

"This woman is quite healthy, sir," he began his observations. "She appears fit and has no current issues that are externally noticeable." The man wrote something on his notepad as he continued. "Without a conscious patient, however, I won't be able to determine if there are any other concerns with her health."

"Has she been with another man?" The question burned out of my throat, but I had to know. My gaze found Angel's sleeping form once more. I had to know just how far her betrayal had gone. I'd drain the corpses of anyone who'd thought to touch *my* fucking wife and toss them into the bay without a second's hesitation.

The doctor shook his head. "There's no evidence of recent sexual intercourse," he replied, pausing before lifting his head away from his notepad. "And as for your other ... concern, I saw no evidence of childbirth either." My chest eased, but only slightly because in the next moment his words sent another wave of anger washing through me. "Her birth control implant appears to be nearing the end of its life—if she would like to continue, I recommend bringing her in to have it removed and a new one placed in."

Birth control? My eyes snapped down to the woman slumbering so peacefully at my side. Oh, no, that wouldn't do. Now that Angel was back in my grasp, she would perform her side of our little deal. Of that, I would make sure.

"Remove it," I commanded.

The doctor paused and gaped at me. "H-here?"

Lifting my attention away from my wife, I focused on the spindly man. "Yes," I growled. "I want that thing out of her *now*."

Dropping his notepad, the doctor turned my way. "Sir, that requires a safe and clean environment. I will need to cut down into the dermis to remove it with a scalpel."

"Do you have one?" I demanded.

The man continued to gape at me as if he couldn't believe the words he was hearing. "Y-yes," he finally answered, "but I—"

"Then you'll perform the procedure."

"Without her consent?" He stared at me.

My lips twisted into a cruel smile. "You're here, aren't you, doc?" I asked. "Don't start acting like you have a conscience now."

The doctor trembled. "Th-this is unethical," he said. "I-I can't possibly—"

"It's also unethical to give drugs to an already unconscious patient." My anger was quickly rising. I got off the bed and stood to my full height, rounding it as the elder doctor stumbled back. The big eyes beneath his glasses rounded even further. I reached out and slammed him into the wall opposite the bed, gripping his throat tight. "I recommend that you do everything I tell you to and you don't ask any more fucking questions, doc. You were brought here to perform your duties, not offer unsolicited advice."

"As a doctor—"

"As a doctor, you've already betrayed your craft and whatever bullshit oath you took when you got your fancy little degree." I stopped his pathetic attempt at maintaining his self-righteousness. There was no room for it in this world. I leaned into him and tightened my hold until his face grew red. "Take. It. Out." The words slipped through my gritted teeth like shards of glass.

Nothing would be between my seed and my wife's fucking womb. If she were pregnant this time then maybe … just maybe she would be too tied down to leave again.

The doctor wheezed out his agreement finally and I released him. He collapsed before me, gasping for breath as he felt around his throat. I stepped away and strode to the door, opening it.

"Get on with it," I ordered.

The man didn't speak again as he picked up the bag and set it on the bed before he got to work. Turning, I placed my back against the hard wooden door and watched as he removed her arm from beneath the throw and then prodded at a place at the inner part of her upper arm. Despite his obvious fear, his hands were steady as he reached into his bag and withdrew a leather case. He withdrew another needle and then took the medicine out before applying the numbing agent. As he waited—or so I assumed—for it to take effect, he began unrolling the leather case. Metal flashed as he removed a sharp blade and with one quick glance back at me, he set its sharp point to Angel's skin and cut quickly.

I shoved away from the door frame, moving forward until my hands gripped the bottom of the mattress and I watched him carefully remove what looked like a tiny little rod. It was barely longer than an inch. My nostrils flared as I maintained my stance while the doctor quickly put it into a small plastic baggy and then slathered something else across the small incision before covering it with a bandage.

That was it. Angel's last little betrayal had been taken care of. That *thing* she'd put in her body to stop me from taking what was mine was gone. When she woke and realized, she'd likely be angry, but it didn't matter. I'd gotten what I wanted—just like I always would when it came to her.

"That will be all," I informed the doctor. He nodded once and said nothing more as he began packing his things. I took a step around the bed to her side as the doctor stood up with his bag in hand. "You may take your payment from my man in the hallway," I said. "You understand what will happen if you breathe a word of this, yes?"

With an almost mousy squeak, the man jerked a nod back at me and said a quick, "Yes" before fleeing the room.

With the door closed, I was left alone—finally—with the woman I'd spent the last five years searching for. It was a heady feeling. All that I'd been seeking was right here before me, splayed out on the bed I'd prepared for her. I smoothed a finger over her cheek as she breathed deeply.

My hand descended, pushing the blanket out of the way as I uncovered her body. Her breasts were barely a handful, but her greedy little nipple was hard against my palm as I gripped her tit and squeezed.

Soon, I'd deliver the punishment she deserved for her actions. Soon, I'd have all the answers that had since escaped me. Even if it meant I had to break her to get them.

5

ANGEL

I came awake slowly, the darkness fading and reality encroaching. *What the hell…?* My body locked up when I realized something as my lashes lifted and I finally opened my eyes. I was naked. Not just naked, but tied down and bared to the cool air of the room I was in.

The flare of fear hit me a split second before my memories did. How I'd passed out. How I'd come to be here. The only thing I didn't recall was where exactly *here* was.

Looking down to where each of my hands were tied with some sort of jute rope—soft, but strong—it was hard not to feel the *thing* that was pressing between my thighs. I frowned, trying to make sense of it. I was seated in a chair of some kind. My wrists were restrained to the arm of each side and my ankles and calves were tied to the legs. I felt twinges all over. The upper part of my left arm. My stomach. My head. It all faded, though, as I realized that my thighs were spread wide and tied open. I looked down and between my legs was the rounded head of a Hitachi wand.

What the fuck? I looked up, scanning the room. Dark, masculine tones. Hardwood and burgundy curtains. It was sparsely decorated in anything that could have hinted at its owner. No pictures, no trinkets, nothing that could detect that an actual person resided in it.

"You're as beautiful as ever, darling," a voice suddenly said. And although the voice was familiar, the suddenness of it made me shriek in shock. My whole body jerked. I tried, immediately, to close my legs, only to realize that it was virtually impossible to keep the wand that was sticking straight up through some sort of hole in the seat of the chair off of me if I did so. It wasn't on, but I still didn't want to touch it. It rested against me lightly with my legs spread, but even trying to close them brought it right up against my clit—pressing hard and insistent.

I cursed and squeezed my legs together anyway around the top of it, my knees not touching despite my straining efforts as I jerked my head up and met the sinister gaze of a man I thought I'd never see again.

"Gaven." I said his name as he lifted a cigar to his lips and put it between his teeth. He reached into his pocket and withdrew a lighter.

Shock ricocheted through me, though it shouldn't have. He looked just as he had in my memory. Tall. Dark. Wickedly handsome. A vile glint in his eyes that spoke of danger. My breathing grew ragged. He'd captured me. Old memories resurfaced. Could I handle what he had planned? Could I escape a third time?

Cobwebs clung to my thoughts, fogging over everything in my mind. Gaven, though, kept pulling me back in. His hair was lighter at the sides, just above his ears—gray just starting to pepper the strands. It made him look even more formidable than I recalled. There were new lines around his eyes and lips. Not laugh lines but ones likely induced by stress. My chest seized. I drifted down to his chest, the massive expanse covered by what looked to be an expensive suit sans tie. Just the jacket, pants, and button-down—all dark, of course.

"That won't be what you call me," he said casually as he lit the end and put the lighter back in his pocket. I blinked and looked up at his face once more.

Though he was the only man who'd ever truly seen me naked, who'd been inside of me, I still felt self-conscious. Sure, at this point in my life, I could masquerade as the confident, sexy vixen. I could pretend that I was experienced, but deep down, I wasn't. I never was. Because he was the one man I'd ever had … and I'd never intended to have another after I'd left.

His words hit me. "What?" I demanded.

Gaven was seated across from me in what appeared to be a far more comfortable and less filthy-minded piece of furniture. It was a wide settee, covered in a velvety-looking green fabric. Unlike the seat I was currently strapped to, no one had altered it or fitted it with any vibrating sex toys like the one currently pressing between my legs.

"You will refer to me as 'Master' from now on," he stated. "And you will not refer to anyone else who comes or goes inside of this apartment as anything because you won't be allowed to converse with them. You've lost that privilege."

Despite my discomfort, I forced a laugh. *He didn't actually think I would just bow to him even though he'd managed to capture me, did he?* Nothing had changed, or rather … too much had. I shook my head. "I'm not calling you that."

"You will," he said without heat, as if it didn't matter what I said, what I claimed or wanted.

It probably didn't. Not anymore. It'd been five years since I'd seen Gaven Belmonte and in that time, I'd tried to convince myself that my attraction to him had all been in my head—it'd been nothing but a young girl wanting desperately to turn the beast she was being forced to marry into someone she could live with for the rest of her life. Now, as I sat across from him—bare save for the rope that kept me secured, I had to face the God-awful truth. I was wet, and it was because of him.

Gaven was no less handsome than he had been the day I'd met him and then, not long after, the day I'd married him. His strong jaw, his ice blue eyes. Cold and dangerous. Something inside of me that I thought I'd long ago buried flared back to life. All those nights alone in whatever city I'd managed to hide away in came rushing back to me. Every time I'd masturbated, pressed my fingers down below and curled them into my pussy, or stroked my clit, I'd thought of him. Every time I'd seen a couple— didn't matter where they were in their life, newly-weds, with children, arguing, or even the old ones— I'd thought of him.

"There are things about me, *sweet Angel*," Gaven said, "that you don't know. Things I would have gladly shared had we been given the appropriate amount of time to get to know each other. Now, unfortunately, five years have passed and *my wife* has only just now come home." The way he said 'my wife' made it sound like both a prayer and a curse, as if he hated it and desired it at the same time. Guilt ate away at my heart.

No! I told myself. *You have to be strong. It doesn't matter what he wants with you. It doesn't matter what he does to you. You need to find a way to escape and disappear again so that he can never find you.*

"I was prepared to wait and ease you into my lifestyle," Gaven continued, his tone casual as he reclined further on his settee. "I see now that it was wrong to do such a thing. Perhaps had I corrected your behavior before, something like this would never have—"

I try to stop him. "Gaven, I—"

"Silence." He didn't yell or bark. He didn't stand or tower over me, threatening me with his size and strength. He didn't have to. That one word, spoken with a deep, masculine vibrato made me stop. It made my lips shut and my eyes settled on him. There was a rage inside of him—something I had created—and when he turned those stone-cold eyes on me, I had to swallow roughly to keep from shrinking back and lowering my own. It was hard to maintain eye contact. Finally, I couldn't anymore and my head tilted down to my lap and my gaze settled on the edges of my knees.

"You've had your time to speak," he said slowly. "Five years of it. You could have come back during that time. Explained yourself. Requested my help—the help of your husband—but you didn't. You ran. You hid. I want nothing from you now save for your obedience."

I shook my head and bit my lip. I couldn't fucking explain myself. If I told him the truth then he would be in danger and as much as I'd tried to convince myself that it didn't matter, I'd agreed, in the end, to marry him. To have and to hold. In sickness and in health. I didn't want his death on my conscience, not when I knew keeping him in the dark could prevent it. It was a small sacrifice. One he didn't seem all that keen to let me fucking make.

I also had to acknowledge that I'd never gone back to the place I'd grown up. I'd never gone home, never attended my own father's funeral … all so that he would remain free from suspicion.

He continued after several beats of silence. "You will remain here, in this apartment, and you will do exactly what I tell you to." I heard the floor creak as he stood. Listened to the movements of his footsteps across the floor as he approached me and the inhale as he breathed in and released the smoke from his lungs. Hard fingers gripped under my chin and lifted my head so that my face was tilted up towards his.

"You have a long time in here, baby," he said. "Until you can repay even a fraction of what you cost me, you belong to me. And, Angel?" I meet his eyes. "I intend for you to take forever to pay back your debt to me. After all, we did agree to devote ourselves to one another for life. To have and to hold … *until death* do we part."

"You can't keep me here," I huffed. "I *will* find a way to get free."

He grinned. "Oh, don't you worry about that, love." He turned the cigar around and placed it against my lips and blinking in confusion, I parted them. "Inhale," he ordered. On instinct, I did. I felt the smoke invade my lungs, fill me up, and then felt a fogginess in the back of my mind. When he pulled the cigar away, I coughed. I coughed and coughed and shook my head as he turned and lifted an ashtray from the settee, crushing the cigar, which wasn't even half finished into the bottom.

"What…" Another cough attacked and I felt my legs relax. Something was wrong. That cigar … my head … it wasn't normal.

"Do you like one of my new products?" he inquired

"New products?" I repeated, more confusion swamping my brain.

"Yes," he said. "Despite your betrayal, I've managed to maintain quite a bit of power. I've begun spreading my business acumen to other markets, and this is a new type of drug we're marketing. It's designed to make you relax. For you especially, darling, it'll make you lose all of your worries and just accept what's happening. Be grateful I offered this. I can still be kind if you're a good girl for me—that is, if you can manage to be good for longer than what it takes to stab me in the back."

The bitterness of his tone was not lost on me, but the foggy smoke made it difficult to think. "I didn't stab you—I wouldn't…" A groan rumbled out of my chest. Why was it so hard to form sentences?

"What's happening?" I asked, even as his words finally sank into my mind. As soon as I inhaled that smoke, my mind had hazed over. The air over my flesh felt colder somehow before it turned hot. Incredibly hot. A million pinpricks of fire rose to the surface of my skin. My head tilted one way and then another as if my neck was struggling to support it. I couldn't seem to focus on any point in the room.

"It's fast acting," Gaven explained as he finished what he was doing and turned around to face me. He pulled a small black square from his pocket and held it in his hand. "It will enhance a few things for you."

"B-but you were…"

Hadn't he been smoking it? He'd taken a single

inhale, at least. Had he just been holding it between his lips for the rest of the time? Why wasn't he reacting the way I was? My head rolled forward and looking down, I realized that I'd let my legs fall open once more, putting the full view of my pussy on display. Air wafted over my open, wet flesh. A gasp escaped me and I snapped them shut again—as much as I could, anyway.

A low chuckle reverberated from him. "Oh no, we can't have that." Gaven's thumb pressed over the central button on the remote in his hand and the wand between my legs flared to life.

I screamed as both of my knees shot outward and my lower spine pressed against the back of the chair, but it was useless. Though keeping my legs open didn't press the wand so hard against my clit, there was no removing it. I tossed my head back and screamed again as the vibrations increased. The damn thing was hammering against my clit, sending what little cognition I had left in my brain into the stratosphere.

I couldn't think. I couldn't breathe. All I could do was *feel*. Feel how soaking wet my pussy was. Feel the hard, fast stimulation buzzing between my legs. Shit. Fuck. What was I supposed to do? I'd known that if Gaven ever caught up to me, that he'd be angry, but I never expected that he'd do this. Keep me captive in some room and torture me like this. I'd expected nail-pulling, beating, or even water-boarding.

Hate.

Pain.

Violence.

He was a killer, after all. But this? Sexual torture? That hadn't even been on my radar. And oh, was this fucking torture.

Gaven stood there and watched me squirm as I tried to wriggle, unsuccessfully, away from the press of the toy. My lips parted and I panted with the effort it took not to lose my ever-loving mind. Just as it was about to send me over the edge, the vibrations ceased. I gasped for breath and curled inward. I could feel the sweat coating my body, thankful for some relief and yet, also mildly disappointed that I hadn't reached that glorious threshold. My chest shuddered as I sucked in air so hard it scraped through my dry throat. My breasts trembled with the effort, my nipples pearling into hardened points.

"You haven't been exposed to this drug," Gaven explained carefully, as if he hadn't just nearly forced me to come apart under his seemingly indifferent gaze with nothing more than the press of a button. "Tolerance and body weight are also taken into consideration. Someone of my mass needs to inhale a lot more of this for it to be effective—you, however, are quite susceptible, darling. You've toned up, become quite a bit smaller than the last time we saw each other." I looked up and glared at him, but his eyes weren't on my face. They were on my body and his lips were curled down—as if he was displeased by the words coming from his lips. "You'll find yourself quite lulled by this drug—well, that is, until I take it away."

Toned? Ha. It wasn't exactly by choice. I had to be fit. It was either learn the skills necessary to survive or risk being found, taken, and possibly killed. But despite his words, I wasn't thinking of that right now. I was shaking. Trembling actually. I could feel the heat of his gaze under my skin. This was a problem—a big one. I needed to get out, to get away.

I'd considered that Gaven might catch up to me someday. I'd had plans in place. Now, though, the harder I tried to think of what I'd planned to say in this situation, the more it evaded me. Another groan worked up my chest. I was so fucking hot, I'd swear flames were licking at my skin. My head tilted forward, and I struggled to keep it up.

If Gaven planned to keep me drugged for long stints of time, I was fucked. Ronald needed me. I still had him to consider, but more than that—staying around Gaven for any length of time would put him in danger, especially if what he said was true and he was still involved in the Price Empire. I had no doubt that my sister would sniff out my whereabouts and the second she knew I was with him again, all hell would break loose. I couldn't let that happen. I had to convince him to let me go.

"Gaven," I said, my chest pumping up and down. I didn't care, now, that I was naked and bare before him, that he could see the hard points of my nipples or the rounded sides of my hips or even the evidence of my arousal coating my pussy. "Gaven, whatever you think you're going to get from me—"

"I know exactly what I'm going to get from you, Angel," Gaven said, cutting me off. His boots made hard sounds on the floor as he strode closer and then bent down. This time, instead of lifting my chin up, his hand curled into my hair, gripped hard, and yanked until I had to arch my back and thrust out my breasts to keep it from hurting. He grinned down at me, his smile twisted and angry—but even beyond that anger, I knew the truth. He was hurt, and he was punishing me.

"I'm going to get the last five years of my marriage back," he stated. "Every wicked thing I had planned for you, you will do. You will remain in this chair and take your punishment until you learn to do as I ask, and when you do, you will learn to continue your service to me for the rest of your life. Misbehave, and you'll be right back here. Locked up. No freedom to do anything—not even go to the bathroom by yourself. Is that clear?"

"You can't..." I gasped.

"I can't what, love?" he demanded.

"I don't..." I didn't want to say it. The words almost stopped in my throat. Lies instead of truth had to make him understand, even if it hurt both of us. "I don't want you anymore," I stated. "My father's dead. Your dream is over. It's gone. Jackie owns the Price Empire. Find another mafia princess to marry and breed. You need to *let. Me. Go.*" The last three words came out on a hiss as the hand in my hair tightened.

"I can't marry another woman when I'm still married to you, Angel," he said coldly, and it was like a punch to my chest. "I don't want another princess. I already own one. I own you. I said you're here to repay me for the last five years you spent running from me. I told you I would hunt you down, and now I have. You lost the game. So, no more fighting me—it'll only exhaust you. As for the Price Empire—well, I have my own power now. I can live without the rest. All I want from you, now, is your *submission*."

"My what?" Gaven released my hair abruptly and took a step back. "Gaven…"

He pressed the button on the remote again and turned the damn Hitachi wand up until the sound was all that filled my ears.

I shuddered as I came on the spot, my body seizing as the grip of the Hitachi still rested against my sensitive clit. My juices slicked down my inner thighs as my orgasm stole the very breath from my lungs. Tears formed in the backs of my eyes. Fuck. What was I supposed to do now?

Gaven watched for a brief moment before putting the remote back in his pocket and turning for the door. "Stop!" I half shrieked. "You can't leave me like this! Gaven, *please*!"

He paused with his hand on the doorknob and looked back, raising an eyebrow. "This is your punishment, Angel," he said. "I told you—you aren't allowed to call me by my name anymore. To you, I'm your Master and until you can call me by that, you'll remain in here. I'll be back in an hour or so. Don't worry, the wand is fully charged. I took the liberty of making sure this didn't need to be plugged in so you couldn't pull it free. Enjoy the orgasms, though they might start to hurt after a while. I expect they'll be the last ones you experience until I don't feel like punishing you anymore."

No, no, no! He couldn't be serious. I struggled in the chair and screamed when all that did was press the vibrating wand between my legs even harder. I was over-sensitive and could feel another orgasm creeping up on me. It was impossible. It was too fast. He couldn't leave me like this. Especially not for an hour!

But Gaven didn't look back as he strode out into the hall and shut the door behind him, leaving me shuddering in the throes of yet another forced orgasm.

6

GAVEN

I didn't go far. There was no way I was capable of doing that, not while the woman I'd been working to track down for the last five years was so close at hand, and also not while I carried the key to her torment and pleasure in my grasp.

Evangeline Price had changed in the time since we'd married. While she'd once been an innocent young woman forced into an arranged marriage with a man twice her age, I had no clue who she was now.

It was only by the doctor's own admission that I knew she hadn't secretly had a child from the one night I'd had with her and that, according to him, she hadn't had sex—recently anyway. She'd proven to be conniving and quite the slippery target. There was still so much I didn't know, so much left to find out about the woman that I would control and own for the rest of our lives.

Even as I sat in my office in the next room over, I

couldn't help but appreciate her cries and sobs as they filtered through the wall. Had we been in my Boston home, I wouldn't have heard a peep. But here, in this makeshift penthouse loft on the outskirts of the city, while the outer walls were made of brick and steel, the inner walls were thin—allowing me the pleasure of playing with her, both body and mind.

My computer screen was turned towards me, the cameras I had planted around every angle of the room allowing me adequate visuals on what she was experiencing. Once more, I watched as her hair slipped over her back and her head was thrown back as she was catapulted into yet another—I'm sure— agonizing orgasm. Even in the recording, I could see how her body trembled. The tears streaked her face and she fought against her bindings.

It didn't take long for her to begin screaming and cursing. My lips curved as she called me every name in the book. Asshole. Pervert. Motherfucker. Deviant, wicked, villain. Yes, that's exactly what I was. Her villain. Her husband.

Every once in a while I'd reach into my pocket and I'd turn off the wand. I'd listen to her gasp in relief as her body was given relief from the pleasure and pain of coming so often. A few minutes later as I finished going over the documents of the drug trade deal I'd set up for the Price Empire, I slid them to the side and reached back into my pocket. I hadn't smiled this much in so long. My lips curved once more as the wand between her thighs flared back to life and a fresh scream was ripped from her throat.

It was like my very own personal symphony. Her cries and begging. Her broken sobs. I relished in them. All the while, my cock hardened in my pants, pulsing with the need to take her. I was a man of restraint, though. I waited five fucking years for her; I could wait a little longer to train her to my preferences.

So, instead of going into the room adjoining this one and removing her from the personally made throne of forced orgasms, I leaned back and reached down to my zipper.

I stared at the image she presented on the screen as I took my cock out and palmed it. Long and thick, I stroked my shaft up and down in time to the undulating movements of her hips as I turned the Hitachi wand back on and watched her body move against it as she sobbed through yet another stunning release.

It was like magic—owning her this way. Cruel, perhaps it made me, but she had been far crueler. Leaving me with little more than a few words and no explanation. It didn't matter that I'd pieced the reasoning behind her betrayal after she was gone—her sister had obviously had something to do with it. I knew it, and so did Matteo. It was why the man had come to me.

None of that mattered now, though. Angel would soon find that her options had never allowed for her to run away. Her options should have been to come to me. To tell me the truth. Seeking my protection and help. *That* was what I allowed her. Not the betrayal of leaving. The first time she'd tried to escape me, I thought I'd scared her enough to avoid such a stupid decision again. I'd been wrong.

Now, as she sat there, her naked body shivering against the waves of pleasure coursing through her, I watched and waited. My cock pulsed in my grip as my eyes locked on the woman on the screen. Her head was still turned upward, hair sliding back down her nape and over her shoulders. Her tears were magnificent. Beautiful. Pre-cum leaked from the tip of my cock and I paused, rubbing a thumb over the head as I resisted the need to stroke myself hard and fast—to reach the release that was right there.

I would punish her, but I would also punish myself as well. I had, after all, no one else to blame for her disappearance, for being unable to capture her for so long. The wand between her legs was buzzing away, pressed firmly to her clit as she cried.

Her nipples were pebbled into tight little points at the tips of her tits. They trembled, making my eyes lock upon them as I imagined streaking her in my cum. Painting those rosy tips in my seed as she looked up at me with glistening eyes and swollen lips.

Soon, I promised myself.

I gritted my teeth as she jerked and screamed through yet another orgasm, the chair and her bindings keeping her pinned in place. It was enough for me.

My cock jerked against my fist as I slid my hand up and covered the top with my palm. A low growl rumbled up my throat as I came, imagining her taking me into her little mouth, swallowing around me as I dumped my load down her throat.

A little over an hour later, as the clock on the wall ticked past six p.m., and I'd come a total of three times watching her torment, I decided that she had suffered enough for the time being. I set the papers down and got up, leaving my office to return to the bedroom I had set up to be her prison. Whether my Angel realized it or not, I'd been planning her capture for quite some time and I was going to enjoy every little piece of it.

I unlocked the door and strode back into the room just as her lips parted and she moaned through another forced orgasm. Shutting the door at my back and flipping the lock, I watched and waited for her body to stop shuddering before I turned off the wand and really took in the sight of her.

Her gasps filled the air between us. Her chest was flushed a bright pink and her face was soaked in sweat and tears, streaks cascading down to her trembling chin. My cock jerked in my pants. Her makeup was ruined, smudged around her wide eyes, and dripping in lines down her face.

Tilting my head to the side, I took another step into the room. Her adorable shyness was gone now, the exhaustion of her body obvious in the way she didn't even attempt to close her legs. I could see even from here how red her pretty little clit was. The poor abused thing. She fought against touching the wand, whimpering as she tried keeping her legs spread and her spine as far pressed back into the back of the chair as possible.

"*G-Gaven*," she begged. "Please."

With a frown, I pressed the button again, eliciting yet another scream from her. It didn't take long for her to realize what she'd done wrong.

"Master!" The word erupted from her lips. "Please!" I pressed the button and stopped the vibrations between her legs with a cold smile. She collapsed against her chair.

"See, love," I said as I approached. "I knew you could be trained."

Her head tipped back and her eyes cut towards me with a vicious glare. Something that was also new about her. Before, Angel had been such a modest and cautious creature. Her face always turned away if I ever looked at her directly. That innocent, virginal part of her was as attractive as anything I'd ever had before. This rebellious look, however, wasn't bad either.

"You're a bastard," she accused, the curse a hiss despite the fact that I held the key to her release.

I chuckled as I pocketed the remote and leaned over her, tipping her chin up with a finger beneath it. I didn't mind the curses she threw my way. After all, I had her now. I was the one in charge. If all she could do was curse at me, then I'd let her, even as I took everything else from her very fucking soul.

The tear tracks that had dried to her pretty

cheeks fused her lashes together. Despite having heard her moans and cries for myself, seeing the way her body had reacted to each orgasm on the camera feed, I still couldn't imagine how many times she'd come within the last hour. Her poor little pussy had to be sore and swollen. I grinned. This was only the beginning.

"That I am," I agreed readily as I released her face and reached down to untie first one arm and then the other. She reached up as if to push me away, but her arm flopped uselessly into her lap as if even that was too much effort for her. I carefully finished untying her and then lifted her limp body from the chair.

"What the fuck were you thinking this would accomplish?" she demanded, her tone hard even as her body relaxed against my chest. Well, perhaps relaxed wasn't quite right. It was more as if her body couldn't seem to do anything else but lose all tension. Forcing someone to come repeatedly seemed like such a sweet release, when in fact, it was a wicked, cruel torture. No doubt, every inch of her precious skin felt like a livewire had been infused with her very body.

"Catching up on lost time," I said as I strode to the bed across the room. The second I laid her down, however, she tried to roll away, shrinking away from my touch with a scowl.

"We're not married," she snapped. "Not anymore."

"Unless either of us has signed divorce papers—

and I certainly don't recall signing—then we are, in fact, married," I informed her as I grabbed her wrist and brought it up to the cuff attached to one post of the bed.

When she realized what I was doing, Angel yanked against my grip. "Stop this!"

With little effort, I ignored her demand and dragged her struggling arm up, snapped a cuff around one wrist, and then circled the bed and performed the same action on her other. "This is rape!" She fought against the bindings I'd placed her in, turning her wrists this way and that, wriggling her perfect little body across the sheets as she tried and failed to free herself.

I took a quiet step back and admired her form. Then I reached down and smoothed my fingers up the inside of her thighs, collecting a fair amount of the cum that was drenching her flesh onto my fingertips and bringing it to my mouth. The second she felt my touch, she clamped them shut. It was too late, though. I smiled as I sucked her taste off of my digits.

I climbed onto the bed. Angel gasped and scrambled back until her spine hit the headboard. The small incision on her arm that the doctor had made caught my attention. It was slight, barely noticeable, and she hadn't said anything about it yet. Now that her mind wasn't fogged over with the drugged smoke or the pleasure coursing through her clit—she looked down at it. Her brow puckered with confusion.

Would she know what it meant? I debated on allowing her to realize what I'd done. Something wicked in me, though, wanted her to think she was safe. So before she could contemplate the small wound further, I made my move.

Pressing the full weight of my body over her, I pinned her squirming form to the bed and let her feel the hardness of my cock between us. Her nostrils flared with anticipation as I directed her attention back to me. Gripping her legs, I forced them apart and leaned down as she trembled in my grasp.

The smell of her invaded my senses. I pushed my fingers back over her swollen pussy. She stiffened, her body going cold even as I gathered the evidence of her arousal onto my hand. Slowly, I brought my fingers up to my face and separated them, showing the clear fluid that told me the truth.

Her cheeks tinted pink. Her lips popped open and then her eyes widened as I brought my fingers back to my lips once more, parted them, and sucked them inside. The taste of her on my tongue really was everything I recalled. Sweet. Heady. Delicate.

I finished sucking my wife's juice from my fingers and then withdrew a handkerchief from my suit pocket, wiping the remains from my hand. "There are things we didn't get a chance to explore when we were together, my darling," I began. "I was hoping to gently guide you into the lifestyle I live, but it's clear that you don't care for gentleness." She likes my punishments.

"Gaven..." Her lips trembled as I shot her a dark look.

"One," I stated, cutting her off, "is that you will refer to me as your Master from now on. You may call me 'Sir' in mixed company—but not to worry, I won't be allowing you out of this room for some time. Not until you can prove your good behavior to me."

"This is ridiculous," she snapped.

"Only good wives are given the privilege of calling their husbands by their name, Angel," I said honestly. "And you have *not* been a good wife."

She sucked in a breath. "Well, then you're in luck," she replied. "Because we're not together anymore."

"Oh?" I tilted my head to the side and examined her.

"You *have* to let me go," she insisted. "I'll sign whatever divorce papers you want. I want out. I'm done."

"Oh no, darling. The time for that is over. Perhaps you've been living in the outside world for too long, but you should understand the reality of your situation. You belong to me, Angel. Any attempt to escape will be met with more punishment." I gestured back to the chair. "You've been away for too long. This is merely the beginning. You can consider yourself nothing more than a pretty object for me to please and punish at will, is that understood?"

Her soft hair slid over her shoulders as she shook

her head. "I'm not a fucking object," she snapped. "You may be angry at me, but you have no fucking clue what you're doing. You think I'm the same naive girl who was forced to marry you? Well, you're wrong. I'm much different than I was then. You don't own shit—and you certainly don't own me."

I left the bed and strode around it before I settled on the side as she finished spewing her bile my way. Grabbing her chin, I tipped her head back and hovered over her. *This was fine*, I thought. Her anger, her spirit, her fight. I actually preferred it this way. Perhaps if she wasn't a fighter, I might not have had the fucking self-control to keep myself from fucking her until I broke her.

It was true that my sexual lifestyle was far darker than anything I'd shown her, but this ... this was pure revenge. For the woman who'd stolen my sanity and then fled with it in the middle of the night. The woman who'd lied to me, betrayed me and left me to pick up the wreckage.

"I want you to consider something, Angel," I said. "In the last five years, I've planned for this moment. I've plotted and prepared for the second you would land right back in my lap, and I know exactly how to keep you where I want you—legally and interminably mine."

"What is that supposed to mean?" Her eyes fused to mine.

"It means..." I let my thumb smooth over the side of her face even as I kept her chin in my grip, "that you are quite a disturbed young woman with a history of psychotic breaks and violence against your caretakers."

She frowned. "What the hell are you talking about? I've never—"

"I have years of hospital records to prove that you require someone who has both the means and time to dedicate to your health." Her lips parted as my words began to sink in.

"They're not real." Her protest was feeble at best and, at most, shocked. It never occurred to her that I could prevent her from ever being able to go back to Evangeline Price. Perhaps she thought that after all this time, she might one day be able to be herself again. If she wanted that, now was the time to tell me the truth. I waited a beat, but she said nothing. Instead, she just glared at me.

I sighed. "Of course, it's not real," I agreed. "But—after all the years you've been running from me, quite expertly, I might add—you should know that the perfect paperwork is just as much a weapon as a gun."

"Paperwork like that would only..." She stopped before finishing her sentence, but I already knew her meaning. It will only draw Jackie's attention. That was fine by me, though. Soon enough, I'd take care of Jacquelina Price, and once she was gone, if Angel still wanted to run then I'd ensure she never could.

Angel shook her head—in denial or inner turmoil, I couldn't say.

"Because of your mental health, I'm afraid," I continued as her face grew paler and paler, "you own nothing. Your licenses have been revoked. Your original identifications all showcase that you are nothing more than a young woman who requires a full-time relative to look after you. And as your husband, I am your sole provider and your guardian. If you were ever to leave these premises or go somewhere without a guard approved by me, any attempt to seek help would find you promptly returned to me and back in that fucking chair for another round of torture. Only this time ... I won't leave you for just an hour."

I'd sit here and watch her come for many hours. Days if I had to. I'd wait until it was so painful that she'd pass out and then I'd wake her up only to start all over again. I'd hook her pretty arm up to an IV to make sure she wouldn't get dehydrated and I'd relish in watching as she came and came and came. No breaks. No stopping. I would show her what it meant to abandon me. What would happen if she dared to do so again.

"You ... you wouldn't..." She breathed the words as if she couldn't understand.

I tightened my hold on her face. "I warned you, Angel," I whispered as I leaned close. My lips hovered just before hers. "I said I would hunt you to the ends of the Earth. What I failed to mention, however, was that when I found you, I would ensure you could never leave again. Welcome home, *wife*."

7
ANGEL

I was trapped. Never in a million years had I even considered that Gaven would take this route. That he would strip away everything that made me ... *me*. I'd underestimated him. Somehow. Some way. I'd merely thought of him as a killer. Yes, even after the way he'd taken my goddamned virginity, I'd still assumed that once I was no longer the key to his plans, he would lose interest. That was a very dangerous assumption to make, I realized. This was a far more precarious situation than I'd ever expected.

Though on the run I'd switched random aliases, I'd always considered and hoped that one day I could go back to being who I was. That I could be Evangeline Price once more. With Gaven's words, though, that dream became a complicated web. The only way out would be to find someone who could disentangle it. I had the contacts. I could do it, but even then, I had no doubt that he would think of something far worse and far more confining.

It was as if time had reversed and I was suddenly transported back hundreds of years into the past. It was more difficult in modern law but not impossible. Those considered a danger to society and themselves had no rights. No autonomy. No escape.

Gaven's hands fell away from my face as I sat there in stunned silence.

"Now that you understand your situation," he said, "perhaps I can progress with your new rules."

I didn't look up as he moved from the bed. The mattress rose as he stood. "You will remain naked in this room at all times," he continued. "If and when you are introduced to anyone who comes to this place, you will remain silent unless asked a direct question. When I return, if you are not restrained, then you will greet me on your knees, legs splayed, palms up on your thighs. You will sleep with me each and every night."

My mind rioted and rolled as his words slung arrows into my chest. What was I going to do? Could I escape? Did I explain to him why I ran? No. I couldn't. He was still in danger, and he had no clue. I needed more information. I needed to know just how he'd gotten the power he so obviously had. He had his own men—capturing me wouldn't have been possible without them. The drugs, too...

He was different. No longer a simple killer but a mastermind with a strategy.

I tilted my head back and stared at him as he moved across the room, loosening the buttons on his white dress shirt and sliding it from those wide shoulders of his before setting it on top of the dresser directly across from the bed.

"Does anyone else know I'm here?" I asked.

Gaven paused, his head lifting as he met my gaze in the mirror that hung over the dresser. "Are you concerned that your clientele will be looking for you?"

I blinked. "You know what I do?"

I'd been cautious to keep my new business far from the Price Family and my sister's knowledge. In fact, I'd avoided the North American criminal world for the majority of my five years in hiding and on the run. It'd only been in the last six months that I'd chanced the return. I'd naively considered that perhaps they were done looking for me. That they had given up. I should've known a man like Gaven Belmonte would never be done with me. He wasn't the type to give up on something he considered his property, and as his legal wife, that's exactly what I am. His property.

In the reflection of the mirror, Gaven continued to watch me. Finally, after what felt like forever, he turned and leaned against the dresser. Though it was difficult, I forced my eyes to remain on his face and not drift down to the sharp cut of his chest. As angry as I was with him, as spiteful as I'd acted, my chest tightened at the sight. Masculine. Chiseled. Beautiful. But beneath all of it, there was also a monster. A devious, sinister monster intent on ripping me apart for the offense I'd dealt him.

"If you're asking if your family knows that I have you, then no." His words made my spine stiffen, but at the same time, relief filled me.

"That's not what I said," I replied.

One corner of his mouth curved upward. He flipped back around, and I watched his hands go to the belt at his waist. With precise movements, Gaven unbuckled the clasp and slipped the leather from the loops of his trousers, setting it on top of the dresser before he moved back to the button and zipper. Unable to stand it, I ripped my gaze away and stared down at my lap.

He was right to be angry at me, but I was serious when I said I'd sign divorce papers. The longer we remained in the same vicinity, the higher the chances she'd find me. Jackie. My sister. My blackmailer.

"Your whereabouts are on a need-to-know basis," he finally said. "Those that need to know do, and those that don't need to know, don't."

His words were frustratingly vague, but I sensed that any more pressure from me would only irritate him, so I let it go. I was well aware of how he looked at me, his eyes roaming, watching, seeking. I knew exactly what he was trying to do. Gaven was a good assassin, but he was far more adept at other things aside from pulling the trigger.

"Now," he stated, "for the rest of the rules."

"How long will I need to follow these rules?" I asked before he began again.

His face didn't change. "Until I determine you don't," he said. I resisted the urge to press my lips together or let any hint of my emotions show on my face. I was highly aware of my anger, but even more aware of the fact that anything I did now would only serve his purpose. He wanted information on what happened the night I ran away, and I wanted to keep it a secret. Forever, if at all possible.

"You know," I said, "this doesn't change things between us." I gesture down to my naked body. "It doesn't matter what you do to me—or what you force me to do for you—I'm not going back to being the Angel that you knew, the one that you picked out like a shirt from a catalog. I'm not the innocent little girl you knew anymore, Gaven."

He hummed in the back of his throat. Gaven's mouth curved upward at the edges as he tilted his head back. The underside of his jaw shadowed his throat, but his face and the smugness it presented were fully visible. "You were never truly innocent, Angel," he replied. "You were just inexperienced. You flourish under my commands—you and I both know that. I don't need to force you to do anything, love."

Despite my earlier resolve to keep my emotions in check, my body automatically tensed at those words. Other than scowling, though, I didn't respond. He didn't seem to be too offended either, because he easily continued. "But since we're on the subject, why don't you answer a little question for me." His gaze bored into me. "What happened that night, Angel?"

Gaven's brows drew down, and the arrogance he usually held around him like a cloak receded the barest of bits. I couldn't tell for sure, but his features seemed to soften somehow. His mouth wasn't quite as tight and his jaw was not nearly as clenched as it had been. Perhaps it was my imagination, or maybe I wanted to believe that this man who claimed to still be my husband didn't completely mistrust or hate me.

What happened that night?

So much, my mind supplied. The memories poured into me—flashing one after the other. The wedding. Gaven's arms around me. Then the darkened hallway as I slipped out—for what? I couldn't remember. A glass of water or the bathroom. I didn't know. All I knew was that it had been the worst mistake of my entire life to leave the safety of his arms.

My father's body. His open, unseeing eyes— sometimes, I still saw his face in my nightmares. His and … Jackie's. His true killer's eyes—staring at me as she laughed.

To tell Gaven, though, would doom him. If he knew then Jackie would stop at nothing to get rid of him, and after seeing the way she'd killed our father and what she'd done to me … I knew she would. There was nothing soft in her, no loyalty save for what she gave herself. But Gaven wouldn't go down without a fight either. The truth promised nothing but death and destruction. It would cause an all-out war, and though he was strong and powerful, even Gaven wouldn't be able to avoid the outcome.

I shook my head. "It doesn't matter what happened in the past," I said instead. "What matters is that I don't want to be with you now, and with my father gone, I'm useless to your plans. There's no point in keeping me, Gaven, you have to know that."

Gaven went silent for several long moments. Then he sighed. "I'd hoped you would've at least gotten rid of that lying habit of yours while you were away," he said.

"Lying?" I gaped at him. "I never—"

"Say those words," he interrupted with a dark look, "and you will regret it, Angel." All earlier softness vanished as if it had never been. "You've lied to me as well as yourself. You ran when I could have helped you. You lied when you signed the marriage contract, when you took my fucking ring and became mine. If you don't want to tell me the truth now, then I'll just have to ask again at a later time. For now, let's continue with your new life rules."

I scowled but couldn't respond. There was nothing more to say. Until I found an opening, I would have to listen to him. Just enough to get him to loosen the reins so that I could escape again. I'd done it twice and even if he kept catching me, I was obviously getting better. It'd taken him half a decade this past time. Next time, I'd make sure it'd be a life-time. Even if it meant I had to run to the furthest reaches of the world, I would get away. I'd keep him —and myself—safe from my psychopath of a sister.

"I'll repeat what we've already gone over to ensure your understanding," Gaven stated as he launched into his new role as Dominant and Master. "You will not wear clothes in this bedroom or this apartment unless you are given permission. If given permission, you will wear only what you are provided with. Nothing more. Nothing less. You will not leave this bedroom unless you are given permission. You will not speak to anyone who comes in and out of this room or apartment. You will be provided with three meals a day. You will eat them. I won't have you harming yourself while you're in my custody."

"Oh, but the harm you do to me doesn't count?" The dryness in my tone was automatic.

His glare hardened. "If you think what I'm doing to you is harmful, then you'll be in for quite the shock if you break any of my rules, *wife*."

I shut my mouth and returned his glare.

He continued. "As I've stated before, you will refer to me as Master. If and when I decide to take you out in public, you will refer me as your husband or Sir."

"I can't call you Gaven?"

Gaven arched his brow. "Do you want to?" he inquired.

I shrugged. "It seems odd not to."

"Calling me by my given name is a privilege you've lost, Angel," he replied. "Perhaps when you've proven to me that you can behave, I'll let you do so again. For now, no. You will call me Master while we are in, and husband or Sir when we are out."

I knew what he was doing. In the five years I'd been away, I'd done my research on Gaven Belmonte. All the things I would have learned about him if we'd stayed together, I'd had to teach myself through other means. The man I'd married was no ordinary hitman. He'd been right when he said that he'd gone easy on me before. We'd only been married a mere matter of hours before I'd thrown everything away and gone on the run. I'd hardly known him—much less the type of man I was crawling into bed with.

Now, he was showing his true colors. He was a Dominant. He attended BDSM clubs. He had submissives at his beck and call. Oh, I hadn't been able to resist the temptation of spying on him. I'd kept away from North America and run when I thought he'd gotten close, but I'd wanted to know if or when he would go to someone else. Surprisingly, he never had. Or if he did, I'd never caught him.

So, now, I was being punished for that as well.

"And last, but certainly not least"—his voice was cruel and filled with relish. I already knew what he was about to say—"You will adhere to any and all sexual training, Evangeline Price. You will be trained as my submissive." He gestures across the room to the bookshelf against the far wall. I'd paid it little attention since I'd gotten here since it just seemed to be one of those things people put in a room to fill it out. Now, though, I let my gaze rest upon it in curiosity. "I've provided you with as much reading material on the subject as necessary. If you find yourself bored while you're confined to our bedroom, you may peruse those."

"Sexual training..." I repeated.

"Yes." He sent me a quick look. "We are husband and wife, after all," he said. "You'll need to perform those wifely duties of yours to my specifications."

Cold, direct, and demanding. That was the man I married, the Gaven that stood before me. "Just because we're married doesn't mean it's not rape," I pointed out.

Gaven's eyes flashed with something volatile, and before I had a second to inhale, he stalked across the room and was in front of me. His hand lowered to my face and then slipped back into my hair, fingers dug into the back of my skull as he yanked my head back.

"Oh, Angel," he said. "How little you think I know you. You and I both know that anything we do in this room, on that bed, any sexual activity between us will be consensual. You can spout those pretty lies all you want, but in the end, you'll never be able to deny me. I'm your husband, and soon enough, I'm going to be your fucking God."

8

GAVEN

Smoke lingered in the air above my head, drifting from the burning red end of the cigar sitting in the tray at my side. On the screen, Angel moved around the room. It'd been a few days since we last spoke. Despite my rules and intentions, I found myself unable to go to her on many occasions. I stayed up all night, working well into dawn just so I could watch her when she woke. I'd decided that leaving her to her own devices—albeit locked in— was an appropriate way to let her get accustomed to her new circumstances.

I had other work to do as well now that she was back where she belonged. There were meetings— other Families to contact. Now that the woman who would carry the Price heir into this world was back in my possession, the things I'd been putting off for the last few years needed to be put into action.

Since Raffaello's unexpected death and Jackie's subsequent takeover of the Price Empire, the Price

Family's influence had ebbed and flowed. It hadn't gotten worse, but it certainly hadn't grown. Not like I had. With Raffaello's right hand now mine, the undercurrents of potential war were rising to the surface.

I could have let it go. I didn't necessarily need the Price Family's assets to attain the power I sought. The principle of it was, though, that I was owed something more. Plus, I had the suspicion that if Jackie were to find out that Evangeline was back in the picture and that she would soon be taking her place at my side as she was meant to, there would be a whole new world of enemies to prepare for.

Angel hadn't said as much, not when I'd asked, but I was by no means a stupid man. It hadn't taken the full five years to piece things together, but I was sure that Jackie was the true culprit behind Raffaello Price's death. She'd framed her sister, cast her out, and used the chaos to seize control. It had all been smartly planned on her part. I could respect a cunning woman willing to do what it took to be on top, but I couldn't allow her to be a threat to my own, and Angel was just as much mine as the child she would soon be carrying in her womb.

Movement on the screen brought my attention back to the present. I turned my gaze to the images of my wife as she huffed and puffed, pacing back and forth across her room.

She was bored. I'd watched her off and on for hours. She read many of the books that were stacked against the far wall across from the bed.

She'd tried to hide in the bathroom, but it hadn't taken her long to find the cameras there. I was more surprised that she hadn't tried to disable them. She very well could have, but perhaps my punishments were working. So long as she didn't try to escape, I would give her small freedoms such as this.

So far, she had been allowed to watch television. She's fallen asleep and woken up again. She's eaten the meals brought to her.

Now she paced. Back and forth. She turned, and my eyes skimmed down to her full, round ass. It was nice, I had to admit to myself, to have her right where I wanted her. Her tight little body was completely on display for me.

Sure, she attempted to cover up within the first day. When no clothes could be found, she'd tied the sheets from the bed around her body. The next day, she'd discovered no sheets or blankets available. Nothing would keep me from viewing what I owned.

On the screen, she finally stopped pacing and turned, looking up at one of the cameras placed in the corners of the room. Angel's arms arched up and crossed over her chest, plumping her breasts up, not that she seemed to notice. She glared at the camera with fiery intent.

That, too, I'd missed. Her grit and determination. Her fight. I'd once thought Evangeline Price would be far easier to control than her sister, but what made my insides tighten every time I looked at her wasn't the thought of simplicity, it was the arousal of my baser instincts. Of holding down and forcing a woman with such ferocity to bow to me.

A weak, vulnerable woman was useless to a man such as myself, but a woman with absolutely no softness was not desirable either. Angel was the best of both. Strong but beautifully hungry for affection.

I loved this. Having her in my space, naked and dependent on me. The reminder of her there, on my computer screen is enough to have my cock hardening in my pants. Still, at the same time, there's a pang in my chest. The high-protocol BDSM life could be fun, but the truth of the matter was that she and I weren't part of that.

The truth of the lifestyle all relied on the trust between a Dom and a sub. For us, trust had been broken, all but erased. Her lies and her betrayal burned in the back of my mind on a constant low heat until it was ready to drive me to the brink of madness. Yes, I wanted her. I desired her. Craved her, but more so than just her body.

Evangeline Price was the woman of my dreams. In my core, I wanted to devour and corrupt. Now, though, things were different. I hated that. Hated her for that.

We weren't a true Dominant or submissive. We weren't true Master and slave, and we wouldn't be until she finally opened up and told me the truth. Until she trusted me enough to let me into her deepest parts. Not her pussy but her fucking mind and heart. Until we had that trust, this was all just like shadows dancing on the wall. A pseudo-relation-ship watered down.

"Gaven!" Angel called my name on the screen. "I want to talk."

I leaned to the side, watching as Angel continued to glare at the camera—through it. In my pants, my cell buzzed, alerting me to a call.

With a sigh, I withdrew the device, glancing at the screen before answering. "Belmonte," I barked into the receiver.

"Damn," Archer said, "for someone who asked for a favor, you sure sound grouchy."

I pinched the bridge of my nose between my thumb and forefinger, forcing back the dull throb beginning in the front of my head as much as I could through sheer willpower. "Just tell me what you've found," I ordered.

"Don't need to," Archer replied. "I just sent you a file. You'll be able to see what I've found for yourself."

I grabbed the mouse and clicked away from the cameras. Angel could shout for me all she wanted, but I was the one in control here. I would give her my attention when I saw fit. Pulling up the secured email Archer would have used, I found the file waiting for me. "I see it," I said, opening the folder and then scrolling to the file attached.

"It lists everything your girl has been up to for the last five years—or at least what I could find. Funnily enough, when I talked to Scarlett, she said she recognized her."

"Hadrian's woman?" I clarified.

"*Yup.*" Archer popped the last part of the word, and the sound of his fingers tapping across a keyboard filtered over the background.

"She recognized Angel?" I sat up straighter. What would an ex-international thief have been doing to run into my wife?

"She said she met her in some bar in Cabo," he replied. "Scar said they didn't talk much, but she had a feeling that the girl was running from something. She's got good instincts like that. Kinda funny, though, that she would have come that close to someone you've worked with."

"I wouldn't say that I've worked with the Scarlett Thief," I replied dryly.

Archer chuckled. "No, of course not. She hates your guts."

I hummed. No doubt if Miss Scarlett had known that Angel was running from me, she would have helped her. I scrolled down the line of dates, photographs, and timestamps collected on the document before me. Cabo. Italy. Fuck, even China. Angel had been all around the world in the last five years, it appeared. Another country pops up and I scowl.

"She was in Australia two years ago." Rage surfaced, as well as the old memory. I'd almost fucking had her then. Two years ago, I'd gotten a tip from one of my many contacts. A woman matching her description had been seen in the Sydney area. I'd sent men ahead, but once I'd gotten there myself, the woman in question had disappeared. I'd never truly known if it had been her or another ruse. The information in the file, though, along with CCTV footage told me that I'd been close. Because of my delay, though, I'd missed my chance to have her two years earlier. A curse worked its way up my chest, but before it could slip free as I turned my attention to other points in the file.

"There's nothing in here about the men she's fucked." The words were vile on my tongue, but I needed to be sure. I needed to know just exactly what she'd been up to, and who she'd been involved with. The doctor hadn't seen any signs of childbirth or recent sex, but that didn't mean she hadn't played around while she'd been overseas.

"That's not a mistake," Archer confirmed. "It looks like your girl was pretty much on lockdown. She's practically lived the life of a nun for the past five years. Any man I'd found her with on CCTVs hasn't been confirmed. Some of them are dead, married, or ... well, let's just say they play for a different team."

"What about the man she'd been with in Queens?"

"Yeah, I got him too." Another email popped up on my screen as he spoke and I switched my focus as I opened yet another new file and scanned the contents.

"Ronald Wiser," Archer said. "He's a bit younger than her usual clients, but—"

"What's his job?" I interrupted.

"Scientist—boy's practically a genius, at least on paper. He's into the research of progressing the medical field. As of now, though, since you picked her up—there's been no sign of him on the map. He's disappeared. His mother filed a missing person's report last Friday when he didn't show up to work for several days or respond to any of her calls."

"He went underground," I determined.

"That's a good assumption," Archer replied with his agreement. "Don't really know why yet though."

"It doesn't matter. Forget the boy," I said, my voice deepening as I stared at the face of the man my wife had been meeting with the day I'd captured her. My hands curved into fists. Rage coursed through my veins. If she'd truly lived like a nun for the last five years, then he wasn't a threat. Logically, I knew that. Still, I disliked the man simply because he was part of her current life—a life that hadn't been reliant on me.

"Tell me, exactly, what kind of work she was doing."

Archer sighed, seemingly blissfully unaware of just how close to unhinged I was becoming. "Did you not completely read through the first file?"

"I understand that she's kept herself alive and on the run via a remote business. I know she meets with clients—what I don't know is what she does for them." She couldn't be an escort, but what else would allow her to hop from country to country on short notice?

"She's an accessory," Archer said. "Or rather—I suppose she'd be considered a type of cleaner. She's on the dark web and everything. Your girl is business-minded. She gets into contact with people who need assistance hiding or running from someone or something and helps them get out of their situations. If you scroll to the bottom of the document, you'll see a list of some of the people I believe she's helped in the past five years. Think of it like a witness protection program for criminals—or people who don't trust the government."

Before he's even finished speaking, I've switched my computer screen over and moved down to the last few pages of the first document. A list of names, dates, places, and certain organizations appear— some familiar and some not. Mob wives. Scientists. Political enemies. B-list celebrities from across the world. Socialites. There are dozens of men and women alike.

"She's hidden all of these people?" My brows drew down as I considered the list. It's long. Impressive.

Archer's voice echoed over the receiver. "Not necessarily hidden them all, but many came to her for assistance. It looks like her primary job was creating new lives, but for others, she helped to gather evidence to be used in defense of their abusers or enemies. She appears to be particular about her clients and Ronald Wiser is her newest one. He's previously worked at Carpovel Pharmaceuticals, but now that he's gone underground, there's no telling what exact kind of mess he's gotten himself into that he needed her help."

"And you're sure there was no other relationship between the two of them?" I demanded.

"Doesn't seem like it," Archer replied. "I'm sure I'll find him soon. It shouldn't be too hard, but I've spent the last few days looking into your girl's past and hacking her email server on the dark web. That took most of my time, seeing as the power walls I had to get behind. She's——"

I cut him off. "Did she keep in contact with any other clients?"

"Hmmmm." Clicking reached my ears. "Like I said, man, as far as I can tell, she's been as single as a pringle for the last five years. Scar said she didn't seem particularly interested in anyone who hit on her when she was working that bar in Cabo—in fact, she suspected that the job, too, was another way for her to gather evidence for a female Latin American politician being blackmailed by an ex-lover."

Despite Archer's assurance, a wicked jealousy stabbed into my chest. My hands clenched into fists against the surface of my desk. Needing to regain a bit of control, I pushed back against my seat and blew out a long breath. Archer's information revealed more about her life since she'd left me. Beyond her beautiful face, she was clever. She was resilient.

"If you want, I'll keep on the lookout for Ronny boy," Archer continued. "And I'll give you a ring when I have more, but until then—over and out, my friend." With that, the phone call ended and I was left alone with my thoughts.

I set the cell on the surface of my desk and tilted my head back, my eyes focusing on the ceiling above my head. Considering all that she'd been through, I knew she had an inner core of steel. At eighteen, she'd been forced to marry me—a man nearly two decades her senior. She'd gone on the run and had managed to evade not only her sister, but me, for nearly five years.

Her innovation was impressive. She'd taken her skills and used them to solidify her safety, which I had to respect. She'd managed to turn her interests into a weapon and shield, playing in the shadows of the criminal underground without me at her side. It both enraged and aroused me. Her intelligence was a turn-on. It only served to solidify the need I had for her. When she finally did submit to me—the strong, incredible creature that she was—it would be the biggest accomplishment I'd ever had. The highest victory a man like me could achieve.

Evangeline was a woman of strong fortitude. Someone who could handle our dark world and I would be her Master, her Dom.

All I needed to do now was ensure that she accepted her fate.

9

ANGEL

I felt like a caged animal. Hell, I fucking *was* a caged animal. The longer I was locked in this room, the more insane I swore I would go. It had been several days since Gaven had come back. The only reason I knew that was because I'd been delivered food three times a day, every day. Breakfast. Lunch. Dinner.

I'd never been claustrophobic, but now I was concerned that I would soon develop the fear. I was restless. Hungry for stimulation. Anything really. Even if it meant that Gaven came back and tortured me in that way of his. There was only so much TV a girl could watch, and it didn't look like the reins of my new confinement were slipping. There wasn't even an opportunity to escape.

The cameras made sure of it.

They had to be using them, too, because otherwise—how the hell would they know when I was distracted enough for them to deliver food? It was always when I was in the bathroom or asleep. When I woke up, breakfast would be there already. When I showered, lunch. For a while, I tried to sit in front of the door, waiting.

Nothing. Nada.

The second I'd given in to the urge to pee—I'd come back to fresh food. So, yes, someone must always be on watch. I could have destroyed the cameras, but then that would bring him back. Honestly, though, after the days of boredom and confined frustration—I was debating on it.

It was odd, too, that after so long dressing to cover myself, it only took a few short days of constant nudity for me to grow accustomed to being naked. Then again, the room was now bare of anything to cover myself with—so it wasn't like I had a choice there either.

I wasn't quite sure how Gaven had managed to remove the blankets and sheets without waking me, but I wouldn't put it past him to put more of that drug in my food. My skin tingled with the need for something—*anything*. Pacing had grown old, and the books he'd left for me to read had left me feeling ... certain things that I didn't want to think about.

Whatever Gaven did to my body, remaining strong and resistant was my goal. To a certain point, anyway. I knew that feigning acquiescence too quickly would be suspicious. I had to maintain myself for at least a little longer to give him the illusion that he was breaking me. Once he thought he had control, then and only then could I escape.

After calling for Gaven multiple times and getting no response, I finally gave up and plopped down in one of the chairs to the side of the four-poster bed. Across the room, the chair that I'd woken up in was placed against the far wall—almost as if it was meant to be a constant reminder of what he could do to me again. After that first night, I'd half expected more deviant actions from my husband.

I considered my options.

One. I could try waiting for food delivery again —see who entered the room to drop it off. That had failed, but if I just stopped drinking the water they provided for a short time, then I wouldn't need to use the restroom.

Two. I could go on a hunger strike. Gaven obviously wanted something from me and starving myself would anger him enough to make an appearance.

Or … three … I could give him a show.

My head turned as I glanced at the bed. I couldn't say that number three was something I would mind doing. I'd love nothing more than to torture Gaven as much as he'd tortured me. Even if Gaven wasn't the one constantly on watch— whoever was in charge of the cameras would inform him of my actions.

Breaking his rules would send him running my way, and considering that all of his rules were about asking for permission—I had a feeling that making myself come without his permission would anger him.

My body heated at the thought.

I'd been on my best behavior since Gaven had left. Perhaps it was time to flip the script. Standing abruptly, I strode over to the bed and crawled onto it.

Don't think of whoever could be on the other side of those cameras, I told myself. *Just close your eyes and do it.*

My chest heaved up and down as I worked up the courage. Opening my eyes, I looked up—straight at the camera pointed directly at me. Without hesitation, I spread my legs as far as I could and leaned back against the headboard.

Slowly, I pressed my palm between my tits and moved downward, over my belly and towards my mound. My skin tingled as I pictured that it wasn't one of his men—but Gaven himself—on the other side. How long would it take him before he barged in here? Would I manage to come before he did?

I wanted to see.

My fingers reached my pussy and I found myself already wet. Just the thought of Gaven made me this way. Closing my eyes, I tilted my hips up further as I started rubbing myself. Up and down, gently and then firmer—with more pressure. My fingers slicked over my entrance easily, picking up my wetness as I gathered it and then pulled them up to the top of my pussy.

Using my own juices, I rubbed circles around my

clit, circling the little nub until a groan escaped my lips. My head moved back against the headboard as heat stole over my skin. I felt flushed as I toyed with myself. Hungry. I needed to be filled with something.

My free hand moved to my breasts. They hung heavy on my chest, my nipples already pebbled into tiny little beads. I pinched one, squeezing it between my thumb and forefinger. Electricity raced through me and I cried out, arching against my own hands. My thighs trembled as I worked my clit harder.

Wetness gushed from my cunt, soaking the bare mattress. It'd be uncomfortable to sleep in a pool of my own juices—but if it pained Gaven to watch me masturbate then it was worth it.

I opened my mouth and let the sounds coming from my throat free. Moans poured from me as I worked myself into a frenzy. My stomach muscles cramped and tightened as I drove myself higher and higher. I pinched my nipples harder, pulling and plucking them away from my chest until they were dark and rosy and sore. I liked that soreness. It reminded me of the time Gaven had clamped my tits in the cheap, shitty motel I'd run to when I'd been eighteen and afraid of the wedding I was being forced into because of my father.

Gaven had found me and showed me just how he planned to punish me for defying him. Even now, the memory spurred my fingers faster. They flew over my clit, rubbing the nub in never-ending circles as my body undulated against the air and mattress. I could feel my pussy contracting—the greedy thing.

Gaven's fingers had been so hard against my cunt as he'd thrust them into my core. I'd been frightened, confused by the sensations he was eliciting within me. I'd never known a man so harsh or cruel. He'd forced his way into my body, proving just how deeply he could own me.

Like the villain he was, Gaven had forced more than just his fingers into my virginal hole. He'd fucked me, broken through, and fisted my cunt, stealing my innocence for himself. I'd come like that too, driven to the brink of madness by him as he'd forced my body to heights I'd thought were only imaginary.

Even now, my pussy was growing swollen with anticipation. Too much so. I couldn't take it anymore. My fingers left my nipples and moved down. I thrust two fingers into my cunt, their passage eased by the soaking wetness slipping from my own body, down the crack of my ass, and onto the mattress.

Whimpers rolled out from between my lips. I cried out as I felt myself nearing the edge of relief. So close…

Still, nothing from Gaven though. Tears pricked at my eyes. Was this not enough? What would it take if he didn't come when I was so blatantly taunting him?

I was so absorbed in my own body and the feelings of pleasure coursing through me that when I next opened my eyes, I didn't anticipate what I saw. A dark shadow lingered at the end of the bed, hovering like a monster in the night. I screamed in shock and jolted back against the headboard, slamming my spine into it as my hands fell away from my body.

Gaven's icy blue gaze cut into me. "Oh, don't stop on my account, Angel," he said, his voice low, dangerous. "You've gone this far—you might as well gain a little bit of pleasure before I punish you."

My chest rose and fell with the shock of his sudden appearance. I'd planned it. I'd hoped for this, but now that he was here, I found myself trembling under his sharp glare. Swallowing roughly, I pushed down the fear and tilted my head up.

Hoping he didn't see the shaking of my hands, I defiantly met his gaze and spread my legs once more. "What's wrong, *Master?*" I asked, taunting him with the word. "Are you angry with me?"

Gaven's eyes fell to the place between my legs as I rubbed my fingers over my pussy and then tweaked my clit. Heat burned through me. With him actually there in front of me, my arousal heightened. More juices leaked out of me and slid over my folds.

"More than you could possibly know, Angel," Gaven replied.

Still, despite his words, he didn't try to stop me as I touched myself further. He remained at the end of the bed, never stepping closer, nor turning away. He watched, enraptured by the movements of my body and hands as I teased myself and played over my cunt.

"You ignored me," I said, my voice breathless as I slid two fingers back into my entrance. "I was bored."

"Bored?" Gaven hummed in the back of his throat. "Bad things happen when you're bored, it seems. You forget your place."

"What is my place?" I asked, continuing the ministrations of my hands. "To be a toy you put in the closet?" I forced a laugh as I craned my head back a bit and thrust my chest out. His eyes snap to my tits. Good, just what I wanted. "The toy wants to play with herself. So, why can't she? Her Master doesn't seem all that interested anyway."

"Her Master is not done punishing her." Gaven's low growl sent tingles through my body.

I panted, thrusting my fingers into my hole as my orgasm threatened to overwhelm me. "Then perhaps he should get off his ass and get it over with," I gritted out.

"Is that what you want, Angel?" Gaven asked. "You want me to punish you?"

"I want my freedom," I said. "But since I can't have that…" My fingers sped up, circling my clit as I fucked my own pussy. I added a third digit and stretched the three of them apart as I whimpered.

The room was quiet. The only sound that could be heard were the squelches of my fingers fucking my pussy and the low breaths and moans that escaped me. Waiting was impossible. My orgasm was almost there. I was on the edge, just one more little pinch of my clit would send me over the edge, and yet, still, Gaven hadn't stopped me. He hadn't even tried to.

"Are you really going to just watch?" The words were barely a whisper, practically a plea.

He arched a brow. There was something to be said for this scene between us—me, nude, fingering myself before him as he stood at the end of the bed, completely clothed. The dark fabric of his suit cut against his frame, making him appear darker in the room than he would have been, had the light been on.

When I'd started this play, there had been light pouring in through the windows, but now—the sun had set and darkness had invaded.

"I'm giving you what you want, precious," Gaven replied coolly. "I'm waiting for you to finish. I hope you make it good, too, love. Because it'll be the last orgasm you have for quite a while."

My hands slowed at those words and, finally, he moved. Gaven left the end of the bed and strode around to the side. "Oh no," he said, reaching out and grabbing ahold of my wrist as he pushed my hands back between my legs. "Finish what you started."

"I want you to do it," I whimpered.

"No."

I blinked at the denial, surprised. "No?"

"That's right," he said. "I won't be helping you

to defy me. If you want to come, then you'll have to fuck your cunt yourself."

Anger whipped through me. "You think I can't make myself come without your help?" I pushed my fingers back into my pussy.

"I never said you couldn't," Gaven replied. "In fact, I'm sure you're very close, aren't you, my needy little girl?"

His filthy words poured into my ears, making me shiver as I stroked myself, moving faster than before. My throat grew raw with the harshness of my breaths, but I didn't care. Sparks were already dancing against the inside of my flesh.

Gaven leaned over as his hand sank into my hair. He moved up from my neck, his fingers spanning outward before he gripped it suddenly tight and I cried out at the fire that it lit within me as pain rocketed through my skull.

"Go on now, Angel," Gaven insisted. "Fuck your greedy little cunt and come all over the bed. *I dare you.*"

My teeth clinked against each other as I clenched all over, and my orgasm bloomed in my lower belly. My limbs shook as it crashed into me and a low moan spilled out. Wetness gushed out of my pussy and over my fingers as I finally slowed down and just let myself ride the tidal wave of pleasure.

My body coiled with the wash of ecstasy and the sensation of Gaven's hand in my hair as he watched me come undone. The sweet release of it waned, and moments later, as my eyes opened and looked up to meet Gaven's angry gaze, I realized just how dangerous the game I'd started was.

I'd teased and taunted a lion and now, he was pissed. And hungry.

10

GAVEN

The second Angel's eyes opened after her orgasm and she looked up to meet my gaze, I made my move. Using my hold on her hair, I pulled her from the bed. She gasped and cried out as I tightened my grasp, and though she stumbled a bit as her feet hit the floor, she managed to get them under her rather quickly.

I strode from the room, dragging her behind me as we entered the bathroom. Once there, I finally released her—shoving her into the wide, glass shower.

She thought she could taunt me? I would show her exactly what happened to little girls who thought they had control over their Masters.

"Get on your fucking knees," I ordered.

"Gaven—" My hand snapped out and circled her throat, stopping her from speaking further.

A buzzing sensation—tingles—raced through my veins. "If you don't want to spend weeks with a ball gag in your mouth—only taken out when it's mealtime—and the biggest fucking plug I can find in your tiny asshole, then I suggest you do as I say, Angel. Now is certainly not the time to defy me. Not more than you already have."

Her eyes widened and she swallowed against my grasp before nodding. I released her and watched as she sank to her knees before me. In my suit pants, my cock pulsed with hunger. It'd been that way since I'd gotten the call that my precious wife had been up to no good. When I'd seen for myself what she was doing, I knew that a fresh punishment was in order. I'd left her alone with her thoughts for too long, and she'd decided that defying me was her only option.

Setting my finger to her chin, I lifted her chin so that she was looking straight up at me. "I'm not going to lie to you, Angel," I warned her. "I want to hurt you. What happens next isn't for you, it's for me, and you'll take your punishment and thank me for it afterwards. I'm angry enough that I could do so much worse, but I don't want to permanently scar you. When you wear my mark, it'll be when you actually want it." When she begged me for it because until then—this was all just an elaborate ruse, carefully constructed. My chest burned at that knowing, too, because, at the end of the day, I didn't want a pretend partner. I wanted realness. I wanted a submissive I could trust. I wanted her to rely on me, to stop fucking lying to me.

Angel remained silent. Smart girl. She must've sensed just how close to the edge of darkness I was.

Even now, I found myself greedy for her pain. My fingers left her chin and I moved upward, undoing the row of buttons that held my shirt closed. Keeping my gaze pinned on her big, wide eyes, I finished with my shirt and slid it off. Reaching around my back, I took the sleeve of the opposite arm and pulled it down roughly. The dress shirt dropped to the floor and I kicked it from the shower stall, stepping further in.

Her skin pebbled with light goosebumps. Fear danced in the depths of her eyes. She watched me cautiously, nervously. *Good*, I thought. I wanted her on edge. I wanted her to be afraid of what I would do to her. Her fear was a connection that held the two of us together. No matter what else she tried to do, she would constantly hold onto it. Perhaps it was mere hope on my part, but as I gazed at her, I had to wonder if there wasn't more than just that. More than fear but a glint of something … deeper.

She was holding herself back from me, but this —the scene from the bedroom, had been a purposeful taunt. One I hadn't exactly anticipated from her. Seeing her spread her legs like that on the camera and touch herself had been a shock. The woman before me, naked and on her knees, was not the same woman I'd married five years ago.

I'd known that much logically, but seeing her actions had brought it home far more than any theory had. She was different. Stronger. Braver. It made me a bad, bad man, but I liked that.

I'd never wanted a dumb or weak woman as my

wife, and I'd known when I met Evangeline—when she'd originally been offered to me all those years ago—that she was anything but. She was independent and had a core of steel deep down inside of her. Even if I wanted to cause her pain, it was never meant to crush that personality of hers.

So, as I stepped back into the shower and reached for the shower head, removing it from the wall, I reminded myself not to take this too far. If I truly unleashed the amount of rage I had carefully contained on her, then I could go beyond breaking her. It would hardly take any strength to simply snap her in half, shattering her completely.

Although we didn't have the true dynamic of a submissive and her Dom, she isn't fighting me now. She trusts me on this base level. If she's going to be my Queen after all of this is over—after her sister has been taken care of and the Price Empire is back within my grasp once more—then I need to be very mindful of how I punish her.

Aiming the shower head at the wall and cranking the handles, I waited until the water began to heat up. Her eyes followed the movements, curious. I crouched down before her and her chin dipped as she trailed the movements.

"Sit up," I commanded, and she arched up slightly, her thighs parting the barest of inches. I pushed them out further and wedged the shower head between her legs, right against her clit. She gasped and tried to scramble backwards, away from the powerful sensations.

Anchoring my hand on her shoulder, I stopped her with a hard squeeze. "Don't. Move," I warned her.

Her lips parted, and her eyes unfocused as the spray of hot water slammed into her clit, and she shuddered. I'd made sure to put it on just the right amount of pressure and shove it back far enough that it wouldn't suddenly come arching up and slap either of us in the face. As long as she remained in position, this would prove to be a very good method of pleasure for her. Pleasure now … and discomfort before the pain.

It was all about the build-up, after all. I stood back to my full height as her thighs clenched around the shower head and she looked up at me, her eyes already watering as she shuddered. I undid my belt but left it hanging on the loops of my waistband. My fingers found the button and zipper of my slacks and I freed myself.

My cock fell into my hand and I stroked it once, from the base to tip before I directed the head towards her. "Open and suck," I ordered, and before she could respond, I pushed myself directly into her waiting mouth.

She choked lightly, her eyes widening as her hands left her thighs and moved up to mine. She grasped onto my slacks, as water poured between her legs. I didn't give it to her gently. I shoved all the way back, taking her mouth roughly until I felt my shaft entering her throat.

Tears leaked from her eyes, trailing down her

cheeks. Nails clamped onto my slacks, stabbing at me through the fabric. Her throat convulsed around me and I resisted the urge to groan. Her body was flushed with heat, red staining her pale skin. As I looked down at her, I noticed the smattering of freckles that crossed over her shoulders and down towards her chest. They hadn't been there five years ago, which told me she'd spent a lot of time outdoors in little clothing.

Irritation wavered through me that I hadn't known that. I reached around and clamped a hand on the back of her skull and pulled her deeper, pushing until her nose was smashed against my groin. Her nails turned into fists against my thighs and she shoved back roughly. I didn't care.

Angel's little throat worked against me, convulsing as the steady stream of water beat against her clit below. Pulling out quickly, I waited as Angel coughed and hacked. Streams of spittle dripped from her swollen lips, connecting the two of us as they wrapped around my cock in strands.

"Again," I said. It was the only warning she got before I tightened my hold once more and slammed her back down. The scream of surprise that echoed up her chest vibrated against my cock as it entered her throat. This time, I couldn't stop the groan that rose up from me.

"That's it," I moaned. "Right there, love. God— your mouth is like a vise."

Angel's lashes fluttered against my skin as she tried to glare up at me. I grinned back at her. "Your throat is just as sweet as a cunt," I told her. More red stained across her cheeks as she took in that comment.

Oh, yes, whether she admitted it or not, she loved my filthy mouth. Down below, I felt her legs shift. The muscles of her thighs tightened and released. After several moments of holding her against me and refusing to give her air, I let her back up for a quick breath. More spit dribbled out of her lips as she turned her head down. It dripped down her chest, painting her breasts in the filthy strings of my precum and her saliva.

"You're going to kill me," she said hoarsely, coughing as she dragged in breath after breath.

I liked seeing her struggle, witnessing the spark of fury in her eyes when I took her despite her feeble protests. "Why would I kill you, sweetheart, when I can think of much more torturous and pleasurable things to do to you?" I taunted her. Pleasurable, at least for me. "Now, open your mouth."

She shook her head and tried to back away once more, but I refused to let her. Grabbing ahold of either side of her skull with my hands, I pulled her back down and felt the barest scrape of her teeth. It might have scared another man—the thin threat of being unmanned—but I wasn't shy of pain myself.

With a laugh, I looked down at her. "Sink your teeth into my cock, little one," I warned her, "and I assure you, I'll pay it forward. You remember how I took your virginity, don't you?"

Her cheeks hollowed out and her eyes glittered

with anger. "Imagine my fist in your ass this time," I said. "Imagine you spread open for all to see with one fist in your cunt and another in your ass. You know I'd never let any other man touch you." I couldn't bear the thought. She was fucking mine, after all. "But I'd be more than happy to let them watch as I make you come in the most humiliating of ways."

It would be the ultimate act of control. Forcing her to lose herself as a crowd of men looked on. I already knew that Angel might not have minded a hint of exhibitionism—my filthy little girl. She seemed to enjoy a little bit of degradation and humiliation. I was the one that didn't want to share her.

"It's up to you," I said, "but I'm not pulling out until I'm good and ready. You wanted to torture me, baby. Now, you get the cock you craved and you'll take it until I've finished spilling my cum into your belly and you're walking around with my seed sloshing around inside of you. If you want a little blood with my cum—I can be more than accommodating."

Her teeth carefully pulled back and the sensation of her soft lips pillowing around my shaft returned. I grinned, feeling victorious. "Good girl." I patted her hair softly, stroking the sides.

If Angel finally understood her situation or not, after that last warning, she seemed to give up on fighting me. I sawed in and out of her mouth with ease, thrusting all the way into her tight, resisting throat and then pulling out until I could paint her in the strings of saliva and precum once more. Gripping her hair tight as she coughed, I grabbed ahold of the base of my cock and held it against her cheek.

It arched up against her soft skin. "Open," I commanded. "Lick."

Blinking, Angel's eyes looked up at me with caution as she parted her lips and her pink tongue came out. She stroked up the underside of my shaft, licking from base to tip like it was a lollipop. The sight of her, so focused on pleasuring me despite the constant barrage against her clit turned me on like nothing else.

It was as if she'd forgotten the pleasure from below in favor of servicing me. That was what I wanted—for her to lose herself in worship. She suckled at my head without a command, circling the slit that contained my cum with the tip of her tongue. She laved me up and down before parting her lips and sucking the head into her mouth.

Her lashes lowered and she suckled. She didn't even seem to realize what she was doing. I wasn't controlling her anymore, but letting her play and in essence, her natural submissive came out. Wanting to take care of her Master, she reached up and took my cock from my hands, stroking it up and down, gripping me perfectly as she licked and suckled at me.

It was enough to nearly have me come undone far too early. After a few minutes of her careful ministrations, I knew I had to put a stop to it. Wrapping her hair around my fist, I yanked back abruptly when she would've taken my cock into her mouth once more. "Enough."

Hazel eyes snapped up to meet mine. Her dark lashes trembled against her skin. With the toe of my shoe, I pushed forward between her legs. The shower head moved back and I could tell the second it hit her entrance because her lips parted on a gasp and her body quickly jumped against my hand.

"Let it happen, Angel," I said, moving the toe of my shoe further, nestling it against the shower head. "Lower yourself down."

She blinked, confusion covering her features. I pushed down with my free hand on her shoulder, forcing her down against my shoe as I tilted it up and lifted my foot, pinching her little clit against the hard leather fabric. Petal pink lips parted as a gasp escaped her.

"Does that feel good, sweetheart?" I asked. "Do you like it when a man steps on your clit?"

She whimpered in response, the sweetest of sounds to my ears. "Do you want to come?" I taunted her. I just bet she did. With the water slamming into her cunt and my Italian leather loafers pinching against her clit, she was probably closer than ever.

I adjusted my hold, directing her face upward so I could see every dirty, filthy detail of her submission. Her nipples were red and beaded at the tips of her breasts. Her stomach was hollowed in, sucking in with each breath she took. Her pulse fluttered against the inside of her throat, moving rapidly like the beating wings of a hummingbird.

"You know what you have to do, don't you?" I asked. "If you want to come…you need to be a good girl, don't you?"

Her eyes settled on my cock, and she tried to move forward, but I held her steady. "Ah, ah." A smile graced my lips. "I didn't say you could have that, did I?"

Another whimper echoed up the tiled walls. I closed my eyes for a brief moment, relishing in the sound before reopening them and refocusing back on the woman on her knees before me.

"If you want to come," I said. "Then you'll have to beg for my forgiveness. Ask me to forgive my filthy little wife for touching what doesn't belong to her, for making herself come all on her own."

"If you hadn't left me alone, I wouldn't have—"

My grip on her hair tightened and I yanked hard, stopping her words. "Now, now," I said, chiding. "Let's not place the blame and take responsibility for our actions. I'm taking responsibility for you now, love. The least you can do is do the same for your own actions."

She shuddered as I lowered my toe and then tapped against her clit once, twice, three times—an unspoken warning. Her hands latched onto my pants. "You can't just expect me to remain locked up in this room without—"

"I expect you to follow my rules—both spoken

and unspoken," I said, cutting her off. "Now, are you going to apologize and ask for forgiveness, or do we need to step this up?"

Her eyes narrowed. "You and I both know that you're going to step it up regardless," she snapped. "This is hardly a punishment. You're not done with me."

"No," I agreed. "I'm not, but your apology and sincerity will determine whether or not I'll let you come at the end of your punishment or not. So, how about it?"

Angel's hair slid over her shoulder, the dark blonde strands catching my attention as she dipped her head. A beat of silence passed, and then another and another. I'd nearly given up hope that she would understand the error of her ways and that I would have to use much harsher methods to punish her than I truly wanted to when she finally looked back up at me.

"I'm sorry ... Master," she said carefully, rounding the words out with her lips as if she wasn't quite sure yet whether they belonged in her mouth or not. "Please forgive me."

"Forgive you for what, pet?" I asked.

"For being naughty," she replied. "For breaking your rules and touching myself without permission and making myself come without permission."

My hand on her hair eased and I stroked her. I reached up and shut off the water and felt her whole body ease. "Good girl." I took a step back, and she frowned as she leaned forward, more confusion etched into her face. "Now, stand up and go lay yourself over the bed and prepare for your punishment."

I held up my hand and allowed her to take it as she got to her feet. On wobbly legs, she stood. She continued to watch me with that frown on her face, but she moved past me, stumbling lightly—enough that my grip on her tightened and I only released her once she was out of the shower stall.

I let her go all on her own as I took a moment to clear my head. Greed was a vile thing coiling in my lower stomach. It swarmed me, an angry monster that demanded I stride in there and take her without any concern for her pain or pleasure. I would— eventually. I'd show her just how wrong she was to underestimate me, to think that she had control over her body. I was its ultimate owner. That was a fact.

Now, though, as she waited for her punishment, I needed to prepare.

11

ANGEL

Anxiety crawled through my system. My lips felt sore and swollen and as I walked across the bedroom towards the bed, I reached up and touched them. They were wet. I looked down and realized that I was as well. My legs were soaked with more than just water from the shower head.

There was something wrong with me. There had to be. It was the only explanation for the floaty feeling currently coursing through me. Despite knowing that, however, I found myself following Gaven's orders. It felt undeniable, after all, this chemistry between us and though I shouldn't have been, I was curious. I went over to the bed and stopped at the end. My fingers found the mattress and I bent over it, arching my back and pushing my ass out so that when he entered from the bathroom, he'd find me just this way—with my head down and my ass on display for him.

Even if it was only in the furthest recesses of my mind, I must admit that I missed this part of our relationship. The back and forth—the push and pull—I'd never had that with anyone else but him. In the lonely years that had followed, I'd thought of him as I'd touched myself late at night. He asked me if I remembered how he took my virginity—the answer had to have been obvious to him. Of course, I did. How could I forget?

It'd been a moment to remember. With his tie gripping my throat, my legs spread and bound open for his hand as he'd fucked me with his fingers. He'd added more and more lube—practically emptying the bottle until he'd managed to collapse his thumb and slide the whole of his palm into my pussy. It'd been a shock, a stretch. It'd been painful—but out of that pain had bloomed pleasure.

I hadn't felt anything like it since. Not until now.

Quiet footsteps reached my ears as Gaven entered the bedroom from the bathroom. I held my breath, waiting, but he didn't say anything as he strode across the room. The soft swish of Gaven's belt being pulled from the loops of his pants echoed into the quiet room. My heart thudded in my ears, a rapid fluttering beat.

Yes, there was a tinge of fear there, but there was also anticipation. I couldn't deny that and so close to the pain and pleasure he promised, I didn't want to.

A snapping noise—leather slapping against itself—made me jump, and the low rumble of Gaven's amusement followed. "Are you frightened, baby?" he asked.

"I think you like frightening me," I replied.

Pain bloomed against my flesh as something sharp landed on my ass and I cried out, arching against the suddenness of it. "That wasn't an answer," Gaven stated.

I panted and twisted my fingers into the mattress. "No," I said quickly. "I'm not frightened."

The leather from before touched my ass, except this time it was gentle. I jumped more from the shock of it than anything else as Gaven slid what I could only assume was his belt over the spot of pain he'd left behind. The gentle back and forth movements of the leather made me feel more insane because it wasn't enough. I needed something far more stimulating and the bastard knew it.

The belt was removed and it swished through the air, landing with a crack on my ass. I cried out again before sinking further into the mattress. My head bowed as my spine arched and my ass automatically came back up for more, and more, Gaven gave me.

Using his belt, he hit me again and again. Each blow was quick and precise. He never hit the same spot twice—instead peppering my asscheeks with spanks and then lowering the strikes to my thighs. I could feel myself leaking, pussy juices sliding from my insides down my thighs. It took considerable effort not to squirm after each hit.

The pain flushed through me, rising in a giant tidal wave before slowing and morphing into something else. My eyes slid shut as I took it and let it roll through me. Over and over again, he struck me, delivering each blow with harsh hands. Finally, when the spanking was over, warm hands touched my flesh and a groan left me.

He squeezed the mounds of my ass, pressing his fingers into the likely reddened flesh. "Your skin is hot to the touch," he said casually, as if he were talking about the weather. It reminded me just how depraved this whole thing was. A grown woman bent over, allowing herself to be punished and spanked and somehow finding pleasure in the act.

Gaven slid a finger through the crack of my ass and I stiffened as he stopped, hovering over my ass. With a hum, he moved further downward. "Ah, so you liked your punishment," he said as he reached my cunt.

More heat spilled through me that had nothing to do with the spanking. Embarrassment burned into my cheeks. "It's alright to like it, love," Gaven continued. "Many strong women get off on submission. You will too." He said it as if it was already a sure thing, a fact that he spoke into existence.

I gritted my teeth but didn't respond as his finger slid into my pussy, not nearly thick enough for what I wanted, but just the barest hint of pleasure combining with the ache from the pain he'd caused. It was electric—what he did to me—something completely otherworldly.

The control I'd managed to maintain on myself as he'd struck my ass slipped loose and I found my hips swaying as I tried to thrust back against his finger, fucking myself onto his hand for the barest bit of satisfaction. The flat of his palm came down on the top of my ass, halting the movement.

It was far different—the pain of his belt versus that of his hand. Somehow, the skin to skin contact made it altogether something *more*.

"Don't seek out pleasure I'm not willing to give, Angel," he said in warning.

I bowed my head against the mattress once more. "What are you going to do next?" I asked the question as a means of distracting myself because, despite his words, it was nearly impossible not to fuck myself against his finger as it sat inside of my entrance.

Gaven hummed again, the sound thoughtful. Sweat beaded on my temples and slid down my face. My arms and legs trembled with the effort to keep myself up and in the position he wanted me in. Despite the sound he'd made, though, Gaven didn't immediately respond. Instead, his finger twisted against my insides as he gathered my juices and pulled it out. He trailed up back to my asshole and then circled it with his finger, drenched in my precum.

My spine stiffened as he circled the dark hole again and again. My breaths came in quick spurts. In and out. I felt lightheaded, dizzy, with the unknown. His actions were both a threat and a promise.

When he pushed against my dark hole, I yelped and tightened up all over. A hand settled on my lower back, pressing me down into the bed. "Don't fight it," he said.

"It hurts," I muttered.

"No it doesn't," he replied. "I haven't done anything to hurt you yet, love. This is merely discomfort."

Discomfort was fucking right. I squirmed and wiggled against his hold as his finger slid into my ass. It was *wrong*. My sphincter contracted around the foreign digit in my hole. I rolled my head back and kicked against the mattress and another slap landed on my backside. The finger sank deeper as I cried out at the pain.

"You'll have something much thicker than a finger in this ass soon enough, Angel," Gaven said. "So, I suggest you get used to it.

"No," I groaned. "I don't like it." It made me feel strange. Little sparks rose up beneath my skin and flooded my limbs. I crossed my arms over my head and buried my face in them as he continued his movements.

Moving out and then back in, Gaven thrust his finger into my asshole without stopping. Whimpers left my lips. I whined. I writhed against the disgusting sensations. It was so very … odd. I felt hot and dirty.

"Do you feel like a whore taking my finger in your ass, Angel?" Gaven's words rocketed through me, burning more embarrassment and humiliation into me. I couldn't help but tell the truth.

"*Yesss*," I hissed at him.

He fucked my ass harder as the wetness from my pussy soaked into my hole. It grew dry and harder for him but he didn't stop.

"You're clenching down on my finger like you want more," he said.

"No, I don't!" I protested.

"Oh, but I think you do," Gaven replied. "I think you secretly like having my finger in your ass like a little whore. Only sluts love having something in this hole of theirs and you're no different, love."

The burn of humiliation swept through me at his degrading words. I twisted my head back and forth as tears touched my eyelashes. *No. No. No.* That couldn't be true. I didn't like it, that's not what these sensations meant.

"Is your cunt fluttering, baby?" Gaven leaned over me as he withdrew his finger. His hand moved to my pussy and he gathered more wetness there before smearing it between my asscheeks. "Do you want something?"

"You said if I were good," I moaned. "You said if I begged for forgiveness, you'd let me come."

"I did," Gaven agreed. "I didn't say how or when I would let you come, though."

"My ass isn't for fucking," I huffed.

"Oh, but it is," Gaven argued. "In fact, your ass will get a lot of fucking before I'm through with you." My breath caught on those words and I clenched my hands into fists.

"I'm going to fuck you wide open, Angel," he continued. "Slide my cock into your darkest depths and then fill you up with my cum in every way and when I'm done I'm going to shove a plug inside and make you walk around, carrying my load like the filthy little whore you want to be for me."

I speak through gritted teeth. "I'm not a fucking whore…" Despite the harsh denial on my tongue, the filthy words leaving his mouth had an effect on me. My stomach was on fire, burning with hunger. My pussy was pulsating with need. My clit practi- cally *throbbed* with the desire to be touched.

Gaven wasn't put off by my rebuttal. In fact, he didn't even grace it with a response as his finger slid right back into my asshole and I clenched around him all over again. This time, though, he didn't spank me. Instead, he merely withdrew and added another finger.

I cried out and arched up. "Stop!" I begged. "Please, it feels wrong!"

"Every time you try to push me out of your ass, I'm going to put another finger in, Angel," Gaven replied. "So, I suggest that you relax, or else, you'll have my whole fist pounding your asshole in a few minutes."

I cursed at him. I begged. I pleaded, but I knew … deep down, he meant every single word. So, finally, after several minutes of silence from him and begging from me and three thick, solid fingers pushing into my asshole, I stopped trying.

I forced my ass to relax and breathed through my nose as he shoved them inside. Back and forth, they fucked into my darkest hole—my filthiest part. Tears touched my lashes, but I quickly rubbed them away.

"There we go, good girl. Just take your punishment and it'll be over soon." Gaven's words of praise made my head cloud over, but that slight pleasure was marred by the fingers that invaded my asshole. I squeezed my eyes shut and just counted down from one hundred. Soon, though, they weren't as uncomfortable, and in fact, as my asshole relaxed and loosened for him, I found myself arching against the thrusts of his hands.

My lips parted as I panted. When he withdrew them, I almost moaned in sorrow. *Just what was he turning me into?* I didn't dare move or think he was done with me. It was clear Gaven had something planned and there was only one way to find out.

He left the bed and returned a short while later. The sound of a bottle popping open was followed by the squirt of something liquid. I jumped as cool wetness touched my asshole. A small little nozzle was pressed against my hole and I gasped as that same cold liquid flooded my backside.

Gaven's hand fell back onto my lower back, urging me silently to remain still as he filled me.

"Shhhh," he whispered. "It's just to get you ready for your plug."

"Plug?" I tried to look back, but it was hard to see anything as he kept his hands low.

"When I pull it out, I want you to clench and try to keep as much of the lube in as you can," he ordered.

I gritted my teeth, but knowing him—if I resisted, then it would only cause me pain, and not the fun kind. So, when he pulled the lube free, I did as he commanded and clenched down, squeezing against the weird liquid sloshing against my insides. Some of it still leaked out, I could feel it smearing against the inside of my asscheeks.

Gaven left once more, long enough this time that I found myself leaning forward into the mattress as my head bowed again. When he returned, I didn't even have the energy to prop myself back up. I just left my ass up and waited for him. He would do what he wanted regardless.

Cold metal touched my backside. I blinked, my eyes sliding open as I turned my head. "What is that?" I demanded.

"Your final punishment," he said. "Now, open for it."

I winced, but did as he ordered and let myself ease my clenched asshole. The strange metal was smooth but wide. It burned as it entered—stretching my hole around the widest part. "Master!" I arched back, a sob escaping.

"I know, sweetheart," Gaven said, gently stroking

my ass. It was quickly growing sore, but that soreness was shifting into something memorable. Later tonight, when I fell asleep, I'd do so with the reminder of what we did today. "Almost there…"

"It hurts…"

"It's a punishment, Angel," Gaven said calmly.

I hated that response. I clenched my teeth and on the next push, the metal plug was pushed all the way in and my asshole closed around a small dip. I sighed as relief moved through me.

That relief, however, was short-lived. A hard, metal rod protruded from my ass, connected to the base of the plug, and it pressed against the inside of my cheeks. Gaven reached up and twisted it, causing the plug inside to expand and open. I screamed, jolting forward against the mattress as if I could run from the thing in my ass, but it was too late.

Gaven grabbed a hold of my hips and dragged me backwards. Then with fast movements, he finished twisting the bulb and my asshole contracted as it expanded inside. It didn't hurt, per se, but it was a shocking sensation. My insides were clamped down on the thing inside of me. It burned. It ached. It made me feel impossibly full.

"There, there, shhhh." I didn't realize I was crying until Gaven's voice reached my ears. "You did so well, love. So fucking well. You took the pear with grace."

Pear? Was that what this thing was? What the fuck kind of pear went inside a person's asshole? Gaven didn't explain and I was too focused on the strangeness of it inside of me and the pressure I felt against my belly to ask.

He must have sensed my quickly deteriorating mind because Gaven gently pulled me off of the bed and lifted me into his arms. I'd stopped expecting kind treatment from the man who had me locked up —the same one that I'd been forced to marry five years ago—but at this moment, he acted as if he wanted to prove me wrong.

Striding across the room, Gaven took a seat and cradled me in his arms as he stroked my face and hair. I felt like a child in his arms, small and fragile. Yet, there was no denying the inherently sexual spark between us. His cock had been tucked back into his pants, but it still rested—rock hard—against my side as he held me on his lap.

His fingers moved through my hair, pushing the strands back and away from my face as my pussy leaked and my ass throbbed. I was impossibly aware of the foreign object inside of me and after several minutes, I finally felt strong enough to lift my gaze to his.

Crystal clear blue eyes found mine. His face was etched with hunger, a greed so deep that I was shocked he hadn't yet pressed me back to my knees and taken my throat in the same manner as he had before. Instead, he was forcing himself to hold me, to *care* for me through the shock of what he'd done. *Why?*

Why now was he showing me consideration? It wasn't fair. Did he know that? Was it all part of his plan or was this the real Gaven? My heart thudded rapidly against the inside of my ribcage, a violent and needy creature. I bit down on my lip. *Hard*. My insides trembled and my mind was a riot of confusion. If Gaven truly cared for me beyond that of what I could bring him as a princess of the Price Syndicate … then it made the place we now found ourselves both tragic and beautiful.

"Do you feel better now?" he asked.

I blinked at him, his question detangling my feelings better than any other antidote could have. I sucked in a breath and offered him a bland glare. *Better?* No, I did not feel better. I had a strange plug in my ass that was stretching me to the limit and building up a constant uncomfortable pressure. His thumb came up and brushed away the wetness of tears from my cheek.

"I know you're new to these things, love, but I promise, everything I do is to help you understand your role."

"My role…" I repeated his words as his hand descended from my face. Gaven's fingers touched my throat and I arched my head back, keeping my eyes locked on him. His face was focused, his lips twisted with the curve of pleasure and victory. *Was that I was to him?*

It was clear he was pleased by his actions. His hand moved down more, trailing from my throat to my breasts. He pinched one nipple and twisted it until I gasped and shoved it further into his palm. Between my legs, fresh wetness slid down the crack of my ass, towards the base of the plug. I squirmed in his lap.

He released my nipple and followed my abdomen until his fingers pressed between my legs.

"Yes," he said as I quickly grew distracted by the thumb he slid over my clit. "As a submissive, it's your role to please your Dom."

"And…" I breathed. "It pleases you to hurt me?"

His eyes caught on mine and he arched a brow. "You like everything I do to you, Angel," he replied.

"I told you no," I protested. "I told you to stop."

"Normally, I'd allow you the use of a safe word," Gaven replied. "We discussed it previously—do you remember?"

I stiffened at his reminder, but I did, in fact, remember. It'd been the night of our wedding—when he'd explained what safe words were and how they would be beneficial to us. We'd never gotten to the point, though, of using one.

"Now, though, I don't want you using such a thing to escape from your punishments."

"What if I really get scared?" I asked. "What if I think you're going to kill me?"

Gaven's thumb paused over my clit and his eyes darkened. His brow creased and he leaned forward, hovering over me as he glared down at me. His hand left my pussy and shot up to my throat, circling and squeezing.

"If I wanted to kill you, Angel," he said, his words distinct and cold, "I could do it at any point and there would be nothing to stop me. No action or word could keep me from ending your life."

His fingers pressed into the side of my throat, clamping down tight—not cutting off my airflow, but making me dizzy nonetheless. A beat passed and then another and another. Finally, his grip eased and I felt my clouded mind clear the slightest bit.

"Red," he said. Confused, I stared at him, waiting for an elaboration. It took a moment to get one. "That can be your safe word."

"Red?" I repeated.

His hands curved under my body and lifted me from his lap as he stood. I swayed into his chest, my arms wrapping around his neck.

"We're not a true Dom and submissive," Gaven said. "There's trust in that relationship—I don't trust you." My heart slammed into my ribcage and I dipped my head. Of course, he didn't trust me. He had no reason to. I closed my eyes at those words, though, surprised by myself and how much they actually fucking hurt. "But I'm not a complete monster," he continued. "And if anything—I respect the unspoken contract, so you're right. From now on, you will have a safe word. You may use the word 'red' whenever you truly feel as if it's something you cannot handle."

"What if I say it and you don't stop?" I asked as he strode across the room and stopped at the side of the bed.

His blue eyes touched mine again as he eased me down and laid me on the mattress. My body compressed into the surface and I retracted my hands from his neck. "Go to sleep, Angel," Gaven finally said after what felt like forever.

He moved back, stepping away from the bed.

"I thought you were going to let me come?" *Was it over now?* I didn't understand.

"I did," he replied. "I allowed you to come while I watched. That was your reward for being so brave."

I sat up, but my fingers curled into fists. "What about you?" I asked, gesturing to where his cock still tented his pants.

"I'm always in control, Angel," Gaven replied. "Even of myself."

Before I could ask what the hell he meant by that —if that was an answer to my earlier question or a warning—he turned and left the room. My insides coiled and immediately retracted at the pressure against my ass and lower stomach. I jumped at the sensation. He'd left me, and he'd left the reminder of him behind—stretching my dark hole open, a constant sign of what was likely to come in the future.

Gaven claimed not to be a monster, but what else could he be but a cruel beast hell-bent on tearing me apart from the inside out to make me regret my actions?

Well, I wouldn't, I thought to myself. I regretted nothing. Not running. Not saving him. Not anything I'd done to survive while I'd been gone either.

I'd done it all and I hadn't broken from it.

From the shattered pieces of my life, I'd picked myself up and I'd fought on.

I wasn't weak. I wasn't without my intellect. And whether Gaven realized it or not, he wasn't completely in control. Not always. The second it slipped, I'd be there and I'd find my path to freedom. I'd done it before, and I could do it again.

12

GAVEN

Evangeline Price was in my head. A dangerous place to keep her, but she was there, nonetheless. More days passed and through her own merit—eating when she was ordered to, no more fits like before—she slowly earned privileges back. Sheets and a comforter for the nighttime. A nightgown—a thin one without underwear—that outlined her body perfectly as she stood by the window and watched the sunset each and every night.

She'd grown accustomed to the pear of anguish in her ass and had taken it splendidly again and again as I removed it for her to clean it and allow her breaks to wash and other things. After the third day of it being inserted, I decided that it was likely time for me to prepare her in other ways.

That decision was how we found ourselves at a standoff with her arms crossed over her chest as she glared at me with that spark of resistance in her eyes.

"No." She shook her head. "Gaven, I'm not doing it."

"It wasn't a request," I replied calmly as I held the package up. "We can either do this the hard way or the easy way. I assure you, it will all go much smoother if you simply give in."

"I can do it myself," she said, her face flushing as her eyes followed the package in my hand.

I shook my head. "You don't get to make that decision," I said.

"Gaven…" I should have punished her for her continued use of my name, but it was hard not to like the sound of it on her lips. In fact, I wanted to hear it more. I wanted to hear her scream it. "Please, it's humiliating. I've been good. I haven't tried to escape. I've eaten everything I've been given. Please, if you insist, I'll do it, but don't make me—"

Her little attempts at taking back control were amusing, but I wouldn't give in on this and she needed to know that. I gestured to the bathroom. "Come on now, love," I said. "If you're good for this, perhaps, I'll give you a reward."

"Will you let me out of this God-forsaken room?" she asked, eyeing the package before swapping to my face.

I arched a brow as she chewed on her lower lip. I already knew the answer to that. I had plans for her later this week, plans that would give her a bit more freedom than she was used to. If she took it as her reward, who was I to tell her otherwise?

"Perhaps," I hedged.

Her teeth sank deeper into her lower lip as her eyes danced from the package to my face and back again. Finally, she turned. Her shoulders slumped as she made her way into the bathroom and I knew I would have to come up with a better reward for such a good girl.

"Go to the sink and bend over," I ordered, watching her hips sway as she followed my commands.

Casting a look back at me, Angel complied. Her head dipped in front of the mirror as she bent over the sink and grabbed either side of the marble countertop. The sight of her rounded ass positioned out and tilted up in my direction made my insides churn with desire. I inhaled sharply and approached.

My fingers clenched around the package and I carefully set it down on the counter next to her before smoothing the flat of my palm over my wife's ass. "You've been behaving so well lately," I murmured as I reached between her cheeks and twisted the pear inserted into her tiny little hole.

The sound of her breath hitching echoed throughout the smooth walls of the bathroom's interior. It was like music to my fucking ears. I closed my eyes and relished in it before finishing the task of twisting the pear completely so that it closed on the inside and allowed me to pull it free.

A low moan rumbled up her throat, deeper than

her natural voice, and the sound shot straight to my dick as I slowly worked the smooth metal pear back and forth. I eased it out of her hole, listening to her keen and whimper as it stretched the tight ring of muscles back open. Finally, after several long seconds, it popped free and she sagged against the counter with another sigh—this one of relief.

Beginners often found the pear of anguish difficult to take, but I'd been kind enough to find one that was smaller than average. Though I was sure to my Angel, it probably hadn't felt like a kindness. Still, I enjoyed getting creative with my punishments for her. Deep down, I think she enjoyed it too.

I stroked her ass, cupping the mounds as I pulled her cheeks apart and stared down at her slightly open hole. "I bet it was uncomfortable to sleep in that," I said.

"No fucking kidding," she huffed.

A chuckle was drawn out of me at that. Rarely did I find amusement in anything, but this was why she was perfect for me. No matter how much I pushed her to the limits, Angel managed to overcome them each and every time. The day her father had offered her hand to me in marriage was the luckiest goddamn day of my life and she didn't even know it. What had started as nothing more than a tool to achieve my wildest dreams had strangely become something that I struggled day in and day out without.

Her. My wife. Angel.

"It'll be worth it in the end," I assured her,

moving a finger down closer to her hole. I circled it and she tightened all over again. "When I fuck this tight virgin ass of yours, you'll thank me for stretching you out first."

Her breathing hitched again as I played with her hole, rimming it with my finger before putting more pressure on it and sinking one digit deep. Dirty blonde hair slid over her back as her head popped up and she whimpered. There were filthy fucking noises that escaped her throat, but no resistance. Yes, she was getting used to this, just as I'd wanted.

I pushed a second finger into her ass and scissored them apart, causing her insides to tighten and clamp down around me as she expelled a harsh noise. Her hips shifted against me, feet moving restlessly. Laying one hand firmly at the small of her back, I held her in place and thrust my fingers into her asshole.

In the mirror, with Angel's face craning back, I could see the flash of white teeth as she gritted them and bore down on my fingers. Pain morphed into pleasure and surprise then, ultimately, shame. A pretty pink flush moved up her cheeks and her lips parted as she moaned low and long.

"That's it, baby," I urged. "You're taking my fingers so well. You know what comes next."

Her head dipped once more and her face was hidden from view as I pulled my fingers free and then moved to the side to wash my hands before picking up the package from earlier and ripping it open. The contents spilled out across the counter, making her jump slightly where she stood, still bent over, but she didn't lift her head. I smiled. What a nervous little girl.

Removing the small tube that came with the supplies. I snapped on the provided gloves and lubricated the end well before finishing the preparations. A moment later, I returned to Angel.

"Reach back," I ordered. "Hold yourself open for me."

"Do we really have to do this?" she whined.

I didn't speak and instead answered her by delivering a sharp slap to the side of her thigh. She yelped and immediately jumped back, her hand snagging on one asscheek and dragging it open for me.

"Good girl," I murmured as I set the end of the short nozzle to her hole and pressed it inside. She clenched around it and whimpered again. "This might feel cold." I compressed my fingers around the end of the tube and water washed into her insides.

Her gasping breaths filled the room and I stood there, watching as her dark hole contracted and released against the nozzle inside. This was an intimate act—cleaning out her insides for my use later. It was one I would've relished had we been more than the pretend Dom and submissive that we were acting as. This act would have been followed by trust and care, but it was now tinged with the reminder that she'd betrayed me and run away.

Instead of trusting me enough to tell me what

her sister had done—what she'd likely witnessed—Angel had done the one thing I thought we could avoid further. She'd fled, and she had yet to show any remorse. No, she didn't regret her actions, and neither of us could move forward until she did.

"It feels weird," she said, her cheek pressed to the counter as her fingers tightened against the cheek of her ass.

"You'll get used to it," I replied.

"I have to do this again?" Her head snapped up and she looked back, eyes wide.

I nodded as I squeezed the end again, sending a fresh wash of water into her ass. She groaned and lowered her head once more. "You're evil…" she complained.

My lips twitched. Only my wife could say such a thing and make it sound as if she were complaining about my socks being left out. I pressed and released the end of the enema until I was sure it was done, only then did I move forward and relieve her of the nozzle in her ass.

"Clench and keep it inside," I commanded.

"My stomach feels weird," she replied as I pulled it free, but she still did as I said.

"Give it a few minutes and then you can go to the bathroom," I said, moving to the side and cleaning up the supplies and torn package left behind.

Half an hour later, she was freshly cleaned—inside and out—wet from a recent shower and sitting on the bed as I towel-dried her hair with my shirt sleeves rolled up my forearms. Her head leaned to the side as her eyes slid shut. The few water droplets left behind smoothed over her bare breasts and between them to her hollowed stomach. My lips turned down at the reminder of how much weight she'd lost since I'd last seen her. Another check-up was likely in order.

My eyes scanned over to her forearm and it appeared that she had yet to notice the small cut there—and by now, it was practically healed completely. If she didn't realize yet that her body was no longer under the foul chemicals of birth control, then she would soon learn when my child was sitting inside of her belly.

I finished my task quickly and then set the towel to the side. Her eyes opened and flicked up to meet mine. A quiet beat passed between us. I wanted to order her to turn around and present her ass to me. I wanted to spank her fucking blood red and then take advantage of her now completely stretched and cleaned asshole. I wanted to be the monster she thought me as.

In vengeance. In betrayal. In hurt and pain.

I gritted my teeth and resisted the urge, instead choosing to give her a modicum of reprieve from me. "We're going out tonight," I stated.

Her eyes flared and she blinked up at me. "We as in … you and me?" she clarified.

I nodded, turning away from her angelic face as I strode across the room to the bathroom, where I'd left my jacket after I'd taken it off to help her into the shower. My sleeves were slightly damp, but I'd be changing anyway.

"I'll have a dress dropped off later," I said as I retrieved the coat and brought it into the room. "You'll put it on without complaint."

"IF it means getting out of this room," she replied. "I'll fucking crawl on the floor."

A wicked grin overtook me at that comment. "Is that so?" I tilted my head to the side.

She seemed to realize what she said—and *to whom* she'd said it. "I didn't mean that literally," she said quickly, but it was too late.

"I'll see you later tonight, love," I said with a devious smirk still on my face.

"Gaven, wait—" The mattress creaked as I heard her stand up behind me.

I stopped at the door, my hand on the knob. "That's not my name, Angel," I reminded her. "I've let you get away with a lot, but you should know that the more you resist calling me by my title, the more I'll have to punish you for it later."

There was silence, and then, "Yes … Master."

My insides cramped with pleasure. The feeling of it was so intense, it damn near sent me to my knees. By some sheer force of will, though, I remained standing. More than that, I found myself able to turn the knob and stride out of the room, closing and locking the door at my back. She'd never know what hearing that single breathy word from her did to me, and until she trusted me, she never would.

13
ANGEL

Master.

It took some getting used to, but every time the word left my lips, I couldn't deny the tingle it gave me, like a rush or a thrill that echoed deep in my core. Even, hours later, as I lay on the no longer bare mattress in the room I saw only as my prison cell, the reminder of it on my tongue made me think of him.

Footsteps stopped outside the locked door. I didn't even bother looking up until the sound of a key scratching in the hole on the other side alerted me to an intruder. I stood up as the door cracked open and instead of Gaven, as I'd come to expect, an older woman came in. Her gray hair was pulled back into a severe bun at the back of her head, and her simple black dress covered her from her collar to her thighs. If the long matching white apron wrapped around her waist hadn't told me that she was a maid, then the sensible and no-nonsense expression on her face would have.

She didn't blink at my nakedness and I didn't even remember the fact until she was already halfway into the room with the door shut once more. A flush stole over my cheeks and I crossed my arms over my breasts. Embarrassment rode me hard, but the woman didn't even bother to glance my way as she bustled into the room with a long white bag in hand—a hanger sticking out of the top side.

The older woman strode right past me and only stopped when she got to the bed and laid out the bag in her hands. As her wrinkled fingers moved for the zipper at the top of the bag, I edged towards her.

I contemplated asking her questions. Where was I? Were we still in New York? Somewhere else? How many men worked here? There was very little I'd managed to glean from the singular window the room boasted—just that we were far from any other buildings and that my room was high up—surrounded by trees.

As I approached, however, my gaze flickered to the cameras. It would be smarter to just let this woman do her job. There was no telling what kind of trouble I could get her into if I tried pulling her into my mess. So, instead, I diverted to the chair on the side and grabbed the single nightgown I'd been given. It wasn't much, but at least I could feel somewhat respectful of the older woman currently straightening the sheets around the bag she set down.

The woman didn't speak. Her eyes cut to me as I stepped up to her side and stared down at the bag's contents before she returned to her task. With deft movements, she yanked the zipper down and extracted a gown before laying it next to the bag on the bed. My eyes widened.

"Holy shit..." I murmured. Growing up as Raffaello Price's daughter, I'd been allowed more than my fair share of luxuries. I wasn't unaccustomed to priceless brand-name clothing and jewelry, but this gown was on another level. It looked like something that should have graced the body of a model strutting down a runway in fashion week.

The entire gown, from chest to hem was made up of a shimmering midnight blue fabric that glittered. It looked like diamonds had been crushed up and sewn into every inch of the surface and when I reached out and touched it, I found that it was as soft as silk, but didn't cling to the skin of my palm the same way silk would have.

I was so focused on the dress that I hardly noticed the maid turning for the door until the sound of it opening snagged my attention. Flipping around, I gaped as she bustled quickly out of the room and then returned a split second later, with several boxes stacked in her arms. The door shut behind her, and out of habit—I eyed it.

Soon, I promised myself silently. Soon, I'd escape, but first I had to glean some information from

Gaven. I had to make him think that I'd fallen into his trap and given up my freedom. He was still too suspicious. Even if his hands had become more gentle when he touched me, I had no doubt that it was all due to my seeming lack of resistance.

The woman grunted as she moved past me once more and dumped the boxes on the bed next to the dress she'd revealed. The labels on the tops of them made me wonder what the hell Gaven had planned for tonight. It was obviously something important if the evening gown, the Tiffany jewelry, and the Louboutin boxes were anything to go by.

She flipped it open, revealing striking, red-bottomed black heels. Wrinkled fingers flipped the flimsy white pages of packaging paper out of the way before retrieving the shoes and setting them next to the dress. Still, the woman didn't speak. Her lips remained firmly shut as she bustled about the bed and removed smaller jewelry boxes from on top of the larger ones. My mind spun.

I took a step back and then another and another until the backs of my legs hit the chair I'd pulled my nightdress from and I sank into it with a palm to my forehead. The woman worked with dizzying speed, setting all of the pieces I was to wear tonight out on the bed before grabbing up the now empty dress bag and the empty boxes and carting them out of the room.

There was little point in me trying to gain any information from this woman. She was obviously well-trained and had very little interest in me as she worked diligently. As she finished her job—several long minutes later—in setting out the gifts from my husband, she nodded my way and then disappeared the same way she'd come—right out the door.

When I was once again alone, I finally stood and moved back over to the bed to peruse the items I'd been given. The dress was alone—a clear indication that it wasn't a choice—but there were multiples of the other items. There were more shoes than the original pair I'd seen the maid pull out. Multiple pairs of Louboutin's, Manolo Blahniks, and more. There were boxes from Tiffany & Co., Cartier, and Harry Winston.

"Where the fuck is he taking me?" I wondered aloud.

The age-old adage 'curiosity killed the cat' repeated in my mind even as I spotted a white envelope that had been left behind. I picked it up and turned it over to find my name—Angel Price—written on the unmarred surface. I noticed that it had been written by hand rather than printed. Ripping the back open, I pulled the letter inside free and unfolded it.

They were instructions.

PUT ON THE DRESS. CHOOSE YOUR ACCESSORIES. *Neutral makeup. I'll pick you up at 7 p.m.*

— *Master*

. . .

He'd even signed the instructions with his title versus his name. For some reason, that made me smile. I set the envelope and letter of instruction back on the bed and reached for the dress. There was still no indication, however, of *where* we would be going, but that didn't stop the burst of excitement at the idea of getting out of this room, even if it was only for a single night.

I touched the fabric of the dress again, lifting it away from the bed and holding it in front of me. It was a deep-cut neckline with the sides cut out as well so that the length of the dress would sit upon my hips. I twisted and turned it, noticing the strips that were meant to hold it up at the back and nothing more. There was no bra or underwear set to go with it. Not shocking. I was coming to learn that Gaven Belmonte was even more of a pervert than I'd known him to be.

With a sigh, I slipped the nightgown over my head and went about pulling the dress on. The bottom half of the gown fell into place easily enough once it was over me, but the top sagged forward as I fumbled and struggled to weave the strips around my back to the front to keep it up. After several frustrating attempts and subsequent failures, I finally gave up and just tied the strings around my neck to keep it from falling down.

Gaven's request for neutral makeup was heeded —not that I really could do anything else with what I'd been given. There was a single palette of makeup was prepared amongst the boxes along with all of the tools necessary to do a full face. Normally, I'd prefer not to put on such makeup while wearing an obviously priceless dress for fear that I'd ruin it with some of the fallout, but unless I wanted to stand in the bathroom with my tits out then this was as good as it was going to get. Being forced to remain naked for so long certainly made me appreciate clothes more than I thought it would.

Standing in front of the mirror, I was reminded of what Gaven had done to me mere hours before. I shivered at the memory, a wash of both humiliation and arousal pooling low in my stomach. My ass felt strange now, after several days of stimulation. I'd never considered whether or not I'd like it back there, but after what Gaven had put me through—I knew one thing for certain.

I was just as much of a pervert as he was.

I finished preparing for Gaven's arrival in record time, and at 7 p.m. sharp, the doorknob turned and he appeared. My breath stopped. My heart leapt into my throat and I was frozen at the sight of him —dressed impeccably in a tailored black-on-black suit. He wore no tie, but he did wear a set of rings I'd never seen on him before—four of them across the knuckles of his right hand. The chunky silver caught my attention, distracting me briefly as he entered the room and came to stand before me.

"You look breathtaking." Gaven's words brought me back to reality and I jerked my gaze up to meet his as he stared back at me, his eyes shadowed with something surprising. Amusement. "Although…"

His hand came up and he fingered where I'd tied the strings of fabric at the back of the dress around my neck. "I don't think this is how it's meant to be worn." He undid the knot easily and the fabric covering my breasts fell forward.

My heart dropped away from my throat back into its place and began to pick up its pace, pounding against the inside of my chest as my nipples pebbled beneath his heated gaze.

"Turn." One word. An order. A command.

I followed, turning slowly until my back was to him. He reached around my body and gathered up the strips of fabric before sliding them up my arms. I glanced down as the upper folds of the gown came together and then I felt them tighten around my spine, crisscrossing over my shoulders and down my biceps—almost pinning my upper arms to my body. With a quick jerk, I gasped and nearly stumbled backwards into the hard body at my back.

"There," Gaven said, his voice low and full of gravel. "Now, turn back and let me look at you."

Pivoting on the heels I'd chosen—something I'd certainly gotten more used to in the last few years—I tipped my face upward. Pleasure filled Gaven's dark face. His eyes were locked on the way the strips of fabric cupped my breasts and pushed them up, creating a dip of cleavage.

My insides trembled as he leaned around me and looked across the mattress where the rest of the unused jewelry lay. "Just a few more details," he said, picking up something.

Cold metal touched my back, making me arch against him as he slipped what looked like a delicate-looking chain around my waist and then fastened a diamond broach into the middle of the dress, where the strips came together before the bottom half flowed down to the cutout sides at my hips. He clipped it into place before reaching for something else and holding it up to my neck.

Unable to look away from his eyes, I held perfectly still as he slid the choker necklace around my throat. "There, now you're perfect," he stated. "Go take a look."

Blinking as he moved away from me, I took wobbly steps towards the bathroom and entered to look at myself in the floor-to-ceiling mirror there. The sight of me made my mind catapult back in time. With my hair raised up into a messy, unsophisticated chignon—the best I could do with my limited supplies—it made the diamond choker against my throat stand out even more.

I had chosen not to wear a necklace simply because it reminded me of the first gift he'd ever given me. This necklace was ... strikingly similar. I reached up and touched it as a shadow appeared in the doorway behind me.

I loathed to admit it—even to myself—but the necklace felt right against my throat. It felt like coming home. Strange considering that I'd only known Gaven for a short time, had only considered his wife for a single night, before it'd all blown up in my face.

As if he could sense the dark turn of my thoughts, Gaven approached and settled a hand on my shoulder. The contrast of his broad, scarred palm on my skin was evident. He maintained the same air as he had five years ago. Strong. Competent. Intimidating.

My eyes met Gaven's in the mirror, and my heartbeat thundered in my ears. His hungry gaze moved down my body in the reflection. Heat rose to my skin. I swallowed roughly. He was a formidable figure at my back.

"Do you think you're ready?" he asked.

I doubted I'd ever be ready for the insanity he constantly pushed me into, but I had to play by his rules if I had any chance of surviving. Turning to face him, I lifted a hand and he took it.

My answer, when it came, was just as much a lie as it had been the night we married. "I do."

14

ANGEL

"Where are you taking me?" I had gained very little information from the walk from the bedroom out to the limo. I turned my head up to the sky, noting that the sun was already falling behind a long line of trees. Warm air touched my skin, a gentle breeze lifting the strands of my hair as I was hurried along. The first breath of fresh air felt like a Godsend, but at the same time, I felt too rushed to actually fucking enjoy it.

Glancing back over my shoulder, I finally got an actual look at where I'd been imprisoned for the last several days. The place that I'd been kept in was obviously a large manor house—not unlike the one where I'd been raised. The face of the mansion had four large columns at the entrance, each one wrapped with what looked like perfectly gardened ivy. There were even flowers. A strange detail, in my opinion, considering I didn't expect Gaven to have a gardener. How long was he planning on keeping me here? Did he expect that it was something I would like?

Gaven stopped at the back of the limo and opened the door without waiting for one of the men who trailed out after us. They were all in black suits, but surprisingly, they hung back. In the past, whenever I'd gone anywhere with my father, they'd been practically on top of us. These realizations, however, didn't have much time to percolate in my head as I was urged into the vehicle and, soon after, joined by Gaven. The door shut, and the car pulled away from the building.

As the man in the front drove down a long, winding pathway, I peered out of the tinted backseat windows, watching trees pass by until we slowed at a set of iron gates. The limo paused and after a few moments, the gates opened and we were on our way once again.

"Would you like a drink?" Gaven offered instead of answering my question. He reached down into the side of the back of the limo and pressed a button. The soft whirr of a secret compartment opening and raising up sounded in the otherwise quiet interior of the vehicle. I silently watched as Gaven pulled two crystal glasses out of the revealed compartment and uncapped a matching decanter full of amber liquid.

"I'll take a drink if you tell me where we're going," I replied.

Gaven didn't immediately respond as he filled the glasses and then passed one to me. A large part of me didn't expect an answer, but surprisingly, Gaven gave me something. "A club opening," he finally said.

"A club opening?" I repeated his words as I put the glass to my lips and took a long sip. The spicy brandy seared over my tongue and I winced as I swallowed. Contrarily, however, Gaven gulped down half of the glass without batting an eyelash.

"Yes." Even though his glass wasn't empty, he took the decanter again and refilled it nearly to the brim.

I nodded to it. "Are you feeling stressed about something?" I prompted.

Cool, steel blue eyes met mine. "If I am, will you offer to relax me?"

My fingers clenched around the glass in my hand. "Perhaps." Being the object of his obsession and the craving for his relaxation and release would be good, I told myself. Getting close to him was a good goal because it would soon have him letting his guard down just enough for me to actually get away.

My offer had nothing to do with the pulse of heat between my legs. Nothing at all.

That was yet another lie I told myself and hoped I would one day believe.

Gaven sipped his drink a bit more slowly the second time around as the driver steered the limo away from what looked like a tree-infested country-side and closer to an urban setting. Several minutes passed in silence and it wasn't until my glass and Gaven's were both empty that he spoke again.

"Come here, Angel." His order was soft, spoken with a clear, succinct inflection—though not angry or otherwise strained.

I stared back at him for a long moment, wondering if I should or not. What would it help? But then again, what would it hurt? Gingerly, I laid the glass into one of the cup holders and scooted across the leather seat towards him. Without missing a beat, Gaven reached over and grasped me around my waist, lifting me up and depositing me in his lap in a fast movement that sent my head tumbling face-first into a gloriously confused state.

What game was he playing at?

After locking me up for so long, could I trust that this was simply a reward from him for being so well behaved, or was there something more he was planning? Something worse in store?

"You said you'd like to relieve me of my stress, yes?" he asked.

With my legs thrown together across both of his thighs and one of my arms draped around the back of his shoulders, I had nowhere else to look but directly at him. "If you think I can…" I hedged.

Gaven's hand moved down, dropping from my face to my throat. One of his arms banded around my back—the heat of him burning into my skin in a way I thought was only possible with actual fire. The other, however, was given free rein as he trained it across my thighs and over the openings in the sides of my dress and further up to my chest and neck.

"I know you can relax me, Angel," he replied.

"The question is—if you're willing to give me what I need, what else are you willing to give me?"

I swallowed. "What do you want?"

His lashes lifted. "The truth." As quickly as I'd found myself leaning towards him, my body filling with warmth and arousal, just as those words slammed into my ears, a wave of cold swept it all back up again and drifted the cozy, lustful hunger away. He gripped me tight when I swayed back and attempted to leave his lap to move back to my earlier seat.

"Don't run away now," Gaven said. "Not when I've got you where I want you."

"We're in a moving vehicle," I reminded him, though the words came out less than firm.

His lips twitched before slowly curving up on both sides. A smiling Gaven was an odd thing. I'd seen him smile before, but it always preceded him doing something absolutely disgraceful—usually to me. As if trained for this very moment, my heart began pounding against my ribcage.

"Don't think about that now," he urged, his head dipping until I felt the heat of his mouth against the side of my throat. "Spread your legs for me." His hand moved lower, spreading over my stomach, warming me through the fabric of my dress.

"I can't," I muttered. "The dress…"

Without hesitation, he gripped the delicate, expensive fabric and began dragging it up in handfuls. When the end of the dress was in my lap and my legs were bare, his hands finally reached my flesh.

"Now…" Gaven gripped my thigh and dragged it wide, sliding over until I was sat, facing away from him, with my legs spread open and his chest against my spine. "Give me something to make me relax, *wife*."

There's only one person getting to relax and it certainly wasn't me because as my legs were hooked on either side of his thighs, his hands were given the freedom to roam, and roam, they did. A gasp escaped from between my lips as he slowly worked his way inward, kneading my thighs on the outside and then the delicate inner flesh before he slid upward, towards my pussy.

My back arched and a whimper left me. Against the strips over my chest, I felt my nipples tighten. Fire danced around inside of me, just waiting to be unleashed, but still he kept himself contained. His fingers played against my lips, stroking up one side and the other and then back down, but he never ventured inward. He never slid them against my clit or thrust them inside of me.

He knew what he was doing. He was driving me to the brink of insanity and he was getting off on it. It was fucking maddening.

"Do you want something, love?" he asked after several long moments like that with me spread out in front of him and his hands all but fucking my cunt.

"*Yes*." I hissed, my hips bucking upward as his

fingers damn near grazed my clit once more. I was fucking soaked.

"I want to do something else," he said with a chuckle. "Do you trust me?"

I stiffened at that question, the untamed arousal that had been swimming through me seconds before fading, even if only marginally. I bit down on my lip. "Don't ask me that, Gaven," I cautioned him. He wouldn't like the answer.

Silence met my warning, then my body was being lifted. A squeak left my throat as I was deposited, face down, over his lap and the back of my dress was flipped up until my ass was bare. A shark slap echoed through the back of the limo and I gasped as heat burned through my backside.

"What—"

"Don't speak." Gaven's low growl had me shutting right the fuck up. It was two words, but the voice in which they were spoken sounded more like that of a barely leashed animal. It was bitter. Angry. "From here until we get to the club, keep your mouth shut," Gaven said. "You may moan, you may cry, but I want no words to come from your lying little lips, Angel."

"Gaven, I—"

Slap.

His hand disappeared from my ass only to come down hard on the sensitive flesh. I screamed at the first strike. The second one was less surprising but still just as harsh. Gaven's palm came down hard, again and again. He spanked me, lighting my ass on fire with his discipline.

I keened, arching up as he pinned me down across his lap. Fresh pain blistered my ass and I breathed low, hissing through my teeth as I waited for it to change. I knew it would, given time.

"Do. Not. Speak." Gaven's words were clipped and quick. "That was your last warning. The next time you open your mouth and try to talk without permission, I'll fuck your ass right here and have you walking into that club with my cum dripping out of it, do you understand? Nod once if you do."

I nodded and then hung my head over the side of his lap as I breathed quickly through my teeth. I could feel his gaze eating up my body. I was pinned by something far larger and more dangerous than myself. A lion and his prey. As if he heard my inner thoughts, too, Gaven's hand slid over my ass, smoothing across the area he'd just abused.

My hands clenched into fists as I remained perched, precariously, on his lap with my naked ass in the air—waiting for whatever he decided to do to it. "This is going to hurt." That was the only indication I got—the only warning. A split second later, his forearm pressed across the small of my back harder than ever and his hand came down.

Slap.

Slap.

Slap.

My legs shot back as I automatically kicked out, the pain a shock to my entire system. I thought he was hitting me hard before. That was nothing compared to this. My nails sank into his pants legs. Gasping, I clutched onto him to keep from shooting off of his lap.

Ten passed. Twenty. Thirty. I lost count. He never struck the same place twice in a row, but instead layered his spanks all over my ass and then even down to my upper thighs until I felt as if my flesh was burning. I squirmed on his thighs, my pussy juices leaking down my legs despite myself.

A gasp broke free and then another and another until I was panting with each slap. Still, he continued, spanking me far past what I thought I could handle and then into a hazy fog where the pain disappeared. It faded and something warm took its place. He struck my ass on both sides, peppering my flesh with his hand until I swore it was already painted red.

Tears threatened the corners of my eyes, and as shame poured through me, I tucked my head against the seat on the other side of his lap. I didn't want to cry. Not here. Not now. And certainly not in front of him. Regardless of what I wanted, I could feel them —the tears—as they leaked down the sides of my face, dripping onto the seat.

He began gently stroking his fingertips over my bare ass cheeks before he struck me again, and another line of wetness dripped down my inner thigh. A shudder moved through me. My legs lowered to the ground and Gaven's other arm settled over my upper back, keeping me stable against him. I blinked back the wetness at the backs of my eyes.

I closed my eyes as the realization hit me. This was what he needed—someone else's pain. *My* pain. It not only turned him on, but also gave him some sick sense of relief. Shame. Embarrassment. Humiliation. All of it drove through me.

Why? Because I liked it. Because despite the wrongness of it all, there was no denying that if Gaven were to reach between my legs and slip his fingers up my cunt, he'd find me open and wanting. I was fucking soaked. My nipples were hard. I craved—I wanted—something harder, darker. *More.*

I wanted him to hurt me.

I sobbed against Gaven and the limo seat at the suddenness of my understanding, and only then did I feel his hands pause. "Angel?"

I whimpered, and when I wanted to speak, I sealed my mouth shut and even went so far as to bite down on my lower lip. "Angel, speak," Gaven ordered. "Where are you at? Do you need to use your safe word?"

I shook my head against his thigh. No. Safe wording was the last thing I needed—or maybe it wasn't. I wasn't scared of him right now, but I was scared of myself. Of what I was feeling and of what I wanted him to do to me.

Gaven flipped me over and I must have been a mess if the way his brows rose at my expression was any indication. He lifted me up and settled me into his lap in much the same way I'd been originally, both legs closed and slung over his as he wrapped one arm around my back and cradled me against his chest.

"Are you okay?" he asked.

I nodded quickly as I sniffed hard and turned, burying my face against his chest. His wide palm smoothed up my back, the warmth against my skin welcomed. "What's wrong?" he asked. "Tell me."

"Can I?" I asked, rubbing my hand under my nose and thankful it came away clean. At least I wasn't fucking snotting everywhere.

His hand cupped my face and directed my eyes up to meet his. "Yes," he said. "You have permission. Tell me why you're crying."

I sniffed. Hard. "I thought you liked it when I cried."

One thick dark blonde brow arched. "I do," he agreed, "but only when I think we're both enjoying it. These…" He drifted off as he caught one of the still lingering tears as it slid down my cheek and then stroked it away with his finger. "These don't seem like you're enjoying it."

I shook my head. "I am," I murmured, dipping my head and pulling my gaze away from his. "That's why I'm crying."

"You're crying because you're enjoying it?"

I nodded. "It's fucked up." I laughed, but the sound was anything but amused. His fingers found my chin once more and forced my head back up.

"Look at me." His command sent shivers down my spine and I was compelled to lift my gaze to his for the second time. "There's nothing wrong about enjoying sex with your husband, Angel."

I bit down on my lower lip before releasing it with a sigh. I resisted the urge to turn my face away, but as the words came out of my lips, I found my eyes drifting to a point over his shoulder—fixating on a piece of the car's interior.

"You know that our marriage is irrelevant now," I said. "Besides, it wasn't something I wanted. I never wanted to be married to you, and you trying to force me back into it isn't going to make that any less true."

Despite the honesty of the words, they burned like acid against my tongue as I spoke them. It felt wrong to dig that particular knife between us, creating a crack that had been mending over the last few days, but it was necessary. I was getting too comfortable, too close to him again, which wasn't conducive to remembering my ultimate goal—to get away and gain my freedom.

I needed to recall that Gaven wasn't treating me gently because he cared. He just wanted me back because I was a way to ensure that he still had a claim to the Price Empire—even if his wife was the supposed murderer of the last head of the family. This was the mafia … I wondered if that even mattered. It had to, or else Jackie wouldn't have framed me for it.

I kept my face averted to remain steadfast in my resolve. Gaven was quiet for a long time. So long, in fact, that I wondered if the limo would arrive at whatever club we were intended for before he spoke again. Alas, that wasn't the case. As his hands clenched on my bare thighs and my pussy still leaked over his lap, Gaven tucked his head against my throat and pressed an open-mouthed kiss to the hollow—right above where the diamond choker he'd given me again sat.

I blinked and then swayed back, looking down at him in shock. "Didn't you hear me?" I demanded. "I said—"

His hand came up and covered my mouth as those midnight eyes of his glittered dangerously. "I heard you, *wife*." He growled that last word, as if he needed to emphasize what I kept denying him. "There's no need for you to repeat yourself."

I pulled my head away from his hand. "Then why—"

"Because," he said, interrupting me for a second time, "it doesn't matter where our story started, only where it's going."

I wanted to ask him where he could possibly see our story going, but as I parted my lips—the question hanging on the tip of my tongue—I felt the limo decelerate, and I looked up, noticing that we'd entered a much more urban area. I blinked as Gaven didn't give me time to formulate a response and instead quickly and firmly deposited me on the seat next to him before he began to adjust my dress.

He pulled the hem down and urged me to shift so that I could also pull the back down . He said nothing else as the driver pulled up to the curb. I

glanced out of the window, taking in the tall buildings that surrounded us, practically blocking out the
sky. They were all massive brick buildings. The limo
came to a stop, and when I expected someone to
immediately open the back door, instead, I heard a
knock and it wasn't opened until Gaven called out.

Moving first, Gaven stepped out and then
reached back, bending down so that I could see his
face—and the dark look in his eyes as he held his
hand out for me to take. "Take my hand, Angel."
That was a command if I'd ever heard one and for
some reason, it was the easiest one to follow.

My fingers slipped through his and he curled
them around mine as he tugged and helped me out
of the back of the limo. I wobbled slightly on the
heels, but his arm came around my waist and held
me steady. With the get-up I was wearing, I'd half
expected a team of paparazzi to approach us.
Instead, when I peered back, all I saw was a long
line of limos, SUVs, and town cars waiting to drop
off their charges at the front of what looked like an
industrial building.

"You said this was a club?" I clarified as I gazed
up at the flat face of the building. "What kind of
club?"

There was nothing particularly insightful about
the outward appearance of the building. For the first
several floors there were few windows, and what few
there were seemed to be covered in thick black
coating that made it impossible to see inside. Only
when I craned my neck back and saw the upper

floors did the windows look a little more normal. What was with that?

Gaven's arm tightened around my waist, and he urged me forward towards the waiting doors as our limo pulled away and the next car took its place. "You'll see soon enough," he promised.

For some reason that lack of answer made me nervous, but a club was just a club, right? There shouldn't be anything to fear.

Then again ... this *was* Gaven Belmonte: hitman, mafia king, and a bloody obsessive husband. There was really no telling what kind of deviant things he had planned for me tonight.

15

ANGEL

While the exterior of the building left a lot to be desired in comparison to the luxury of our attire, it became apparent why we were dressed so ostentatiously as soon as we stepped through the guarded front doors.

Low, sensual lights illuminated the large open room, casting the other club goers in a soft glow. Music filled the room, rhythmic and deep. It seemed to lull those in attendance to sway and move, showcasing high-end jewelry glimmering on women's necks, ears, and hands, while peeks of gold glinted on men's wrists whenever the designer suit jackets and underlying dress shirt sleeves shifted just enough.

Glancing around the room was enough to tell me that even the decor and furnishings within the nightclub were no doubt expensive. Deep red velvet couches, silken drapes hung from the ceiling, and crystal and gold embellishments covered the walls and ceiling in detailed designs. It wasn't anything out of the ordinary for me to see, having been born a Price Family princess, but what caught my attention and triggered my internal alarm bells was the undercurrent of excited tension that seemed to plague the guests as they mingled.

"Come," Gaven instructed, his hand practically burning my skin from where it rested on my lower back. My husband guided me through the room, greeting various people with a respectful nod or minute smirk on his lips. Implications and questions whirled in my mind as he began to slow near a small group of people—three men and two women—all conversing in hushed tones that were lost amongst the music.

When they noticed our approach though, conversation ceased, and their focus turned to us. I'd been in enough uncomfortable situations now that the fresh, probing gazes that zeroed in on me didn't make me shift nervously. I tamped that shit down, and thankfully, the inspection only lasted a few brief moments before the tallest of the group, a man with inky black hair and tanned skin, reached out to shake Gaven's hand.

"Gaven," he greeted in a steady but friendly tone, "it's been too long."

Without hesitating, Gaven gripped the outstretched hand, echoing a similar sentiment at the man. "That it has, Ian, but all seems to be going well for you and the others. How is Miss Perelli, or should I say Mrs.?" I didn't need to look up to see the knowing grin on his face; it was blatantly apparent in his tone, but neither the man—Ian—nor the others seemed bothered by it.

"She's only a Perelli by blood, man. She's got a new last name now ... well,"—he chuckled—"a few of them. She's doing very well, though. Who is this?" With that, all the focus was on me again.

"This is my wife, Evangeline. Angel, these are some of my friends," Gaven introduced, gesturing to each person. "Ian Marshall, Jensen Travis, and Archer Petrov. These two ladies are Katerina Markovski and Genevieve Durand."

Jensen and Archer stood closer to Ian, obviously deferring to him as they cut looks his way before returning their attention to Gaven and me. Genevieve and Katerina both stood against a small, round cocktail table, casually leaning into the stand as they kept their eyes on first me and then Gaven. Crystal glasses glimmered in the light as they absently swirled their wine while the men had foregone any sort of drink.

"Nice to meet you," I said, nodding to the group.

Katerina and Genevieve smiled my way but offered no more greeting than that. The man Gaven had pointed out as Archer grinned and lifted his palm in a wave while Jensen merely nodded.

Once I was introduced and the typical pleasantries exchanged, I was more than content to stand silently and observe the group. The more I knew, the better I would be in the long run. Any snippet of information could be of use for escape. As I listened, though, I found the more they conversed, the less I truly understood. I couldn't help but wonder just who they were to Gaven. He'd called them friends? But did a man like Gaven even have friends?

Perhaps they were partners. Or as close as one could come to having business partners in this life. Clients? Did they have their own criminal enterprises? It wouldn't surprise me. I recognized the name Perelli from my time living with my father. What had happened to the head of the family, Jason, had spread like wildfire not long before my nuptials.

My eyes scanned to the women Gaven had introduced. What were Katerina and Genevieve to Gaven? They were both beautiful women after all, with long, well-shaped legs and curves for days. Both wore makeup that only accented their already naturally pretty features, from their eyelashes to their fuller lips.

A sharp, ugly ache burned deep within my chest at the thought of either of the two women having shared Gaven's bed in the last five years I'd been on the run. Before the idea could take root further, I shoved it away, refusing to allow even the tiniest hint of jealousy to simmer in my gut. It didn't matter if Gaven had had others. I'd left, and I hadn't ever expected him to stay abstinent. Then again, if I was to linger and a woman thought he was for the taking … that would be an entirely different matter.

I shook my head at that thought. Perhaps Gaven's obsession was rubbing off on me. If we'd been together longer, I might have been even crazier than I was now just thinking of tearing into these unsuspecting women for imagined slights and desires over *my* husband.

As if the cruel twist of fate that were my rioting emotions had conjured the darkest villain of my past, a shimmer of something caught my peripheral attention. I turned and spotted expertly styled dark tresses, a cruel slash of a scowl, and a stern brown gaze. I froze against Gaven's side.

No. There was no fucking way. There was only one I knew who looked like an avenging, *raging* devil disguised as an angel carved out of cold-hearted stone in such a manner.

Jackie. My sister.

"Angel?" Gaven's call was ignored as I searched the room for the woman. Just as quickly as she had seemed to appear, though, she was gone. I scanned the crowd again. There was no sign of her.

Had I imagined it? Maybe being out in the open with Gaven like this was making me paranoid. Still … I couldn't shake the feeling of something wrong in my gut. Nor the feeling of eyes on my back.

"Darling." I startled when Gaven murmured in my ear, closer this time and with far more force. I cursed myself silently for my lack of awareness in my bout of alarm.

"Yes … Sir?" My reply only wavered for a split second when his gaze darkened momentarily, knowing right now was absolutely *not* the place to push him. Especially as my ass continued to throb when I shifted and moved or when my dress brushed over the still reddened flesh.

It seemed as if I read him correctly because the warning glimmer in his expression shifted to a brief show of pride. "Everything alright?"

Of course, he realized something was off despite my best attempts to mask it. He was nothing if not infinitely cognizant of everything around him, including me.

"I'm fine." I hesitated for a moment, unsure if I should say something about what I had thought I'd seen, but I didn't want to go back to that room and lose the first night out in God knew how fucking long. Instead, I settled on, "I just need to use the ladies' room."

Icy blue eyes scanned my face for a brief moment, but I held my expression as calm as possible, my cheeks heating only slightly at the intensity and heat of his gaze. I had no doubt if he wanted, he would eat me up right then in there, crowd be damned.

"Of course." Gaven looked over his shoulder, nodding at two men who had been standing by the wall since we'd arrived. I blinked, not having realized that the guards were Gaven's and not the clubs when they moved away from the gilded wall panel.

"Here, let me show you," Katerina interjected with a polite smile, waiting until Gaven had nodded his permission before she guided me away from the group. It was tense and awkward as we slipped between small, gathered crowds of men and women dressed to impress and practically oozing riches and power.

Only when we reached a small hall off the main room did she speak. "There's no need to worry," she said with a light chuckle.

Jerking my head, I looked over at the petite blond, who even in her heels only came up to my chin. "Worry about what?" I feigned ignorance.

"About Gaven and his … potential *connections* to Gen and I." The statement was simple, said in a way that made it sound like she was talking about the weather or reading items off a grocery list, not discussing my husband's potential affairs in our time apart.

"Oh?" Acid crawled up my throat, choking me as we neared the door labeled 'Ladies' in an elegant script.

She offered me a gentle smile. "Gaven's not the kind of man to stray from a commitment once he's made it." Her eyes panned down as she looked at me and then back up to my face. "Certainly not from a beautiful dove such as yourself." I blinked at the odd compliment. Had it been a compliment? "Straying from a wife that looks like you would be such a waste," she continued, "and Gaven has never been one to waste anything."

No, he just wanted to put me in a gilded cage, I thought bitterly. Yet, the unwanted jealousy that had plagued me faded at her words.

"And if it makes you feel any better, Gen and I are quite happily exclusive with one another." Her words penetrated my thick skull and my eyes widened. Oh … *oh!*

"I didn't realize," I said. "I'm sorry if my expression—"

Katerina shook her head and cut me off. "Like I said, don't worry about it. I, like your husband, don't like to share." The unexpected remark mixed with the sharp and hungry expression earned a surprised laugh from me, and I found the tension within me eased ever so slightly.

"Would you like for me to wait for you?" she asked, redirecting the conversation.

Glancing at the door, I made a quick decision. "No, but thank you. I'll be able to find my way back and if anyone tries to bother me, I'm sure my husband's men will be more than capable." Thankfully, Katerina didn't push or, even worse, try to come with me. As soon as she began to walk away, I slipped into the bathroom quietly, plans already forming before the door had even closed.

This was the first time I'd been away from Gaven in an unsecured location in days. This might be my only chance to find an escape route. I took a look around the bathroom. It was big and long— definitely built more for aesthetics than utility. I started down the row of stalls, noting that only a few were closed and locked. It was a surprise, considering how many people had been in the club. Perhaps there were more bathrooms further into the club or this was a private one. Whatever the case, it was big enough that I turned at the end of the row of stalls, half expecting there to be another hidden entrance.

The room, instead, led to a small sitting area with lounge couches and large illuminated mirrors. A couple of women stood there, touching up their makeup in front of the mirror, using small compacts as they waited patiently for their friends to finish. Across from the mirrors were the sinks where two attendants stood, one with a stack of freshly clean towels and the other holding a basket of what looked like various things—extra makeup wipes, one-use mascara wands, mini bottles etcetera.

Passing a cursory glance over the lot, I nodded to the attendants as I wandered toward the sitting room and grabbed a small blotting tissue from the array of items stored in clear or gold containers, using it as a disguise to look around. Unfortunately for me, there were no windows and therefore no back exit out of the bathroom.

That must have been why I'd been led to this one specifically and why I'd been let away from Gaven. Even now, he was careful not to give me too much space. My half-formed plans crumbled as I balled the tissue paper in my fist and tossed it into the trash can with an internal curse.

I took a deep breath and headed back out into the hall. The two men who had followed me from Gaven's side were still there. Neither said a word, but as I moved away from the bathroom, I felt their presence following me. I wove through the club and crowd, heading back the same way I'd come, back to where Gaven was now standing alone at the cocktail table, a crystal tumbler in his hand while an untouched glass of wine waited for me.

Gaven's stance didn't change as I approached, but once I was within view, his gaze settled on me. Goosebumps flared to life as his eyes moved from my face downward. I swallowed, my mouth and throat suddenly dry, and reached for the waiting glass of wine. Lifting it to my lips, I took a long swallow and paused, pulling it back with a frown. It was sweeter than expected, with a hint of fruit and dark chocolate undertone. A slightly biting, but delicious aftertaste coated my tongue.

"Do you like it?" he asked.

"It's … different," I murmured, staring at the deep red color. "What kind of wine is this?"

When I glanced back at him, I saw the curve of his lips shift upward as he put his own glass to his mouth and downed it in one go. He didn't answer until he'd set the glass down.

"Pomegranate wine," he said. "It's unique. I thought you'd like the taste."

I did, but that wasn't what bothered me. An old thought resurfaced—one I hadn't remembered until this moment. Five years ago, when I'd been younger and far more naive and unaware of just how wicked the world truly was, I'd looked at Gaven and seen him as some sort of Hades, God of the Underworld.

Of all the things for him to give me. Pomegranate wine felt like some sort of unspoken trick— and I'd already had a taste. It was too late now.

Neither one of us spoke for what felt like an eternity—instead choosing to stand there, side by side, watching the world around us. The heat of Gaven's body drew nearer, making me shiver, but not in an unexpected way. He watched me cautiously but also expectantly. I only realized why when I finished my glass of wine. He'd been waiting for me.

"It's time, Angel." The low tone of Gaven's voice rolled over me, causing my nipples to pebble beneath the fabric of my dress as I set the expensive crystal glass back on the soft, cream-colored tablecloth.

"Time for what?" I inquired, taking the hand he offered me without complaint or resistance.

Instead of answering though, the infuriating man only smirked as he led me further into the club. We bypassed several women in evening gowns and men in tuxedos to a darkened hall hidden behind silken curtains and guarded by two more men. They nodded to Gaven and held open the drapery for us to pass. There was a small bank of decorative double doors. The doors slid open to reveal elevators. It wasn't until we stepped into the small space that I realized Gaven's two guards weren't coming along.

"Gaven?"

He didn't answer.

"Sir?"

Still no answer. *Where the fuck were we going?* I tried to pull my hand from his, but his grip only tightened.

"There's no need to be frightened, Angel," he finally said. Somehow, it didn't put me at ease.

The elevator doors closed and the lift descended. The lights on the button were only lit on one thing —a small circle with the center labeled "D."

When the elevator stopped, the doors didn't immediately open. Gaven released my hand to lean forward. I watched as he typed a code into the keypad. A soft ding followed by a click sounded, and the doors opened to display quite a different scene than upstairs.

My mouth dropped open. I didn't move, not until Gaven's hand found my back and he urged me forward. My heartbeat increased as he led me into what appeared to be a lobby with doors and windows into further spaces. It was what I saw beyond those windows and doors that made a fresh wave of fiery heat pass through me. Naked bodies writhing in leather-bound manacles. Chains. Whips. Men and women, bare-chested or completely nude. The sounds of moans filtered through the thin glass as well as the slapping of flesh against flesh echoed like an unholy symphony.

"You brought me to a *sex club*?" I hissed under my breath, low enough that no one could hear.

Gaven settled a dark look on me. "This is the club opening, Angel," he whispered, his voice darkening. "Behave."

I snapped my lips shut as a short woman approached, dressed in little more than straps of leather and lace. "Welcome, Mr. Belmonte, we hope you and your companion enjoy yourselves this evening," she greeted, holding out a small package. "These are the items you requested, Sir."

Sir? I narrowed my gaze on her, but she didn't acknowledge me.

"Thank you. That'll be all," Gaven replied. The woman nodded and stepped back into the club, turning and striding away. I watched her go with a mixture of irritation and mild curiosity.

Before I could ask what that had been about, Gaven pivoted to face me once more and pressed the package into my arms. I stared down at it before lifting my gaze to his. "Through that door is the ladies' locker room," he said, gesturing to one of the only doors beyond this lobby that wasn't glass. "Go put this on and meet me back out here."

I had no clue what he'd been expecting when bringing me here, but I'd already known that Gaven's sexual preferences were anything but normal. With one last look out into the main floor of the new version of the club, I turned on my heel and strode for the door in question. Dread filled the pit in my stomach. Would this be the night that I truly learned what kind of things he expected? Was there more than what I'd already experienced? I didn't know, but I had a feeling that I would find out soon.

16

ANGEL

The package was light in my hands as I pushed open the door to the locker room. We were in a sex club, so I had an idea of what it could be. Memories of the first gifts Gaven had ever given me flashed in my mind. The diamond choker that I'd taken apart and sold to start my new life. The barely there scrap of lace. A hidden twist within the delicate fabric. The vibrating bullet that had been sewn into the underwear was nothing in comparison to the torturous wand he'd hooked to the chair he'd strapped me to days ago. Another shiver wracked my frame at the mere thought of that pleasure and pain-filled piece of furniture before I shoved it away, refusing to dwell on it any longer.

I moved further into the locker room. It was different from a normal locker room, more luxurious and elegant. That made sense, I supposed. I strode across the dark marble floors that glinted in the soft glow of the crystal chandeliers, past red velvet couches and loungers towards the rows and rows of dark gray lockers towards the back. There were several closed and locked, so I stepped up to one of the open ones and set the package on the shelf inside, gripping either side as I tried to take a breath.

Seconds stretched into minutes as I tried to calm my racing heart. My eyes gradually rose back to the package. If I delayed for too long, I had no doubt that Gaven himself would come in to find me and I … didn't want to find out what would happen if he did that. Taking the package down from the shelf, I slipped a finger into one folded end and peeled the thick paper back.

Inside, I found a lace bra and underwear set. The cups of the bra were delicate and so white, they were practically translucent. I ran my fingers down them and then, almost hopefully, lifted them out of the wrapping, but nope … there was nothing else inside. I wasn't stupid. The color had been fucking strategic— as if Gaven was reminding me of what my place was supposed to be. Of what we were supposed to be.

Damn him. It worked. I pictured myself wearing this. I pictured his ring back on my finger—the ring that I hadn't taken with me when I'd run after Jackie's betrayal.

With a sigh, I placed the package back on the shelf and reached back to undo the clasp keeping my zipper shut at my back. Before I could start undressing, however, the door opened and footsteps entered the locker room. I turned abruptly, faced with a woman who was slightly shorter than me in a slinky black gown and wavy golden hair with streaks of brown in it.

She didn't look familiar, but when she spotted me, her eyes lit up and she smiled widely. She switched directions from the couches to me. "Hi, you must be Evangeline," she greeted me warmly.

"Hello?" I stared at her. "Yes, I'm … erm, just call me Angel. Who are you?"

"Ah, it seems my husbands forgot to tell you to expect me." *Had she said* husbands? *As in multiple?* "I'm America."

"America…?"

She chuckled. "I'm married to the big guy who owns this place," she said. "I don't know if you remember, but I actually met you a long time ago—our dads worked together."

"Who was your dad?"

"Jason Perelli." I watched the play of emotions over her face—from happy to sour the second she spoke the man's name. No love lost there, I supposed. That wasn't uncommon in mafia families, though. My father had been an anomaly. The name, however, was familiar. It clicked.

"Ian Marshall? That's your husband?" I bypassed mentioning her father—rumor had it that she'd had him killed a few years ago, so I doubted it'd be a good topic to discuss.

"Yes, Ian's my husband," she said, her smile returning. "So are Archer and Jensen—sorta. Ian's my husband on paper, but in my heart, I'm married to all of them."

"Wow." It was all I could say. "You have a big heart."

She laughed at that and moved down the line to another locker—one of the closed ones. "What can I say, my heart is probably as big as their dicks," she replied, pausing as her locker swung open. She looked back at me. "And just in case you're wondering—they're fucking huge and even better, they know how to use them right."

"Congratulations," I said, and meant it. "Big dicks are one thing, but knowing how to use them … that's rare." I finally reached back to unclasp and unzip my dress as America began to undress as well.

"I know it isn't traditional, or 'normal,' but who really is in this life?"

Ice coated my veins. Traditional. *Normal*. The thing I'd tried my damnedest to obtain for myself before it all went to hell. No, Gaven and I weren't normal, not by a long shot. I doubted we ever truly would be.

"Angel?" America's voice penetrated the dark turn that had clouded my thoughts, her tone suggesting that she'd said my name more than once.

When I looked over at her, I was startled to see her already out of her gown and into what could only be described as fetish wear. Her stomach, which hadn't been super obvious beneath her evening gown, protruded slightly, softly rounded in a way that made me realize she was pregnant. I gaped at her. "Are you alright?" she asked.

I hadn't been alright since the moment I'd laid eyes on Gaven Belmonte. Instead, though, I lied. "Yes, of course," I said, pulling my gaze away from her stomach. Her breasts were covered in a deep red bra that looked like shells of lace similar to the bra I'd been given. Red straps crisscrossed over her ribcage and the matching underwear she wore barely covered her pussy. Heat stole over my cheeks and I hurriedly turned away.

"Mare! I see you've met Gaven's wife," Katerina's familiar tone called out. She was followed closely by her lover, Genevieve, the other woman I'd met upstairs.

"Yes, we were just talking," America—*Mare*—replied. I held the fabric of my dress against my front, frowning as I debated on how to change without them seeing me. Though I supposed if I was going to walk out there in little more than see-through scraps of nothing, it didn't really matter, did it?

Genevieve moved to my side, opening a locker between Mare and me. "Are you excited, Mrs. Belmonte?" she asked curiously as Katerina and America talked.

"Please," I said, "call me Angel. And … I suppose so." Excited wasn't the word I would have used, but these women likely weren't aware of the details of my current relationship with Gaven. A marriage … I wouldn't call it. More like captive and captor. For now, anyway.

Genevieve gave me a knowing look. "First time?"

I nodded.

"Don't worry, it might be a bit overwhelming at first, but I'm sure you'll find something you enjoy. I doubt Mr. Belmonte would have brought you here if you weren't in a similar relationship as the rest of us."

Similar? Maybe. With stipulations. This was Gaven's kink, and though I remembered how it had made me feel—curious, aroused, hungry for more— a real BDSM relationship would have required trust and understanding, and that, we didn't have.

"If you're uncomfortable, just tell Gaven," Mare piped up. "That's what safe words are for."

I sighed and let my gown go. It drifted down the length of my body until it hit the floor at my feet. "You're right," I lied easily. Though Gaven had said I could use the term 'red' before, as it stood, I doubted that would always stop him, not when he was holding me against my will and I was still seeking out any chance I could to get away.

"She's right," Genevieve agreed. "You'll have that safety net then if you get pushed too far." Genevieve and Katerina went about undressing at their own lockers, stripping out of their gowns as if it were the most ordinary thing in the world.

I reached for the underwear Gaven had provided and slipped them up my legs. Why wasn't I surprised to find it a thong? The strings settled on my hips and I leaned down to pick up the evening gown I'd worn before hanging it up in the locker before me. As the other women talked amongst each other, I finished pulling on the bra and clipping it into place. The lace cups molded to my breasts and when I looked down, I was shocked to see that my nipples were clearly outlined.

I wasn't the naive little virgin Gaven had first married, but being naked with him and within the confines of my prison—my *room*—was different from being naked in front of strangers. I'd never expected him to be so comfortable forcing me to walk around a club in little more than … *this.*

Shaking away the thoughts, I continued to take off the jewelry I'd worn with the dress and set it inside the locker. Hesitating on the collar, I decided to leave it. If luck was with me, I wouldn't be back for the rest. It was time for me to make my way out to him. I inhaled and turned towards the other women who were all waiting.

"Ready?" Mare asked.

I nodded. As ready as I'd ever be. She offered a kind smile and together, the four of us headed for the exit.

Though I had arrived at the club with no bra and no underwear, now that was all I wore. My breasts were squeezed into the tightest, smallest bra I'd ever seen in my life. Yet, the binding around my middle was perfectly comfortable. The fabric was soft and expensive. Even the lace that covered the cups at the front wasn't scratchy or itchy. The problem was the cups themselves.

I normally preferred full coverage, but these were less than half-cups. They hefted my breasts up, my nipples on the verge of being revealed and the color definitely visible through the thin fabric as they cupped and squeezed me. Already, I knew where this night was bound to lead with this outfit dragged off of me and Gaven's cock thrusting inside me. Just thinking about it made my insides clench. The tiny triangle of lace that covered my pussy did positively nothing to ease my nerves.

"Wait!" Mare called out as I moved towards them and I paused, frowning, thinking I'd forgotten something. She gestured down to my heels. "You might want to ditch those, or you're going to have a really uncomfortable night."

I glanced down and then at the rest of their feet. Katerina was the only one still in heels; Genevieve and Mare were both barefoot. That seemed unsanitary. I grimaced, and Mare must have seen the disgust on my expression because she snickered lightly and shook her head as I lifted my gaze back to hers.

"Don't worry," she said, practically reading my mind. "The floors are clean. Ian would never let me walk around in my condition unless everything was pristine."

"I agree with her," Katerina said. "Most subs prefer to go heel-less, unless their Doms request otherwise. If Gaven didn't specifically tell you to keep them on, I think it's fair for you to take them off."

Gaven hadn't said anything about footwear. So, I quickly turned back and divested myself of the heels, setting them inside the locker before relocking it and joining the group at the entrance.

"Better?" Genevieve asked.

"Actually, yeah," I said, wiggling my toes. "Much."

She nodded and leaned into Katerina. "Kat prefers to keep them on, but she's nice to me."

Katerina smiled gently down at Genevieve who, without her own heels, was several inches shorter. "I'd rather see you bound in other ways, pet," she said.

I turned my gaze away, feeling like I was peeking into something intimate.

Mare stepped up next to me. "Many subs go barefoot," she said. "Doms seem to like the idea of their submissives being in as little as possible, but them being fully clothed—something about the power dynamic."

"It also saves time of having to take them off during play," Katerina explained. "Most who wear them either aren't comfortable being barefoot or wear them for their roles or kinks." It didn't take a genius to notice the smirk and heated gaze aimed toward Genevieve. "If you have any questions or want to talk about the club and lifestyle more, or just to chat, feel free to ask."

"That's kind of you," I said, doubtful that I'd ever actually get that opportunity. "Thanks."

Katerina nodded and then waved. "Bye, Mare. Bye, Evangeline, it was wonderful to meet you," she said as she and Genevieve disappeared from the locker room.

Mare glanced at me. "Are you ready?" she asked.

"That's the second time you've asked me that," I pointed out.

"Yeah, I suppose it is," she agreed. "You lied the first time, though."

I blinked and then met her gaze. Light brown irises flecked in gold swarmed with warmth and understanding. Perhaps it was because of her connection to me—the Perellis and the Prices—but I had a feeling she knew more about my situation with Gaven than she let on.

"It's just the first time I've ever actually done this," I said. "The nerves … you know how it is." I silently prayed she wouldn't press.

She looked over at me with a contemplative expression on her face. The silence between us was stifling, but I didn't try to break it, unsure of what was running through her mind.

"You and Gaven aren't the typical Dom and sub, are you?" she finally asked.

The question was blunt and it proved my theory. Maybe I was losing my edge. I'd thought I'd mastered the lessons my friend had taught me. Two years ago, Scarlett had done her best to teach me every trick she'd had when we'd met in Italy. As one of the best thieves in the world, she understood the importance of masking one's emotions. Now, though, I felt them overwhelming me, spilling out. Ever since Gaven had swept me off the streets and kidnapped me, I'd found that hard-won control slipping more and more.

"Don't worry, it isn't obvious. Not to anyone else, anyways," Mare explained when I didn't immediately reply. "But I see a bit of myself in you, Angel."

"Do you?" I didn't know what to say to that.

"I do, and if you want my advice … mafia princess to mafia princess? Stop trying to escape it." I stiffened at that, but she continued. "We were both forced into a life we never wanted, but there's really no point in running from it. You are who you are, and I am who I am. When I stopped running … when I turned around and finally fought back, I found it easier to live. Gaven Belmonte's reputation precedes him, so if I'd have to guess he's a bit more … hands-on than my men were, but still … trust me. When you finally accept it, the rest comes naturally."

There was a rawness to her words. Gently said, but still, they cut me deep and flayed me open, revealing things I'd rather have kept hidden. My fears. My anxiety. My anger.

Stop running?

Stop trying to get away?

I couldn't do that … could I? It was as if all of my darkest secrets I'd tried to hold onto, to hide within the depths of my soul, had tumbled out for all to see ... or at least for this woman to see.

"If you ever need help, I'm sure you have a friend or two—you don't seem the type to go solo for long. And even if you don't, you can always ask for me. I'd be happy to help you, Angel. There should be more of us in this world willing to lend a hand. It's lonely and dark enough as it is." Before I could even respond, America stepped back and left the locker room with one final smile.

I wasn't sure how long I stood there, ruminating over what she said, but for the first time in what felt like forever, I didn't feel quite so alone. I wondered if she was right. Could I reach out and ask for help? Would that make a difference? I bit my lip. I still hesitated about opening up to Gaven and telling him the truth. It would put him in unnecessary danger.

For now, though, I didn't need to think about it. All I needed to do was walk out there and present myself to my Dom.

To Gaven ... my Master.

17
GAVEN

I needed a drink. Something strong, I realized as I watched Angel leave and head towards the locker room, her hips swaying in that natural way of hers. She likely didn't even realize it, but every move she made was goddamn sensual. *Had it been a mistake to bring her here?*

Almost as soon as I'd had that thought, the object of my need came to me. A rather young-looking waitress stopped at my side, her eyes carefully downcast and the plain collar around her throat marking her as a submissive in service to the club. She offered a drink from her tray and I took one.

Ian had certainly gone all out for the opening of the ground-level club and the Dungeon below it. Nodding to the young woman, I picked up one of the crystal glasses.

"Thank you."

"You're welcome, Sir," the sub said before

moving away, carrying her tray over to another set of men lingering nearby. There were plenty of us—men and women, Doms and Dommes—waiting for their submissives to emerge before they entered the Dungeon's play floor.

Carrying the glass of amber-colored liquid closer to the main lobby of Ian's new club, I peered through the glass to the inside and lifted the alcohol to my lips. Spiced whiskey touched my tongue and burned easily down my throat. All out, indeed.

I sighed and took a seat in one of the plush armchairs nearby. A familiar face walked out of the nearby elevators and moved in the direction of the locker room. I smiled as I spotted America, previously Perelli, now Marshall-Travis-Petrov, as she strode into the women's locker room.

As if I'd conjured the men, Ian, Archer, and Jensen stepped out of the elevator behind her. Archer was the first to spot me as he lifted his hand in greeting.

"Gaven!" he called as he turned and headed right for me—stopping only when the waitress moved towards them. He grinned down at her and took a drink for himself before finishing the journey. He dropped down into the chair to my right and blew out a breath. "What a night, right?"

Above, he'd been far more reserved. Then again, the crowd allowed down here was undoubtedly closer and far more vetted than those above. "That it is," I said.

Ian and Jensen approached, though a bit slower,

now with drinks in their hands as well. They, too, took their seats across from us. "Congratulations again," I said. "The club above was marvelous, but the Dungeon ... well, you have reason to be proud, Ian."

"We all do," Ian replied. "Archer designed the security system himself and Jensen helped build it." I wasn't surprised by that information—the three of them always had a hand in the work of the others. They moved as a unit, following his lead, but no one was ever left behind or out. It came as no surprise to me when they'd eventually married the same woman.

Now they were the proud owners of not only one of the most infamous Mafia Princesses of our world but the most exclusive BDSM Dungeon in New York. I looked around again. Only the richest and those vetted through multitudes of background checks and interviews who lived the lifestyle were allowed access to this level. This was a place outside of the wars and secrets, and there was no reason to hide connections and emotions when dealing with friends or business partners.

"So, how's it been going with you?" Archer asked, sipping his drink and leaning back against the dark cushions of his chair.

"Good," I stated. Silence met my response. Jensen and Archer both raised a brow in question before exchanging a speaking glance.

"And...?" Archer prodded.

"And nothing," I said. I sipped my drink,

reveling in the slight burn as it trailed down my throat and warmed my chest.

"That's bullshit," Jensen commented. "Don't think we didn't see the way you and your *wife* were acting around each other."

Archer eyed me but didn't say anything in response to his friend's comments. Despite their closeness, I was appreciative that he hadn't spread the word when I'd asked for his assistance. Though, I knew the circumstances would have been different had it affected their little group.

"Yes, well, there were complications, but she's back," I said. "And she's not leaving again." Not if I had to break her fucking legs and tie her to the end of my bed.

"I take it she's … resistant?" Ian asked.

"She'll learn." I drained my glass, the alcohol burning worse this time. Either it had gotten stronger or the direction of this conversation was quickly souring my mood.

"Women are strange creatures," Ian said with a knowing look. "When you think you're teaching them a lesson they need to learn to survive, they'll turn around and you'll find yourself the one learning something new."

It occurred to me that for these three men, America had also run from them. I leaned forward in my seat, setting my now empty glass on the table between us. "She's more stubborn than she used to be," I admitted.

That earned a snort from Archer and an even

higher brow raise from Jensen. "Are you really that surprised?" Archer asked.

Before I could reply, Ian spoke. "She's been away," he said. "She evaded you for years; from what I recall, she did a pretty decent job of it if it took you this long to capture her."

I thought of that. Yes, it had been particularly difficult to track Angel down. Every time I thought I'd gotten close, she'd disappear again. I was always one step behind, and I wasn't used to that. When she'd run headfirst into me on that sidewalk the week before, I'd felt such a rush—both of relief and of triumph. Never before had the high of a victory felt so intense. It'd meant more than any job I'd ever managed to accomplish. It was a different kind of achievement.

"You just need to fuck her and make her come," Jensen said. "Once a woman realizes she can't get what you can give her anywhere else, she'll stay put."

I arched a brow. "That worked well for you the first time, did it?"

He blinked, long and slow, and then, it hit him. Red filled his face and he sat up. "Now, listen here, motherfucker, I didn't—"

"That's enough, Jensen," Ian snapped, cutting off his friend. "Don't let him rile you up."

"Yeah." Archer laughed. "It's too easy to do anyway." And as if Ian and Archer had planned it, Jensen turned and laid into his friend. Archer listened to Jensen rant and ramble, leaving Ian and me to consider each other in near silence.

"I have no intention of prying into your relationship with your wife, Gaven," he said after a beat, "but a man has to wonder—with you bringing her here—if you're not hoping to control her with the lifestyle."

"She's mine to do with what I wish," I replied coolly.

Ian's dark gaze leveled with mine. Cold. Impenetrable. He reminded me, more than Archer or Jensen, of myself—certainly, at least, a younger version of myself. "You've always treated the women you've taken as subs rather coldly, Gaven," he said. "Archer tells me that this is the first time he's ever seen you so … emotional."

My upper lip curled back. "I am *not* emotional." The very notion was sickening.

Ian didn't blink. His gaze didn't waver. Fuck. Perhaps I'd been too strong. I forced my shoulders to loosen and relaxed into the cushioned chair. "For a man who was disinterested in prying, you certainly like to comment on things that are none of your business," I said.

"I'm merely making observations, Mr. Belmonte," Ian replied. "If they resonate with you —you're right, that's none of my business."

Damn him, I thought. "What do you want to know?" I demanded. The air grew thick, and I noted that the conversation between Jensen and

Archer had fallen to the wayside. The two of them were watching us without pretense. It was blatant.

Ian leaned forward, setting his glass on the table alongside my empty one before bracing both elbows onto his knees. "Why did you introduce her to the lifestyle, never mind bring her here, if you weren't in a true Dom/sub relationship? You know damn fucking well how it's viewed to mistreat such a relationsh—"

"The relationship I have with my wife is none of your concern, Marshall," I murmured, cutting him off with a lethal tone, but he was unrepentant.

Archer tilted his head in my direction. "Ian's right, Gaven," he said. "What's stopping the two of you from turning this ... *facade*"—he waved his free hand at the last word as he continued—"into an actual Dom/sub relationship?"

"I can't very well trust a wife who betrays her husband the same night she took vows to obey him," I ground out.

Archer whistled. "Well, damn, I didn't realize she ran that fast," he said. Of course not, I'd kept it under wraps.

"What did you do to scare her off?" Jensen asked. "You did make her come, right? The G-spot is—"

"I'm well aware of a woman's G-spot, Jensen Travis," I growled.

Ian hummed deep in his throat, finally sitting back in his seat, his hard expression shifting to be contemplative and thoughtful as he ran his hand over his jaw. Jensen and Archer both eased, visibly relaxing back into their respective seats. Their words had turned teasing rather than offensively tense.

"So, why do you think she's fighting you now?" Ian asked.

That was the great question, wasn't it? *Why?*

I had my suspicions. Angel would never have hurt her father, even after being forced to marry a man such as myself. And it wasn't that she *couldn't*—I had a feeling Angel was vicious enough when pushed to do what was needed ... including killing— but she had loved Raffaello Price. Even I, who had never once ever thought of my family or known such love from a parent, saw that.

Her sister, the conniving bitch that she was, on the other hand, held no such sentiments. She'd been jealous—was still jealous as far as I could tell. Jacquelina Price had quickly shown her viciousness and sly nature following her father's demise. She had snatched up the Price Family out from under me with gleeful intent. She most *definitely* would have had the balls to murder her father, force her sister out, and ostracize one of the most sought-after hitmen in her plot to take over the family business.

"Gaven?" Archer's voice cut into my thoughts, and I looked back at the three waiting men.

"There's more at stake, more players in the game than just Angel and I," I stated simply, not wanting to give away too much information.

Ian smirked, knowing full well what I was doing. "The option is simple then, isn't it?" It was my turn to raise a brow at his cryptic bullshit question. His cruel grin widened when he saw my confusion. "Eliminate whatever it is that's in the way, whatever —or whoever—drove her away in the first place. Then, she'll have no need to keep running, no?"

Mimicking how Ian had sunk back into his chair, I mulled his words over. I had always planned on going after Jacquelina. She had to pay for what she'd done to Raffaello as well as Evangeline. Then there was the fact that she stood in the way of what was rightfully mine. The Price Empire.

Perhaps all I needed to do now was push up my timeline. Maybe then Angel would feel safe enough to come to me on her own, to reveal her truth, to stay.

"*Mare.*" My attention was dragged from my thoughts by Ian's tone. I looked up as Ian stood. Archer and Jensen followed. I trailed their focus to the front of the ladies' locker room to see that America had emerged and was smiling as she walked towards us.

As she approached, her attention switched from her men to me. Her eyes tightened and her lips firmed. "Gaven."

"America."

"You know what you're supposed to call Doms in the club, Mare," Ian chastised her.

America flushed and then nodded my way. "My apologies, Sir. It's good to see you."

"You look beautiful, America." Though she looked nothing like my Angel, I meant the words.

America was a stunning woman. Slightly rounded, curvy, with long light brown strands framing her face down to her tits. I paused as I stopped on her stomach and the obvious bump there.

"Thank you, Sir," America replied.

"Let's go," Jensen said, moving for her as he wrapped an arm around her side. "I have a scene I want to do with you, sweetheart."

"A scene?"

"A naughty scene," Archer replied, bending against her opposite side and pressing a kiss to her shoulder.

Ian lingered a moment behind as Archer and Jensen led their wife away. "If you want what we have, Gaven," he said, capturing my attention once more, "I suggest you talk to your wife. Find out the truth. Someone has to give in first. Trust is the only way a relationship such as the one you're seeking works."

"I've never needed to trust my subs before—not the same way I have to trust Angel," I admitted. "Our relationship is different."

"Because it's forever," he replied. Then, without another word, he followed after his men and his wife, and I was left to wait for the woman I'd sent in long before America.

I sighed and stared down at my empty glass. No doubt she was waiting for a plethora of reasons— was she looking for an exit? Or was she nervous about stepping out dressed in the clothes I'd requested? I had to admit that the idea of parading my wife around the Dungeon in lingerie was both a source of pained jealousy and prideful arousal.

I wanted others to see her, to want her, and to know that if they ever dared to touch her, I would slice their insides open and hang them with their own intestines.

A beat passed and just when I was sure I'd have to send one of the waitresses in to retrieve her, the door finally opened. I stood up as a flash of white appeared. My mouth went dry. Angel stepped out of the locker room and scanned the lobby—seeking me out.

Her eyes found mine, and I felt my cock twitch in my pants. Fuck, but she was delicious. The perfect bundle of innocent white. She wasn't innocent anymore, though. I knew that. She wasn't the same woman I'd married, but that didn't mean we couldn't pretend sometimes.

I was so much older than her, and even if half a decade had passed since I'd last seen her as the virginal young woman forced to marry a man eighteen years her senior, I had to at least acknowledge that she had matured. As she moved towards me, her hips swaying, the white strings of her thong tightening on her sides with each step, I had to stop myself from coming in my pants like an untried youth.

She didn't stop until she stood before me, her face tilted up to reveal the light pink shade that was spread over her cheeks. Embarrassment? I smiled. I liked that hint of humiliation she felt. I knew that if

I were to put my fingers between her thighs she wouldn't be nearly as shy as she appeared. She'd be wet and ready for the taking.

"You look beautiful, *wife*," I murmured. A man passed, a young redhead on his arm. Despite that, his attention strayed and lingered on Angel's ass. A bolt of rage struck me. At the same time, another feeling rose from the depths. Pride. Possessiveness. He could look, but he could never have what was always meant to be mine.

I stepped forward until my front was right against hers. Her lashes lowered as I wrapped a hand around the back of her neck and brought her face into my chest. This stubborn, feisty woman was *mine*. Tonight, I intended to show her just how much she was missing when she ran ... and just how much she would crave me going forward for the rest of our married life.

Because Angel was tied to me, now and forever.

'Til death would we part.

18

ANGEL

The music filtering out from hidden speakers was low and pulsating. It was sensual, a deep rhythmic beat without lyrics meant to enhance the listener's volatile emotions or … in this case, lust.

I was practically twitching with awareness as I entered the main club. I should have known Gaven wouldn't let me out of my cage without an agenda. The man was nothing if not a wicked pervert. The moans. The gasps. The pain-filled and pleasure-filled screams of release. Just the sound of it, combined with the people's voices in the room, put me on edge, reminding me of the limo ride here.

As if he could sense that, Gaven's hand came down on my back, his fingertips brushing lightly along my spine, making me stiffen. "Something the matter, darling?" he asked, though his tone was a bit taunting.

Was he trying to make me uncomfortable? I tipped my head back and looked up into his face, but like always, he seemed to have the majority of his emotions hidden. Well, I wouldn't give him the satisfaction of my discomfort. He'd learn that his precious wife was a new woman—a different woman.

"Of course not," I lied, offering him a small smile. "Thank you for bringing me out tonight, Ga —Master." I quickly corrected myself, mindful of our location and just what that phrase meant to him here.

Here, in this club, he was the Master and I was the slave.

Gaven's gaze narrowed on my face. "Shall we take a look around?" Though it was phrased as a question, it was evident by the way he took my arm without waiting for a response that he didn't expect an answer.

I didn't fight it. Instead, I glided gracefully alongside him, allowing Gaven to take the lead as I perused the area in search of an escape. I couldn't do so right now, but there was no telling if—later—I might get an opportunity. I'd have to take any chance I could get.

The further we traveled into the club's main floor and the further away from his friends we went, the darker the scenes got. Women chained to walls as their male counterparts stood at their backs. Sometimes, a man would stand back and cast a particularly evil-looking whip against their spines, eliciting shrieks of pain. Occasionally, we'd pass by a darker alcove and a man would be much closer with a naked woman bent over various objects— wooden spanking benches, leather couches, and more—as they took them in quick, animalistic thrusts.

My lips twisted with distaste. I'd learned a thing or two in the last few years about the world of bondage and submission, and if this is what Gaven expected from me, he could fucking forget it. Though there were plenty of ways to live the life-style of BDSM, I'd found one and only one that had ever appealed to me, that had actually made sense.

A Dom who didn't understand where the true control lay wasn't a Dom at all, but an abuser. In the end, it was the submissive who gave them permission.

Curiosity had me cutting my gaze to the man at my side as his fingers moved up and down my back almost absently, as if he couldn't stop himself from touching me. At first, I didn't think he'd noticed, but after several moments, the corner of his lips twitched. And without looking at me, he spoke. "Something you'd like to say, Angel?"

I blinked. "Maybe."

Finally, he turned his attention to me and I was settled with the full brunt of his midnight blue eyes. "Nervous?" he asked.

I shook my head. "Just … confused."

He arched a single dark brow. "About what?"

I gestured to the room around us and he urged me back against a wall, out of the way and far from the small crowd of onlookers taking in the scenes—a mixture of Dommes and Doms and their submis-sives all taking in the sights of exhibitionism.

"On what you expect from me," I said blatantly. There was no point in prevaricating with him, not anymore. He wouldn't get what he wanted from me, not for long, but that didn't mean I wasn't curious.

Gaven turned and crowded me closer to the wall. Over his shoulder, my attention caught on a particular Dom, showing off for the onlookers. The man, though obviously well-muscled, had several scars lingering across his bare chest and back. They whitened against his otherwise tanned skin, rippling with the movements as he reared back and struck the woman he had tied against the wall.

She was a larger woman anchored with ropes, her hands tied above her head as a dark-haired man at her back took a nine-tailed whip to her spine. She cried out when he struck her again, her body shaking with the blow. A moment later, though, a low moan reverberated from her throat, letting everyone know she wasn't just in pain. She found pleasure in the sensation as well.

Gaven's fingers found my chin and directed my eyes back to him. "See something you like?" he asked. His low voice rumbled through my ears as he bent his head close to mine.

I swallowed against a suddenly dry throat. Whips and kinks aside, he could absolutely talk me straight into an orgasm with that silky, deep voice of his. Despite the fact that I'd been forced to be in his space for the last several days, somehow, now that I was out of his home and surrounded by others, I realized just how close we were.

His body heat practically burned into me where he leaned close. It'd been so long since I'd been in his presence. Five long, lonely years. Somehow, I was reminded of that now that we were in front of something that appeared so brutal. We'd only known each other a short time. Hell, we'd only been married for a single night before I'd left him and gone on the run, yet somehow, he'd become quite a big part of my past. The greater piece of my motivation to run from Jackie hadn't been what she'd done to our father but what she'd threatened to do to him. My father was gone, and there was no changing that fact, but Gaven didn't have to suffer just because of Jackie's hatred for me.

I shook my head, unintentionally dislodging his grip. Gaven's hand moved downward instead, and this time his palm touched my throat. My breathing hitched and the sole of my attention slammed into his face.

"There we go," Gaven said. "Keep your eyes on me, love. Now, answer my question. Do you see something you like?"

"It looks painful," I replied.

"Pain is in the eye of the beholder," he said. "Everyone's tolerance is different."

I swallowed beneath the grasp of his hand. Though he was careful, his grip still pressed the necklace around my neck harder into my flesh. "You never answered my question," I switched topics. "What do you want from me, Master?"

"I want what I was promised," Gaven said, his gaze darkening the longer he stared at me. "I want my wife. On her knees. On her back. Legs splayed. I want her to give me everything. Her very soul as well as her submission."

The hand around my throat constricted as he spoke. The tips of his fingers squeezed the sides of my neck, causing me to shiver. How the hell could he have such mastery over my body without even trying? It wasn't fair.

"I don't like pain," I reminded him. "If that's the kind of—"

He interrupted my words with a low, rumbling chuckle. "Oh, baby," he said, shaking his head, "if you think you don't like pain, then you don't know yourself. You don't like pain, you fucking love it."

My lips parted and irritation flashed through me. "No, I don't—"

His hand clamped down harder on my throat, cutting me off. Blood rushed through my veins as he tightened, squeezing impossibly hard until the world began to fade—black encroaching on the edges of my vision. I gasped for breath, and my hands came up, locking against his forearm.

"Do you remember how I took your virginity, Angel?" he whispered against the side of my face. "How I wrapped my tie around your throat and tied your legs open for my fist? How I fucked you with my hand, adding finger after finger until your tight, virgin little pussy took it all?"

I tried to shake my head, but his grip was too much. I couldn't breathe. Yet, below, I felt the stirring of my insides as my pussy gushed with wetness. Heated humiliation burned through my flesh, lighting me up from the inside. I closed my eyes against his expression.

"No, no, no," Gaven tsked at me. "Open your eyes, Angel. Look at me when I'm talking to you."

Choking, still unable to breathe, my lashes lifted and my gaze met his. He smiled. Smugly. Wickedly. The way a cruel master would. "There she is," he said. "My pretty little bride. My lying little slut."

Shame. Humiliation. Degradation. I felt it all.

His chest brushed against my breasts as they were plumped up between us. His free hand trailed over my body, running up my side until he lifted one in his palm. More darkness spread into me. His hand relaxed, releasing me briefly—just enough for me to gulp down a breath of air—before tightening all over again. A strained whimper emerged as he pressed his thumb over one hardened nipple.

"You look at the people in this club like they're monsters," he said, his voice quiet. "Because you see me as a monster, and though I am—there's no denying that—the truth is that these people aren't nearly as wicked as you see them. Look over my shoulder at the man whipping his submissive."

His grip eased enough for me to breathe. I sucked down breath after breath and adjusted my eyes, refocusing over his shoulder as he'd told me to. "I don't want to be whipped," I snapped, coughing slightly.

Gaven's low laugh was enticing. Fuck him, but it was sexy. "That's not why I asked you to look, love," he said. "If you'll look closer—she's not being whipped bloody. In fact, her Dominant is taking quite good care of her."

The two of us were slightly towards the back, but still close enough to see everything with an unobstructed view.

"Do you see the way she shakes and trembles?" he prompted. I hesitated, cutting my eyes to his and then back before nodding. The warmth of his body against mine was driving me close to the edge of sanity.

"The lines on her back are red—slightly raised, but her Dominant is obviously well versed in the art of whipping. Her skin hasn't been split open at all. The marks he puts on her tonight won't scar. They won't even last. They'll make her sore, and they might even bruise—but that pain will only be a reminder of how she gave herself to her Master and he gave her what she needed. She *trusts* him. Implicitly."

Now, my attention was squarely on the man holding me captive. "And that's what you want from me?" I asked. "My trust?"

People wanted companionship. They wanted safety. Not Gaven Belmonte. He wanted control. He wanted mastery over everyone and everything; I was

no different. I had to remind myself of that. The
brief night we'd been married was so long ago now.
I'd been young and stupid and resigned to my fate.
Now, I had a taste of freedom—limited, though it
was since it was always with the knowledge that I
had to stay a step ahead of my sister—but I'd grown
accustomed to it, nonetheless.

"I want it all," Gaven said. "Your trust and the
truth."

I stiffened at that. Tell him the truth about the
night my father was murdered? That would only
paint a target on his back. I shook my head.

Gaven quietly leaned away from me, and as his
gaze burned into my face, I shifted my eyes downward. Away. It was the only thing I could think to
do. If eyes were the windows to the soul, then I
didn't want him to see into mine.

"Perhaps this isn't the best place for a conversation this important," he said after a beat.

A moment later, his body was removed from
mine with startling speed. My hand was captured in
his, and his fingers moved down to lock around my
wrist, a manacle of strength. He yanked me away
from the wall and started walking. Unable to free
myself, I was forced to follow—rushing to keep up
with his long gait, which he only eased after a
moment as if realizing how difficult it was for me.

Gaven found one of the men from before—Ian,
I recalled the man's name—standing in front of
another scene. My eyes trailed to the small stage that
had been set up and I found America on her knees

with a cushion beneath her as her long golden hair trailed in various shades of blonde and brown intertwined down her back. One man stood before her, his leather pants undone and his cock proudly straining as he held it out to her. Another man was stationed behind her with a light flogger.

"I'd like to reserve one of your private rooms tonight," Gaven said to Ian, drawing my attention back to him.

I glanced up and then switched from him to Ian as the second man looked my way. Automatically, my gaze turned down. "That can be arranged," Ian replied. "Any particular play?"

"I assume they're all equipped with the usual?" Gaven asked.

"Of course, anything special will need to be ordered," Ian replied.

"That'll do."

Even with my face turned down, I heard the sound of the flogger slapping flesh and America's low, rumbling moan of pleasure, muffled by something in her mouth. I was heating up inside. My stomach churned at the noise. I shifted on my feet.

"I assume this is a punishment?" Ian's voice lifted in questioning. Whatever Gaven said in response was swallowed up by the sounds of America's scene.

I lifted my gaze and turned my head back towards the stage, catching it just as the man at her back hit her again with the flogger. Pink welts lifted along her back, but she didn't appear to slow her sucking down at all as she took the man standing in front of her in her mouth, down to the hilt, with his hand at the back of her skull.

I saw it, but in my head, I switched positions. Both the man standing in front of her and behind her became someone else. Gaven. And America herself, she became me. I remembered what it had felt like to have Gaven in that position. Holding me against his groin as he fucked my throat raw. I shivered as my insides contracted with need.

In the years since, I'd never even tried to find another who could make me feel the way he did. His grip on my wrist tightened and he tugged lightly, distracting me enough that I shifted my gaze to his.

Dark eyes met mine and then softened. "This way, Angel," he said.

I blinked, so overwhelmed by my body's sensations that I barely understood him. It didn't matter though, because I didn't need to understand to be led by him. Gaven pulled me along, leaving behind America's scene and the dungeon's main floor as we headed for a darkened hallway lit only by scones on the wall next to each door.

I swallowed when we stopped in front of one of them and he lifted a card I hadn't realized he'd had in his hand to unlock it. Ian must have given it to him. I didn't notice because I'd been so focused on America's scene, and now ... there would be a scene of my own. Just like I wanted. Only this one would be private, and perhaps that was for the best. Because as Gaven yanked me inside and the door swung shut behind us, I felt my heart rate pick up speed and my pussy pulse with need.

He said he wanted a private conversation, but this room was not meant for conversation. There was only one thing it was meant for. Sex.

Disgustingly filthy, kink-filled sex.

19
ANGEL

Once inside, I took a look around the room. It was decorated in masculine tones: dark red wood, a four-poster bed, and a thick dark carpet under my feet. There were no windows, but cushions were everywhere. All over the bed and scattered at the end in a decorative array on the floor around a big trunk. My breathing hitched as I scanned the space across from the bed and found the 'usual' equipment Gaven had mentioned.

Apparently, 'usual' equipment meant a leather spanking bench and restraints hung on the wall. The restraints themselves were leather and metal—ranging from cuffs to chains to leather leashes. I swallowed sharply and jerked my attention back to the man standing before me.

His eyes sparked with heat as he released my wrist and took several steps back.

"Gaven?" I was proud of the way my voice didn't shake, but that still didn't deter my insides from trembling. For some reason, I had a feeling that something was about to happen between him and me that was going to change things. I couldn't let it. I still needed to get away from him. The longer I lingered here, the higher the chance Jackie would find me. Plus, there was my client—Ronald, who was waiting for my contact. There was no telling if he'd already been found and killed. I hoped not.

I stepped forward, but Gaven stopped me with a raised hand. He turned away and strode across the room to a tall wingback chair that matched the rest of the room's decor. He took a seat and spread his legs wide as he stared back at me.

I felt … entranced. Trapped and bound in his gaze. One hand rose to his face as he scrubbed a palm down his face. The dark shadow of a beard against his jaw had lightened since I'd known him five years ago. Specs of lighter gray could be seen there. I didn't mind. It made him more attractive in my opinion. Regardless of how sexual he was, the fact remained I couldn't let myself be contained by him.

"Come to me, Angel," Gaven said, his voice a shock in the otherwise silent room. I jolted and took a step forward. "*No.*" He barked the word out so harshly I halted and nearly fell on my face. I looked at him in shock and confusion. He'd told me to come to him. Why had he stopped me?

As if he sensed my thoughts, he pointed with his free hand to the floor. "On your knees," he said.

"When I said come to me, I meant crawl. Crawl to your Master, Angel."

My chest rose and fell. His words sank into my head, but they didn't take effect for several moments. He waited—ever the patient Master. I looked to the floor. It wasn't really hard under my feet. Neither was it rough. In fact, it was almost … inviting. As if this place had been designed for this. Then again, it was a sex club—it *was* designed for this.

I sank to my knees, my eyes on the floor as my hair fell in a curtain around my face. My hands landed against the softness of the carpet, as did my knees. Heartbeat throbbing in my throat, I lifted my head and put one hand in front of the other.

I *crawled* to him, just as he had commanded, feeling every bit as exposed as I knew he wanted me to be tonight in these clothes. My ass swayed back and forth as I moved toward him, slowly edging closer with each passing second until I was in front of his spread legs.

Gaven sat up and looked down at me. His hand came down on the top of my head, stroking my hair back. "That wasn't so hard, was it?" he asked.

Silent, I shook my head. Surprisingly, no. It hadn't been difficult at all. In fact, it'd felt natural. As if I was always meant to come to him on my knees.

"You're so pretty like this, Angel." When he spoke, it was in a whisper. "On your knees, ready to serve me. You're the most beautiful woman in the world to me."

His words, combined with the low throbbing of my cunt, made electricity dance through the air over my skin. My mouth opened on a sharp inhale as his hand moved down to my face, thumb stroking over my cheek and lower until he touched my lower lip. He pressed down and then inward, sliding his thumb into my mouth, over my tongue.

Instinctively, I closed my lips and sucked his thumb further into my mouth, licking over the pad there. His eyes locked on mine. The swell at the front of his pants told me more than his expression just how much it affected him. A spark of pride danced within me. I wasn't the only one affected by this thing between us.

Pulling his thumb from my lips with a pop, Gaven spoke. "I want you to tell me the truth of what happened that night, Angel." His words made me stiffen, but he didn't give me time to respond. "It's an inevitability. If you want my protection— and make no mistake, you need it—then you'll have to give yourself to me as you were always meant to."

"Our marriage was arranged," I reminded him. "Why do you care so much?" Was it just because he hadn't gotten what he wanted? Or was there something more between us? Deep down, I hoped that was the case. Even though I knew I shouldn't.

Gaven leaned forward in his seat, hovering over me. With his head bent, the light above us cast his face in shadow. I could just picture the two of us sitting like this—me on my knees with my face turned towards the light and him, the monster in the shadows. Faceless. Cruel. Deviant.

"Because the moment I put my ring on your finger, Angel," he said, "was the moment you became *mine*." His head tilted down as his hand rose and he touched the jewelry encircling my throat. "You might have been gone for the last five years, but that never meant that I didn't claim you. Everything about you—from your defiant attitude to your lush little body, meant to carry my seed—is mine. That is a fact even you can't erase."

I sighed. "I can't give you what you want," I informed him. A part of me, a secretive part, wanted to. She wanted it like she'd never wanted anything in her life. But reality was different from fantasy.

"It doesn't matter what you think you can or can't do, Angel," Gaven said. "You *will*. That's what it means to be owned by me."

Looking up at him the way I was, I found myself wholly swallowed by his expression. Though shadowed, the intensity of his gaze made its way through to bore into me. My soul—that was what he had threatened to take. That was what he wanted. I feared, for a moment, that it was too late. That he already had it.

Then his gaze lifted and the spell was broken. I gasped for breath as he sat back in his seat and his fingers left me. I sucked in breath after breath, not realizing that I'd been holding it in until my chest began to ache.

Gaven lowered his hands to the crotch of his pants and my eyes anchored there, watching him as he unbuttoned and then unzipped, freeing his erection from the fabric. My mouth began to water. I leaned forward, automatically drawn closer, as he fisted himself and held his throbbing cock up, stroking it once from base to tip.

I realized for a moment that I'd never given myself a moment to observe him, to really look at him. His cock was long and thick, veins trailed up the underside, and the mushroom-shaped head was slightly pinker than the shaft.

"Enough lies, Angel," Gaven said, refuting my words. "Open your mouth and take me."

Although I should have resisted and told him to fuck off, I didn't. I couldn't. Instead, I leaned forward and followed my husband's order. My lips parted and I closed my eyes as I sucked the head of his cock into my mouth. My hands came up, replacing his at the base of his shaft. I gripped him tight and sank down over him.

It felt different with me on my knees before him, somewhat willingly this time. He filled my mouth until my lips were stretched around him. The salty taste of his precum invaded, sliding over my tongue as I sucked him down further. A pressure landed on the back of my skull—his palm. I shivered at the sensation.

Beneath the skimpy lingerie I'd been given for tonight, my nipples tightened further until they were hard little points. With every brush against the fabric covering them, I grew wetter and wetter. Pulling back, I licked up the underside of Gaven's shaft before popping off and sucking down a harsh breath.

His palm clenched, fingers sliding through my hair and pulling the strands sharply until a burst of pain shot through my skull. I cried out and Gaven took full advantage, pushing my head back down and impaling me on his hard cock until the head bumped against the entrance to my throat.

I choked, opening my eyes and looking up at him through a misty gaze. His face was impassive, though his muscles weren't. His jaw was tight, a vein pulsing there as he glared down at me.

"Take me deep," he growled. "All the way in your throat like a good little wife is supposed to."

Tears lingered against my lashes. My throat closed tight as he tried to force himself deeper. My tongue squirmed under the shaft and his hand clenched in my hair again. I paused, realizing that it was a sign. I licked at him again and felt a slight tremble in the thighs encasing me between his legs.

It was clear he had no intention of letting me off of him until he came, so I sucked in a breath through my nose, praying that my nostrils remained clear long enough. Then I pressed my palms into his thighs and lifted up on my knees as I bobbed my head against his lap. His cock moved forward, and I squeezed my eyes shut.

More salt filled my mouth. Precum. Reaching up, I grabbed a hold of his base and pumped him up and down with a tight grip. Gaven's responding moan was my reward. He pressed into me further. Filling up not just my mouth but making his way into my throat. I felt owned. Claimed. Debased.

Somehow, my body didn't mind. My inner thighs were soaked with the evidence of how turned on this made me. Gaven was right to call me a slut —that's exactly what I was when it came to him.

I sucked him down into my mouth, flicking my tongue against him as best I could. I bobbed my head up and down. His hips lifted as he thrust deeper into my mouth and throat. Again and again, he slid past that place where my throat started. His cock moved over my tongue against the hard roof of my mouth.

I tried to keep my teeth out of the way, but occasionally, he would thrust so hard that they would touch the outside of his shaft. Whenever that happened, his grip on my hair would tighten and sparks would dance behind my eyelids. If he lasted much longer, I was going to pass out. I choked on him, feeling my saliva dripping from the corners of my lips. My eyes watered and more tears leaked out despite them being closed.

"Ngh." Gaven made a rough sound. Then a low, "*Fuck.*" I peeked my eyes open and found him bent over me, now both hands on the back of my head as he fucked my throat raw.

My cheeks were wet. My lips felt swollen and stretched impossibly wide to accommodate his size. "Fuck, you're such a fucking good cock sucker,

Angel. Your mouth was made for my dick," he said between clenched teeth.

His eyes opened and locked on mine, and suddenly he stood up. A shocked noise escaped me, but it was muffled by the flesh in my mouth. Anchoring himself with both hands cupping my skull, Gaven fucked into me as he stared down into my eyes. It was wild and violent—like the man himself.

"If I find out you let another man have you," he swore. "I'll fucking kill him. If these pretty lips of yours touched any other cock, I'll fucking cut it off. You're mine. My fucking whore to use as I want. My wife."

The more he talked, the hotter I got. He couldn't know what those words did to me. I wasn't even sure I wanted him to. The brutality of them. The honesty. It sank into my ears and set fire to my insides. I whimpered as he sank his cock into my throat and held me still. My nose was smashed against the light bush of hair at the base of his erection, slightly darker than the hair on his head.

With a groan, I felt him come. Hot semen washed into my mouth, filling me up, and there was no other place for it to go but down. I coughed around him, choking, but he didn't let up.

"Swallow it, Angel," he commanded, his gaze glittering dangerously as he stared down at me and continued to come down my throat. "Swallow my seed and remember there's another place it belongs." My lips tightened around him at that comment. He grinned. "That's right, baby, before tonight is through, my seed will be coating the inside of your pussy too. You won't leave this club tonight without a reminder of me inside of you, sloshing around in your belly the way it's meant to."

20

GAVEN

Despite just coming down my wife's tight throat, when I withdrew my cock from between her swollen lips, I found myself hardening all over again. Her face was wrecked. Eyes red-rimmed and watery as she sniffed and wiped a hand under her nose. Black mascara dripped down her rosy cheeks. She sucked in breath after breath, her chest rising and falling rapidly.

I wasn't done. Far from it.

Tucking myself back into my pants and zipping up, I moved around her and strode towards the wall of equipment. Silently, I pulled down some of the restraints and checked them over. Brand new—and would likely either be thoroughly cleaned by the staff later or replaced entirely—the leather cuffs I held were perfect for what I had in mind. The matching leather paddle called to me, but no. I'd rather have my wife's ass reddened by the palm of my hand than something so impersonal.

Turning back to her, my brows arched when I realized she hadn't moved a single inch from where she'd been on her knees before me in front of the chair. I moved past her again, relishing in the way her shoulders tightened, but still, she didn't look at me. I strode to the end of the four-poster bed and separated the leather cuffs, unclipping the metal chain holding them together so that I could anchor them to the chains embedded into the end posts.

After finishing with both cuffs, I lifted up a few of the pillows scattered on the floor and dropped them into the center of the mattress at the end. Finally, I turned back to the woman quietly sniffling and wiping the tears from her cheeks.

"Angel." She jumped at the sound of my voice, but that was all it took. Her head turned and tilted up, chin jutting out as she narrowed her gaze on me. Such a little fighter. Fuck, that turned me on too. Watching the spark of defiance in her eyes as they met mine, it was something altogether different than anything else I'd ever had before.

She fought for what she wanted. She resisted it. But she would fall—I would make sure of it—but still, in the end, I would be there to catch her. I would be there to ensure she was never irreparably damaged and that, at the end of her fall, she would find that I was always going to be there, waiting for her. I held out my hand. "Come here," I ordered.

Her hands landed on the carpet again and my lips twitched as she bent over on her hands and knees once again and crawled to me. Her ass swayed back and forth, stealing my attention for a brief moment before it snapped back to her face. She was sensual in her movements. Breasts hanging between her arms as she put one in front of the other. She might have been the perfect pet—if it wasn't for her disobedience.

When she got to me, I lowered my hand down to her and she lifted up, taking it. My fingers closed around hers and I tugged. She followed my silent order and stood up, getting to her feet. My eyes snapped down to her knees, but as I predicted, there was no harsh rug burn. The carpet here had been specially chosen. Ian was not a man who missed details.

"What are you going to do now?" she asked, her hazel green eyes lifting to meet mine.

"You'll find out soon enough," I hedged, before leading her closer to the end of the bed. "Bend over the pillows."

Glancing back at me once, she followed and did as I commanded. Her lush, rounded ass lifted as she bent down. I took first one hand and stretched it out until I was able to cuff her to the post and then, quickly, I slipped to the other side and repeated the action. Her breathing hitched as she found herself bound to the bedposts.

Something inside of my chest eased. It seemed that only when she was bound and displayed for my pleasure that I finally found comfort. Tied like this, she couldn't run away. She was at my mercy, and unfortunately for her, I had very little mercy to give when it came to the things I desired.

My fingers traced along the outer edges of her thong. I could practically smell her. She was wet. My dirty little girl. Lifting my palm away from her, I brought it down with a quick whoosh. She gasped and her smooth, even ivory skin flushed pink from my strike. I spanked her again on the opposite cheek and she shuddered, her spine moving as she squirmed over the pillows.

Slap. "Don't fucking move, Angel," I warned her, even knowing that it was an impossible demand.

But I liked that too. Giving her impossible demands, and reasons for me to punish her all over again. Control was a heady drug that I allowed myself to indulge in so often that it was my greatest weakness. My addiction. I was in charge of everything from my business, to my men, to the kill. But this woman spread out like an offering before me was different. The control I exerted over her was earned. It was difficult and that made it so much sweeter when she finally caved and bowed before me.

My cock strained against the inside of my pants, ready to go all over again. It would have to wait, though, because I had other plans for my treacherous little wife.

Hooking my fingers into the thin straps of her thong, I stripped the fabric from her cunt and left it hooked around her knees. She gasped and her thighs tightened, but I could already see what she no doubt didn't want to show me. Her pussy was flushed pink, puffy with juice. I pressed a thick finger against her opening and thrust it inside, causing her to arch her back.

With my free hand, I delivered a fresh series of slaps to her ass that had her crying out. "I said not to move," I reminded her.

Panting, she responded through clenched teeth. "Why don't you let me tie you up and put my finger in your ass and see if you can hold still," she snapped back.

With a deep chuckle, I twisted my finger into her cunt, coating it in her wetness before pulling out and drifting upward. Her body tightened as I pressed it against her dark rosebud. "Now, if you wanted it in your ass, love," I said, grinning. "All you had to do was ask." I shoved it in, eliciting another sharp cry from her.

Her ass muscles clamped down around my finger, squeezing impossibly tight. I could only imagine how good it would feel to slide my cock into her tight dark hole and fuck her until she screamed. She wasn't unused to it now—not with how often I'd forced her to wear the pear of anguish this past week. Both a punishment for her and a reward for me, seeing her ass spread around the metal bulb and knowing that inside, it spread her wide open for me.

Soon, I reminded myself. *I would have her in every way very fucking soon.* But not tonight. I withdrew my finger from her ass and reached into my pocket with my free hand, pulling a handkerchief free to wipe myself off. Tonight, I had other plans.

After I finished wiping off my hand, I rubbed the flat of my palm over the pink skin of her asscheek. For good measure, I slapped it again, watching her flesh jiggle as her mouth above gasped. The headiness of her arousal permeated the room.

"I worried," I admitted to her as I reached for the front of my pants once again, "when you left that you might have been leaving with my child inside of you."

Her shoulders stiffened on the bed and her head turned, her cheek pressed to the mattress. "Gaven…" Her voice was tight, full of sorrow.

With a frown, I brought my hand down against her ass—cracking my palm against the sensitive flesh where her thigh met her cheek, causing her to arch upward as a pain-filled moan echoed into the air.

"No talking, Angel," I snapped. "You're not the one in charge here. I am."

"I'm sorry—" she said, despite my words, and with an inhale, I stopped messing with the front of my pants and stepped forward.

I snatched a pillow out from beneath her and then placed my hand at the small of her back. I pressed down, forcing her to arch her ass up even more until that juicy pussy of hers was on display. Once it was, I rained a series of sharp slaps against it.

She screamed as my hand caught right on her cunt and even the little bud that was her clit. She squirmed and bucked against my hand, but I didn't let up. I spanked her sweet little pussy hard, bringing down slap after slap just to show her that I meant what I fucking said.

"Please!" she screamed after the twentieth strike. "Gaven, stop! I'm sorry, please! I'll be good!"

I paused and looked at her face where she panted into the mattress. Her swollen lips parted as more tears streamed down her face. "No more talking, Angel," I repeated my earlier command.

She nodded quickly, wet lashes sticking together as she looked back at me pleadingly. My cock practically fucking throbbed. Her lips pressed together, yet the second my hands left her, and I stepped back, I watched as her whole body sagged into the mattress. *In relief?* Probably. I was a rough man and I didn't hold back on her spankings. I liked watching her body bloom for me—in pleasure and in pain.

I unzipped. "Now, as I was saying…" I stepped up behind her and pressed both of my hands against her red ass, pushing outward until both of her holes were visible to me. "I want you to understand my point of view, Angel." God, she was beautiful. I'd seen so much darkness—bathed in the blood of the shadows—but she … my sweet, deceitful little wife was Aphrodite incarnate. She was something I didn't deserve but would take regardless simply because I wanted her. Craved her. Needed her.

"You left me." The words came bitter on my tongue. My gaze lifted to her face. Her hazel green eyes were red-rimmed still, but sharper in focus as she glared back at me. She wanted to speak, I knew that much from the tight resistant expression on her face, but my hand on her poor little pussy was enough of a reminder not to cross the boundary.

In fact … I removed one palm from her ass and cupped her cunt. Heat poured over my fingers. Liquid fire as her arousal soaked me. Her pussy was ripe for the taking. I grinned. She might pretend not to like it, but her body certainly knew who it wanted. Me. Always and only ever me.

"You're lucky, Angel," I said, playing across her lower lips, spreading them and then sliding my middle finger right through the center of her heat. She arched against my hand and a small whimper echoed back to my ears. "Had you been pregnant with my child and I found out you kept them from me for five years … we would have had a very different reunion."

Her breathing grew rougher the longer I toyed with her cunt, running my finger up and down her swollen and wet entrance. Her reddened clit poked through its hood, practically calling out to me. I gave it what it wanted—a firm pinch that had her moaning. I wasn't a complete monster, after all, not to my wife and the future mother of my children.

Angel sobbed as I teased her cunt, pushing in a single finger before pulling it out and running it down to her clit to circle it, encouraging it to stay out of its hood. I could have played with her for hours, I realized. Just kept her tied and bound and open for me as I edged her closer and closer to release, only to pull back and listen to her cries of disbelief. She begged me with her body, shoving her hips out, swaying her ass back and forth as if that would be enough to tempt me.

Then again, it was enough. She was all that could tempt me. Perhaps it was the low-riding obsession I'd developed for her over the past five years, but whatever it was—I felt like I owned this woman. The only one who seemed to not realize it, was her, and that was confusing to me.

Ever since I'd shot my first man, taken my first life, made my first kill—I'd always gotten what I wanted. I'd risen to the top of my career and then found my way into an even more powerful position. Because of her. My key. My bride. My fucking wife.

Pulling away from her dripping pussy, I quickly shoved down my pants and took myself in hand. Her breathing caught, the sound loud in the otherwise quiet room—soundproof, no doubt, with Ian's attention to detail. I rubbed the head of my cock up and down her slit, waiting, curious.

Had she not realized yet that she was no longer protected against me? I wondered how it would feel to fuck her and fill her with my cum and wait for her to realize what I'd done. I knew very little about women's birth control—it was never something I needed to concern myself with. But I did know that sometimes women didn't bleed on them. Would she realize she was pregnant, or would it not be until she began to grow, ripe and swollen, with my child that she would understand her circumstances?

She likely still harbored some semblance of hope that she could escape me. That I wouldn't understand what had happened that night. I knew that the true killer of Raffaello Price now sat in his mansion upon his throne. *Jackie.* She was the reason Angel had run, and soon she would get her just rewards, but for now, it was time to do what I should've done five years ago.

It was time to fuck my wife and ensure she didn't leave this room without a solid reminder of me growing in her womb.

I settled the head of my cock into place, and with one solid push, I thrust into her cunt. Angel cried out as I fucked into her, her back bowing and her head popping up as she strained against the cuffs holding her in place. Tight muscles wound around my shaft, pulling me in even further.

A low groan spread through my chest and moved up my throat. "So fucking tight, Angel," I said through gritted teeth. "Your cunt is choking my cock."

Angel's body squirmed beneath me. She panted, she gasped, she tightened and released her insides, driving me that much closer to the brink. Every single movement she made rippled along my cock. Her juices dripped around me.

Pulling out, I slammed back in. My hands found her hips, and holding tight, I began my barrage. I fucked her tight, wet pussy with the same violence as I had her throat. With each thrust, she grunted and whimpered. Her hands balled into fists above the cuffs, the muscles of her arms straining as she pulled them tight.

Using my hold on her, I forced her hips back, jerking her into my lap as I withdrew and then thrust back into her tight, welcoming insides. "So fucking good, love," I whispered. "You take cock like a born whore."

A low curse drew from her lips at that, but I didn't mind. She could spit and curse at me all she liked; I would still have her full of me by the end of the night.

Her insides contracted around me, and I struggled not to come right then and there. I wanted her hotter, wetter, and far more out of her fucking mind by the time I dumped my seed into her cunt. Now that the wicked thought had taken root in my mind, I wanted to see the shock on her face when she realized that I'd gotten everything I wanted from her and she'd accepted it—thinking she was safe.

I sawed in and out of her pussy, back and forth, gripping her tight as her inner walls squeezed me. I was drawing closer and closer and I knew that she was too. Unable to put it off any longer, I reached beneath her and pinched her little clit *hard*. That was all it took.

Angel thrust back against me, her head coming off the bed along with her shoulders as she twisted against her restraints. Her legs kicked. She screamed. But inside of her, I felt the hard clamp of her muscles as her orgasm overwhelmed her.

Finally, I allowed myself that release. My hands

on her hips tightened as I dug my fingers into her sides, holding her against me as I came and came, filling her insides. I'd never had a family before and I wasn't entirely sure that I could become a family man—not with the darkness that tainted my soul. But family wasn't the only goal here. An heir was.

The Price Empire would be mine and Evangeline Price would be my Queen. Her body would produce my right to rule, whether she wanted it or not.

My hips pressed into the fleshy underside of her ass and I bowed over her spine, sweat dripping from my temples and landing on the pale skin of her back. She, too, was coated in perspiration. My cock jerked inside of her and a low groan rumbled through my chest. Never before had I ever felt so out of control above a woman tied to a bed. Somehow, though, Angel made me feel both like a God and like a human bowing beneath something much bigger than myself.

When I pulled free of her pussy, I carefully took the pillow I'd pulled away from her earlier and then slipped it underneath her belly. She moaned and tried to tug herself away, over-sensitized most likely, but I didn't let her. The cuffs and my unyielding hands kept her right where I wanted her.

"There, there," I whispered to her, stroking my fingers down her spine. "Hold still for me, love. We have to make sure that Daddy's little swimmers make it."

Her head turned and she glared back at me. "It's

not going to happen, Gaven," she said, her voice hoarse from all of the crying and screaming.

My smile widened. "And why is that?" I asked. Curiosity drilled into me. Would she admit the truth? Would she tell me about the implant? If so, would I be given the chance to tell her that it was gone?

Angel's teeth raked across her bottom lip and she sighed. A play of emotions crossed her face—irritation, anger, regret, and something else … fear. But what did she fear?

I waited, but the answer I sought never came. Instead, Angel sighed and shook her head. "One time doesn't guarantee I'll get pregnant, Gaven," she said. "It didn't five years ago and it won't now."

Ahh, so she was going that route. My smile never faltered. I turned away and found my discarded handkerchief, cleaning off my cock as I zipped up before pivoting back to her. Leaning onto the bed, I reached up and stroked her hair back—away from her face before I cupped her cheek and stared down into her upturned eyes.

There was a flush to her cheeks, a dewiness to her skin that made me want to roll her onto her back and re-cuff her arms so that I could have her all over again. "There are many things you don't realize, Angel," I said, hedging my truth the same way she had. "But I can assure you of this—we won't be fucking only one time, love. You'll have my cum in your belly every day from here on out until you're pregnant with our heir."

She arched a brow back at me, her lips twisting into a scowl. "And what if I don't get pregnant?" she snapped. "What if I can't? Will you divorce me?"

"I only have one wife, Angel," I replied. "I will only ever have one wife and that wife is you."

Releasing her face, I stood up and took a step back, admiring the way her heart-shaped ass was stained red. White cum coated the outer lips of her sex. "You'll stay this way," I say. "Until enough time has passed."

"It's not going to fucking happen, Gaven!" she cursed.

She didn't think so, and had I not had her looked over by a doctor who'd found her birth control implant, then she would have been right. Now, though, we both held secrets and I felt no shame in letting her continue believing she was safe from me. One way or another, I'd have my heir and my empire. It was only a matter of time.

21

ANGEL

I don't know how long I was forced to lay there—mostly naked with my ass raised as Gaven's cum seeped into my insides, some of it dripping down towards my inner thighs. It was as humiliating as it was torturous. For a multitude of reasons, it was wrong. I pressed my face into the cool bed sheets over the comfortable mattress and rubbed back and forth to try and wipe off some of the makeup I knew had to be staining my cheeks.

Gaven was quiet. If it weren't for the creak of wood and leather, then I wouldn't have even known where he was, but I wasn't an idiot—he was as perverted as they came. He was sitting in the wing-back chair that he'd been in before, watching me. Embarrassment overwhelmed me, but on its heels was something I wasn't entirely sure I wanted to admit, even to myself. Heat. Hunger. Desire.

I waited and hoped. I prayed that Gaven would decide to release me from these restraints and, at the very least, give me some time to myself. Time to regroup. Time to figure out a plan. Because if anything, his oath to impregnate me with his heir only made me that much more determined to get away. He could never know about the implant, but I thanked my lucky stars that I'd had that foresight.

It wasn't that I didn't want a child—but a child in this world? *My* child at that … they would be nothing more than a threat to Jackie the same way I was. I didn't trust myself to take care of someone else, and I doubted I would—not until she was gone and I was safe.

My eyelids drooped as time seemed to drag on. Seconds turned into minutes. Long stretches of quiet filled my ears. I blinked, finding my body drifting deeper and deeper into the mattress despite the slight discomfort of my restrained arms. Exhaustion pulled at my limbs, threatening to take me into oblivion.

I didn't know how long I fought it off, but in the end, the oblivion won. I fell into slumber and the room faded around me. A little while later, I felt myself rise up out of unconsciousness, but only briefly as my hands were uncuffed and my body was lifted into a strong pair of arms.

I drifted as I was carried. The soft sway of the man's steps—Gaven's steps—lulled me slowly back into the darkness. By the time he laid me on a comfortable bed with the sheets pulled away to make room for me, I was struggling not to fall back into my own clouded mind. I shivered as I felt thick fingers trail down my side. A whimper worked up my throat as those same fingers moved between my legs, pushing into my sore pussy.

With a groan, I tried to roll away. Exhausted … I was so fucking exhausted. I couldn't do it again. "Shhhhh." Gaven's low, rumbling voice echoed over my senses. His finger twisted inside of me, causing me to flinch before he finally pulled free and I relaxed into the bed. Sheets were drawn up over me and I snuggled into them, latching onto the silken feel as I let myself be tugged back into sleep.

I slept so hard and so long—or so it felt like—that when I opened my eyes again, it felt like hours had passed. It was one of those slumbers that completely took a person over and filled their minds until the whole world seemed new and different when they woke.

Sitting up in bed, I glanced around, finding myself alone. "Gaven?" I called out, coughing once when my voice croaked and halted. Reaching up, I rubbed my throat and blinked the grittiness from my eyes.

I coughed again and then glanced to the side as I swung my legs over the side of the bed. A glass of water, a bottle of pills, and a note sat on the nightstand. I picked up the pill bottle first, sighing in relief at the Tylenol. Popping two of the oval pills out of the container and into my mouth, I grabbed up the water and drank down half of it.

My muscles were sore. My shoulders screamed in achy pain, but more than that—the place between my legs felt raw. Putting one hand behind my neck, I cracked it to the side, stretching it out in the hopes that doing so would relieve some of the tension as I continued to survey the room.

I was still in the private club room that Gaven had brought me to, but with the lack of windows there was no telling how much time had passed since I'd fallen asleep. The one blaring thing my mind locked on right away was the most important—*I was alone.*

Standing abruptly, I wavered on my feet and grabbed hold of the bedpost as I stumbled away from the nightstand. I gasped for breath and looked down at my legs as metal rattling caught my attention.

"That fucking asshole," I muttered as I realized the reason I was alone.

Gaven wasn't an idiot. No doubt he'd known as soon as I woke alone and unwatched, I'd try and make my escape. He wasn't wrong. That was exactly my intention. Unfortunately, the locked cuff chained around my ankle threw a wrench in those plans.

"Shit." The curse hissed out of me as I pushed away from the bedpost and took several steps away, following the line of the chain to where the end was located. Reaching down, I picked it up and then tugged.

The bed squeaked. I glanced towards the noise before diving for the bottom of the giant piece of furniture. My knees hit the floor and a moment later, my cheek as I scanned the bottom part of the posts.

There—on the other side of the bed was the embedded loop that connected the chain.

Wrapping both hands around the chain, I pulled again and again. The bed squeaked, but it never moved. Standing again, I glared at the bed. It was a monstrous thing made of dark red, heavy wood. There was no way I was going to rip the chain off the post. I wasn't strong enough. There had to be another way.

Turning in a circle, I scanned the room anew. This time, I had a goal. I needed to find something, anything, that would help me unlock the cuff circling my ankle. I didn't know how long Gaven had been gone or when he'd be back, but I needed to be gone by the time he arrived.

The chain trailed behind me as I moved around the space, but it didn't allow me to move far. I stopped halfway into the room and growled low in my throat as the bed squeaked again, and I looked down to find the chain attached to me, taut and unrelenting. Anger rose within my chest. I sucked in breath after breath and shivered as I crossed my arms over my chest and rubbed my arms up and down. No wonder I'd snuggled so deep into the covers—without Gaven there to heat up my body, the room felt like a frozen wasteland.

More air blew over my body and I realized I stood there utterly devoid of clothes from my bottom half down, and the only thing I still had on was the barely there little bra that Gaven had forced me to wear. If I was going to get out of here, I would need new clothes or to get back to the locker room to retrieve the dress.

As soon as I had that thought, though, I shook it off. No. The dress would need to be left behind. It was too ostentatious.

I spun back to the bed and glared at the offending furniture as I contemplated my next actions. This was a sex club—so a woman walking around mostly naked likely wouldn't draw much attention. Would being alone and unaccompanied be odd, though?

As I considered that, something shined in my peripheral vision. I paused and glanced over. My eyes widened as I spotted a pair of nipple clamps hanging on the wall of bondage gear. They were metal—just what I needed. I hurried forward and nearly tripped on my face as my chain drew short once again.

Shit. Shit. Shit! It was out of reach. I dragged both of my hands down my face and inhaled sharply. No, I could figure this out. I just needed something long enough to reach to grab ahold of it or knock it closer. I glanced around again, and when I found nothing straight away, I decided to dig a little deeper.

Turning back to the bed, I hurried towards the trunk that I'd noticed the night before. I got to my knees to unclip the closure and flipped it open, pausing with wide eyes as the inside was revealed to me. If I thought the bondage wall was a little unnerving, then this trunk was full of things that made my insides tremble.

I pressed my thighs together as I reached inside and lifted the first thing that my gaze locked on. It was a spreader bar. Long and thick and black with restraints attached to either end. The bar itself was made of hard steel covered in leather. Even better, though, it was adjustable.

Standing quickly, I pressed down on the center notches and the smaller part of the bar in the inner hollow slipped out. I pressed the opposite side and another piece came out and locked into place. Just at a glance, it seemed to be almost three feet. I imagined that this was something Gaven had likely used before—not on me though and, for some reason, that made my stomach turn sour.

Shaking away the scowl that was beginning to form, I went back to the furthest point of the room that I could reach and then a little further, stretching and arching my body as I waved the bar towards the wall. Leather clanked against the metal and I cursed as I flipped the rod and tried using the restraints to hook beneath the chain connecting the clamps.

I knew the sight must have been ridiculous and, mentally, I swore that if Gaven walked in right now, I'd absolutely combust into a fiery pit of death and be grateful for it. Closing my eyes, I sucked in a breath, and then with a sharp jerk upward, I snapped the clamps off the hook.

My eyes opened and I looked up as the damn thing swung up over me, flying through the air. I spun and dove for it as it landed on the floor at the side of the bed. The spreader bar dropped from my grip as I grabbed a hold of the metal clamps and pulled one off from its slender chain.

The metal holding these together was much thinner and weaker than the same chain tying me to the bed. The loops that linked them together weren't fused either, allowing me to wedge a nail into one and bend it outward until I was left with a small metal circle the size of my pinkie nail.

With a sigh of relief, I bent the little metal outward more, put it on the floor, and smashed it with my palm to flatten it more. I had a pretty awesome thief I'd met in Italy a few years before to thank for this trick. If it weren't for her I wouldn't have had any clue how to pick the lock on my ankle.

Once I had the small piece of metal smoothed out until it was at least an inch in length, I turned to the side, lifted my foot, and planted it flat. I wedged one end of the little sliver of metal into the keyhole and wiggled around, bending down to listen for the mechanism. Unfortunately, if it made any sound, it was too quiet for me to hear, so I had to move by feel.

I wiggled and jerked the metal piece up and down until I felt something inside the lock click. When it finally did, I pumped my fist in victory and quickly removed the lock before unbuckling the leather cuff.

Once I was free, I hurried into the bathroom in the hopes that there'd be something else to cover up with. Thankfully, I found a red silk robe hanging on the back of the door. I snatched it off and covered myself, tying the belt tightly to keep it from falling open.

Gaven might have thought he had me trapped and locked tightly away, but I wasn't the innocent teenage girl he'd married anymore. I was a woman who'd been through fucking hell, and I'd learned to survive it. I sure as hell wasn't ready to be captured and locked up forever. I had things to do. Clients who were relying on me and … a sister that I had to deal with lest she find me and kill me herself.

That, at the very least, was one thing that Gaven had made me realize by capturing me and imprisoning me. I couldn't let this go on. If I ever wanted a life free of looking over my shoulder, then she would need to be dealt with.

Swallowing the lump in my throat at the thought, I moved towards the door I'd come in from and tried the handle. My lips stretched tight and down as I realized that, too, was locked. Gaven was nothing if not a cautious man. Of course, he'd lock the door. Not that I would let it stop me.

Turning back to the room, I returned to where I'd discarded the metal clamps. The small rings of the chain wouldn't work on a door lock, but … I unscrewed the small piece that tightened the clamps and let them fall completely open. They were made of thin pieces of metal, but no matter how adequately made, thin metal could almost always be bent and reconstructed.

After finagling out a small but more sturdy piece

from the clamps themselves, I moved back to the door and got on my knees to insert the piece into the lock. This time, I heard the click right before the lock twisted. I didn't even think to clean up after myself. Gaven would realize I was gone the second he entered the room anyway. So, I just left the piece in the door, grabbed the handle, jerked it open, and fled into the hallway.

Time was of the essence, and I was nearly out of it.

22

GAVEN

The epitome of arrogance was thinking you knew all and that nothing could surprise you. As I stood in the empty private room I'd left hours before to meet with Archer, I had to admit, I was surprised. The emptiness of the room was especially shocking considering that when I left it there had been a sleeping woman in the very bed that now sat with its sheets in disarray.

The woman, however, was nowhere to be seen. A low whistle sounded behind me. "Looks like your pretty little bird flew away."

Cutting a dark look to Archer, I didn't dignify his words with a response. Instead, I returned my attention to the room before me. How the hell had she managed to unlock her cuff? The answer was scattered on the floor at the foot of the bed.

I strode forward and crouched down, lifting the thin chain with one metal nipple clamp still dangling on one side. The cuff had been left behind with a piece of metal still sticking out of it.

A low chuckle rumbled in my chest. I shook my head as it bent down and my eyes shut. *How short-sighted of me,* I thought. I hadn't given her enough credit. I reopened my eyes and stood up, turning back to the others.

"Looks like your wife," Ian's brother—though not by blood—Jensen began, looking over the room as he spoke before stopping on me, "wants a divorce."

My fingers closed around the chain, my grip tightening. "She won't get it," I snapped. "The three of you know as well as I do—once a mafia princess marries, she doesn't do so again."

Ian sighed and stepped forward between his friends. Though he wasn't taller than me, he was undoubtedly wider. He gestured to the room and then to me. "I doubt you'll let something like this stop you," he said. "But if she's smart enough to leave the club undetected, then I have no doubt she's smart enough to evade you again." Despite the calm tone, Ian's words were not meant for reassurance.

I'd gotten cocky. I'd thought myself invincible. I thought I'd had her right where I wanted her.

I'd been wrong.

So incredibly fucking wrong.

I shook my head. "The only one of you I need is Archer."

Archer, in response, groaned. "Come on, man.

I've already told you before—Hadrian is a much better—"

I didn't let him finish his sentence. Before the last syllable of that last word had left his lips, I'd reached into my jacket and withdrew my gun. Without blinking, I centered the barrel on him and paused with my finger on the trigger.

"Friend or not, Archer," I said in warning. "I will find my wife and if I require your assistance, you will provide it."

Without hesitation, Ian stepped in the way. "Put. Your. Fucking. Gun. Down." The man's nostrils flared and he seemed to swell with rage as he stood before me.

Archer, unperturbed, poked his blonde head around him. "How the hell did you manage to sneak one in anyway?"

I shrugged. "You have your ways, and I have mine."

He sighed and shook his head. "You know I was gonna help you, you asshole. Put it the fuck away before Ian blows a gasket," he said. "I was just complaining."

The gun was returned to its holster, but Ian didn't move as he glared at me. I waited, half curious and half already knowing how he would react. He moved forward until we were nearly chest-to-chest. "If you ever bring a weapon into my club again without my permission," he said, his voice low and cold, "I'll shove it up your ass and pull the fucking trigger."

Silence stretched between us. My nerves were laced with a barely repressed rage, and though I knew none of it was directed at him, I needed an outlet. Seconds passed until finally Archer broke the tension with a short, "Kinky" sending Jensen into a fit of chuckles.

I inhaled sharply and stepped around the man before nodding to Archer. "Check CCTV footage," I ordered. "I want every single file from the Club's footage the second you have it—anything that pertains to her."

"What are you going to do?" Archer asked.

I scowled as I moved further into the hall. "I'm going to pay my sister-in-law a visit," I hedged.

It was time to cut the head off of the beast—literally rather than figuratively. The second Jackie was gone, Angel would have no more reason to run. Unless, of course, it was never her sister that kept her away, but me.

That wasn't a possibility I wanted to consider, though.

Just when I thought things had gotten easier, that we were coming to understand each other once again ... it all went to shit. Every time I got close, Angel disappeared on me. I grasped at her, only to be disappointed again and again. Another man might have given in and finally let her go. A normal man certainly would have taken the hint. I was anything but normal. I was Gaven fucking Belmonte.

The only outcome I wanted was one where I

woke up again with Evangeline Price in my bed, in my arms. I wanted her belly swollen and round with my child—*our* child. Still, heir or no heir ... she was mine. I'd laid claim and no other woman could affect me the way she did. No one else could drive me to the brink of insanity the way she did. Now, she was gone. Again and again, I would hunt her.

Even if it meant we circled this path over and over for the rest of our lives. Catch and escape. Hunting her as my prey. I would do it as many times as it took for her to realize that I wasn't going away. I was never going to stop. Not until she realized that she belonged with me. That she was mine.

23

ANGEL

Three days. That's how long it took for me to track Ronald down while dodging every CCTV known to man. Even if Gaven hadn't caught up to me, I still felt watched every second of every day. Then again, at least I was free and not locked up, naked, in some room in the middle of nowhere, New York.

Thankfully, in the time I'd been captured, Ronald had managed to stay hidden. He'd followed my commands and found a shitty motel several hours from his home, where no one would ever think to look for a world-renowned genius and scientist.

I slowed the cheap sedan I managed to pick up from one of my own hidden locations of supplies and turned into the Byway Motel's parking lot. The one-story building stretched out with its back facing a long stream of woods and its front turned towards the old highway that likely saw more action and attention fifty years ago than it did now.

A large yellow VACANCY sign with faded red letters was set beneath the motel's dingy name above the pull-in area in front of the office. I bypassed it and headed straight for the lot along the side of the building, parked, and got out.

Dark clouds hovered overhead, and the distant rumble of thunder threatened the already dreary day. The weather here never knew what it wanted to be, though. There was still a fifty percent chance that by the time I retrieved my client and got back on the road, the clouds would have dispersed and the sun would be shining. It made it damn near impossible to predict.

With a sigh and a quick grab of my hand, I picked up the satchel I had stashed in the passenger seat and closed up the sedan, pressing the lock button on the key fob before heading up the side-walk. When I'd last spoken with Ron and gotten his location, he'd told me he was staying in room number 6 and was nearly out of money.

Dimly, I felt a pang of regret. Not just for Ron and leaving him like I had—even though it hadn't been by choice—but because I wanted nothing more than to leave him again. To disappear into the void of the world and never be found again. Jackie had taken so much from me, and I didn't want to risk her finding me the same way Gaven had.

Maybe it was time for me to move on and find a new place to live. I thought I could return to

America after so long, but I was wrong. If I stayed in the United States for much longer, I feared that I would grow too comfortable, which would only lead to being captured again. Unfortunately, I had enough sense to realize that if Gaven got a hold of me yet again after my second escape—technically my third, if I wanted to count the very first time before our wedding—it would result in something far worse than being locked up without clothes.

I shivered as a burst of cool air hit me in the back and I turned as I reached the awning over the motel room doors. The clouds chose that exact moment to open up and dump down over the land below it. The sudden downpour sprayed the fronts of my legs and my face, misting me with cool, wet rain.

I sighed again and shook my head, turning towards the rooms, not stopping this time until I reached the correct door. I knocked three times, stepped back, and waited. Moments later, the tremble of the chain lock shaking loose echoed back to me. Then the old key lock clicked, and the door swung open.

"Oh, Ronald…" I grimaced as I looked over the man. He looked far worse than the last time I'd seen him. His face was covered in days' old stubble, and his eyes were even more prominently sunken in—detailing just how little sleep he'd likely gotten since we'd last been together.

I took my first step into the room and let the door close at my back. "W-where the h-hell have you been, Eve?" he said, stuttering out his question as his eyes flicked over my shoulder to the now closed door.

I turned and flipped the lock and put the chain back into place, knowing that it was his anxiety and paranoia causing him to be so nervous. Then again —he really did have people after him—so was it paranoia if it was warranted?

"I'm sorry," I said, reaching for him. I touched his face with a pained smile. "I was going to suggest we leave right away, but Ron, you need to get some sleep."

"N-no, no," he replied quickly, turning away as he hurried over to one of the two full-sized beds— the furthest one back—and lifted a small grocery bag from the floor. "I'll be ready in two seconds."

I shook my head, but since he was turned away from me, he couldn't see. "No," I said, moving forward, my sneakered feet squeaking against the fake wood vinyl flooring. At least the motel had done *some* upgrades since the 70s. Otherwise, I'd have expected a grotesque green carpet.

"It's pouring rain right now," I said, as if he couldn't hear the thunder booming over the room. "You need more rest than a small nap in the car can give you. Why don't you lie down and take a nap. With me here, you'll feel safer."

He paused and glanced back, his eyes skittering up and down my form. I knew I didn't look as powerful as I had the first couple of times we'd seen each other. He'd only ever met me at my best, wearing power suits and dolled up in dresses. If I were to take a look in the mirror right now, it would reflect little more than a young woman with no makeup wearing cut-off jean shorts and a big, over-sized sweatshirt that read the faded name of a miscellaneous college I'd never even heard of.

That was purposeful. I wanted Ron and I to blend in. Right now, with his anxious demeanor—the sweat stains showing through the undersides of the white sleeves of the same button-up shirt he'd been wearing several days ago—there was no way we looked like two people who were meant to be together.

I nodded to the plastic bag he'd placed on the bed. "Do you have a change of clothes in there?" I asked.

He nodded and I moved forward, gently nudging him out of the way as I opened it and reached inside. Thankfully, he'd been smart enough to pick up what I'd told him to after our phone call. Memorizing the cell I'd given him had paid off. "Here," I said, pulling out the light gray sweatpants and a white shirt from the bag. I ripped off the tags and handed the clothes over. "Go shower and put these on after you're done."

Ronald took the clothes but didn't move immedi-ately, shifting awkwardly on his feet. "I-I forgot underwear," he murmured, a blush stealing across his cheeks.

Now was definitely not the time to be laughing, so I repressed an amused grin and shook my head.

"It's not going to be a big deal," I said. "You can wear these to sleep in, and I'll run to the front and see if they have a laundry room I can use to wash your other things."

His shoulders sagged in defeat, and he nodded. "Okay."

"Oh, wait!" I called out as he turned away to follow my instructions. He paused, and I reached into my satchel, withdrawing a small case I always tried to carry. I flipped it open and retrieved a cheap razor and handed it to him. "While you're in there, you should try to shave."

He stared at the proffered razor for several long beats before he reached out and gingerly took it from my grasp. "O-Okay," he responded.

I nodded and watched him go into the bathroom towards the back of the room. I waited five minutes after the shower was turned on before I snuck in and stole the dirty clothes he'd been wearing—including his underwear—from the floor before heading back out. I left my stuff on the still-made second bed and snatched the key from the dresser before heading out again.

More rain poured down over the side of the awning as I made my way to the front. It was a quick trip, though, thankfully, and twenty minutes later, I'd commandeered the only washer in the laundry room the motel had and was on my way back to the room.

Twin SUVs with blacked-out windows spun into the parking lot, speeding so fast that the second one hit the curb and nearly went up on two wheels as they came to a sudden halt. I froze, horror descending as I wondered if they were there for me or ... *Ronald!*

The doors opened and several men poured out. My eyes darted the last twelve feet or so to room number 6, but it was too late. The men that came out of the SUVs were dressed in dark wash jeans and black button-up shirts, but I didn't miss the bulges at the small of their backs. They were packing.

Quickly ducking behind a cleaning cart that had been left outside a nearby room, I crouched down and glanced around the side of it as three of them moved towards the very room I'd left Ron in and another two headed my way.

Motherfucking shit. My gun was in the room in my satchel, however it did me little good there. I had to think of something quickly. If they were here for Ron, that meant they worked for the corporation he'd left, but if they weren't here for him, then ... that meant they were here for me and Ron was still in danger.

I bit down on my lower lip and considered my choices.

One. I could stand up and reveal myself and see if they recognized me. If they did, then they weren't here for Ron. Nevertheless, I was still without my gun and could not overpower five grown men packing heat on my own.

Two. I could remain crouched here and see if

they would bypass me as they headed for the front office. It was a risk and highly unlikely that they'd notice me.

Three. I could cause a scene. This cleaning cart couldn't have been unmanned. There had to be a motel worker nearby. Perhaps if I screamed loud enough, someone would call the cops. The threat of authorities could scare these guys away—or it could hurry them into getting what they came for and getting out.

Each plan was met with hesitation. They could all go wrong and, at worst, since these men were carrying guns, they could just decide to kill everyone here. It wouldn't do to get a poor motel employee involved.

So, with that in mind, I did the only thing I could.

Considering the type of place this motel was and what kind of customers it likely attracted, I decided to remove my sweatshirt and tie it around my waist. I gripped the tank I'd had on underneath and yanked it down until the cups of my bra were visible and then I pulled it down another good inch to make it clear. When I didn't think that was enough, I pulled up the hem of the shirt and made a quick knot above my belly and below my breasts. The more skin I showed off, the more distracted and dismissive they would likely be. My cut-off jean shorts were thankfully frayed and small. They'd looked perfectly acceptable with the sweatshirt on, but now I pulled the waistband down and reached underneath, gripping the straps of my thong and raising them over my hips.

I pulled my hair out of the ponytail it'd been in and let it drop over my shoulders. I scrubbed a hand through the strands, fanning them out even more and then flipping the pieces at the front of my face to cover one side more. Once I was done adjusting myself, I took a deep breath and stood up.

The two stomping towards the front office paused as they caught sight of me and I forced a light and overly relaxed smile. "Heyyy, big boys," I murmured, faking a thicker, far more southern accent as they looked me over. "Y'all here for a good time? I can provide that if ya need."

The two exchanged looks and then kept walking without saying a word to me. My racing heart slowed as I realized Gaven couldn't have sent them. Even with my fake accent and the skin, there's no doubt he would have made sure each of his men knew who they were hunting. That only left one reason for these people to be here. My client.

As the men stormed off, I forced a casual pace as I continued walking, curiously watching the three left behind as if I didn't have a damn clue who they were or what was happening.

As I approached, the three men from the SUVs stood in front of Ronald's door. "'Scuse me, gentlemen," I said lightly. "My ... erm ... friend didn't say nothin' bout a party."

The taller of the three tossed a look my way and

scowled. "We're not here for you, whore. Get moving."

I faked a gasp of outrage and bristled. "How dare you!" I squealed. "I'm a respectable lady!"

One of the men with him—a slightly shorter man with ginger hair and a scar that ran down the side of his jaw—scoffed. "Yeah, right," he snickered. "With your tits out like that, there ain't no question what you're here for. Your client ain't free no more. Do what the nice man said and move along."

I twisted my hands in front of my stomach, pressing my arms together as it plumped up my breasts. "B-but my stuff's still inside," I said. "I-I can't leave without no payment, neither!"

The ginger man moved away from the other two and blocked me. My eyes widened as the first pulled his gun out and sent me a glare before he twisted the handle of the motel door and when it didn't move—because I'd locked it on my way out—he reared back and kicked it in. I flinched and gasped as the door splintered apart. Inside, I heard Ron's cry of shock and fear.

Fuck. Fuck. Fuck. This was getting out of control fast.

"Oh my god!" I screamed.

The ginger's hand came down and covered my mouth as his eyes jerked up and looked past me. "Now, now, sweetheart," he said. "You must be new to this line of business if you don't know how to mind your own business."

I sniffed hard and squeezed my eyes shut, forcing

tears to the surface. When he removed his hand, I sobbed hard. "Please," I said as the two others disappeared into the room. "That bag's all I have. I need it!"

His eyes panned down to where my breasts were shoved into his chest. "You need it, eh?" He licked his lips and I found myself fighting the urge to recoil as his fingers grasped my arm and held me in place. "Did you already fuck your client, sweetheart? I don't like to share, but if you're still free, I can see about getting that bag back to you ... for a price."

I shook my head and sniffed again for good measure. "N-no, sir," I said, fluttering my wet lashes. "I-I just—"

Curses sounded from inside the room and another scream sounded behind me—a female scream. Fuck. The cleaner must have heard the commotion. As the man's gaze lifted up over my shoulder, I took my chance and reared back, grabbing hold of his shoulders as I swung my knee right into his groin.

With a shocked look, the man wheezed and crumpled onto the sidewalk just as the two men from before came out, hauling a bruised and crying Ron with them. "Eve!" he screamed.

Frustration rolled through me and I dove for the man on the ground, lifting up the back of his shirt and retrieving his gun. I flicked the safety off and lifted it. I didn't give a warning or make any demands. It was clear these men were here for a reason and I would not be letting them see it through.

I aimed and pulled the trigger, putting a bullet in the shoulder of the man who held his gun in hand. He slammed back against the wall, his gun falling from his grip. I switched my attention and aimed at the second man—shooting both of his legs and at this distance, there was no chance of missing.

"Grab my bag!" I screamed to Ron. He dove away from his captors and for the first time since I met him, he actually managed to follow my orders without question or breaking down.

The first man growled and even with a bullet in his shoulder, he leveraged away from the wall and I stepped out of the way—watching him stumble over the ginger who'd been trying to get back to his feet. Both of them went down in a heap as the third man reached for his own weapon.

I didn't hesitate. Turning on him, I lifted the gun in my grasp and pulled the trigger—once, twice, three times until his chest was riddled with holes. This was survival. Pure and simple.

Ron came back out of the room, holding my satchel. "Keys," I snapped to him. "Let's go."

The two of us took off running. I reached back and felt him slap a pair of car keys into my grasp and I hit the unlock button, flashing the lights of the sedan.

"Hey!"

Shit! I cursed internally. The two others were back from the office, but that didn't stop me.

I leapt into the driver's seat as Ron dove for the passenger seat and as the two unharmed men raced across the parking lot, I turned on the car and pressed down on the gas.

"Eve?" Ron's panicked voice rose above the sound of my pounding heart.

"Take this!" I snapped, shoving the firearm into his hand as I gunned the engine and steered towards the two men.

They're eyes widened and while one managed to dive out of the way just in time, the second wasn't as lucky. His body hit the front of the sedan and then the windshield—leaving a large crack as his body rolled over the top of the hood and then down the back, dropping to the pavement.

I glanced in my rearview as I sped out of the lot. He didn't get back up.

24

ANGEL

"You shot someone!" The smell of Ron's sweaty body odor filled the car, along with his high-pitched, panicked voice.

I winced and hit the button on my window to lower it and allow more airflow than what the air conditioning unit in the car provided. Casting a glance his way, I sighed. "Put on your seat belt," I advised him.

"Are we just going to pretend like you didn't kill a man?" he asked, his horrified gaze lingering on me.

It was actually probably two men, but I wasn't going to say that to him now. Not when he was gaping at me like a fish out of water. Irritation bubbled up within me. "Put your seat belt on, *now*," I snapped. "And you're welcome—I don't know if you forgot to notice, but my shooting someone just saved your fucking life."

"This can't be happening." Instead of putting his seat belt on like I told him to, Ron turns away from me and hunches over until his head is between his knees. "I should have gone to the police. I should have done something else. Something other than hiring *you!*"

It really was just like a man to pitch a whole hissy fit and then blame the woman who rescued him. I rolled my eyes and refocused on the road ahead. Somewhere in the back of my mind, though, a small voice reminded me that if it'd been Gaven in the same situation—he wouldn't have needed rescuing. In fact, Gaven would have easily killed each of those men. He wouldn't have hesitated.

Stop it, I ordered myself. *Gaven's not here, and that's a good thing. You want to get away from him, not run back into his arms.*

Even as I repeated that in my mind, I couldn't help but feel exhaustion weigh down on my shoulders, slumping them as my passenger hyperventilated in the seat next to me. Perhaps if things had been different between Gaven and me, I might have been able to call him for help. As the situation remained, though, I had few people that I could actually contact for assistance. And since being captured by Gaven, I hadn't had time to set up a safe house for Ron.

I wracked my brain for a plan as the speedometer raced upward. Trees and dilapidated country houses, a few barns, and some general stores flew past the windows. My fingers gripped the wheel sharply as a thought occurred. There was someone I could contact. I hadn't talked to her in nearly two years, but after leaving Gaven and running from Jackie five years prior—I'd learned to memorize all the contact numbers I needed.

If luck was on my side, the number Scarlett had given me would still be good. If it wasn't … well, I'd cross that bridge when I came to it.

SEVERAL HOURS LATER…

My foot tapped incessantly against the pavement. The clouds seemed to follow us wherever we went and it seemed to make the fact that I was back in the city—far closer to home than I'd prefer—that much more anxiety-inducing. Then again, perhaps my sudden bout of anxiety might have also had something to do with the man that was sitting in the passenger seat of my sedan with his mouth hanging open and drool dripping from the corner of his lips.

I glanced through the driver's side window at him and frowned. It took nearly the entire trip here for him to calm down, but it was clear that the nervous paranoia that had kept him up for several nights had finally taken its toll. Ron was out cold.

A sigh slipped free and I turned back to the closed bookstore sign I was standing in front of. I stared at my reflection in the window and shivered as more rainwater splashed against the backs of my legs while I stood under the pathetic awning.

Luck was rare in this world—rarer, more so for people like me. Somehow, though, I'd managed just enough luck that when I'd finally stopped to call Scarlett, she'd admitted to being nearby. In this very city, in fact. I shook my head at the ridiculousness of it all. Coincidences were just as rare as luck, and I suspected that her easy appearance was anything but a coincidence.

It was fate.

Perhaps all of this was. Gaven. Me. Jackie. My father's death.

I was born the daughter of a mobster and even if I had thought I could escape that life, the world had shown me something else. It had shown me that perhaps my father had been right all along. It was in my blood.

I'd killed a man today—perhaps two—and I didn't feel all that sorry about it for some reason. I didn't feel crushed or frightened by the lack of emotion either. I just felt … apathetic. Not numb, just indifferent. Had I been numb, well, then I could've written it off as shock or something similar.

It wasn't shock. Something deep down in my soul opened its eyes and peered out at me. Something I thought I'd left behind long ago. It was the very thing that had caused me to make a vile request of that man from my mother's funeral. I'd asked him to kill the person responsible for her death, and I had lost no sleep over that.

I'd hoped it was a one-off, but now it was time to face the truth.

I am my father's daughter. A killer. A criminal.

The door to the bookstore creaked open. The bell above jingled lightly, but the sound was swallowed up by the rain. A somewhat familiar face peeked out. Though I hadn't seen her in two years, I still recognized Scarlett's wicked grin and her deep brown eyes.

She gestured towards the inside of the building, and I paused to glance back. I hesitated at leaving Ron out here in the car, but it'd been hard enough to get him to sleep and he needed it. Plus, I really didn't know what I'd do if he woke up and began spouting his angry and frightened bullshit as he had before he'd fallen asleep.

"Eve?" Scarlett's voice echoed behind me.

I turned away from the image of the sleeping man in my car and followed her into the building. Ron would be fine for a short while, I assured myself. No one had followed us from that shitty roadside motel and I wouldn't be long.

I stepped into the building and Scarlett closed and locked the door behind me. A moment later, she enveloped me in a tight hug. I blinked, taken aback for a moment before I caved to the feeling. I wrapped my own arms around her and hugged her back, pressing my face into her shoulder. It felt good to hug someone, to recognize them, and feel a connection to them. Hugging Scarlett wasn't like being wrapped in Gaven's arms. There was no heat, no visceral tightening in my stomach. It was simply

… nice. Not something I'd experienced in a long damn time.

"It's so good to see you," she said, pulling away seconds later. Her hands remained on my arms as she looked me up and down. All around us, the scent of stale paper and dust permeated the room.

"You too," I said absently. "Um … Scarlett? What the hell are you doing in a closed-down bookstore?"

She glanced around as if just remembering where we were. "Oh, it's just a front," she replied with a wave of her hand. "We're only here temporarily. One of my husbands had a job to do, and his employer wanted to meet with him, and well —one thing led to another, and we're renting the space for a short while. You actually caught me at a good time. I only got in a few days ago. I came up for a visit because…"

Her words trailed off as she began moving, releasing my arms as she turned and headed up the darkened room towards a back staircase. It left me little else to do but follow her, so I did.

"Wait." I frowned at the back of her head as her words caught up with my mind. "Did you say one of your husbands? As in more than one?" Who else did that sound like? America, that's who. I shook my head. What was it with the women of this world? Did they all get multiple men and not give a damn? I could barely handle the fucking *one* I was married to.

Scarlett chuckled, tossing her long black hair

over one shoulder as she looked back. "Yeah," she said. "A lot's happened since I saw you in Italy. I've got two husbands now and a little girl. She's fucking adorable."

"You had a daughter?" I scanned down the length of her body. "How long ago?" My stomach tightened. A small piece of my mind wondered what a daughter between Gaven and I would look like. Would she have his midnight blue eyes? His blonde hair?

Scarlett ascended the staircase and I trailed behind her. "Actually, she's my stepdaughter," she admitted. "But I love her like she's mine. Who knows, maybe someday one of my husbands will give her a little brother or sister."

Just as that last statement crossed her mouth, we reached the top of the staircase into what appeared to be a second-floor apartment.

"Be careful what you wish for, Scar," a man's voice echoed back to us, making me jump. "If it's a baby you want, I'm more than happy to provide."

Scarlett's lips curved into a slow, sensual smile as she moved towards the man I now spotted further into the apartment, at a set of tables and desks pushed together and topped with a multitude of computers. The woman I remembered from Italy— elegant, seductive, and always in control—morphed into someone else entirely right before my eyes. She practically drifted across the floor towards him, circling the tables to wrap her arms around his neck and shoulders before leaning down for an open-mouthed kiss.

I waited a beat ... and then another ... and another. They didn't stop until I cleared my throat as discomfort got the better of me. Scarlett lifted her head from the man's lips and looked at me with an almost fuzzy gaze. Her eyes were slightly unfocused and even as she drew her arms back, I noticed that she still stayed near the man.

Two years ago, she'd been a single woman on the prowl—looking for her next sugar daddy or her next victim. I hadn't quite approved of her choice of career, but on my own, it was hard enough to make friends, and well ... those in glass houses shouldn't exactly throw stones.

"Eve, this is my husband, Hadrian."

I moved forward around the tables and paused before them, extending my hand to the man. "It's Angel, actually," I said. "Eve's just an alias."

Scarlett chuckled. "Giving away all of your secrets now, huh?"

I shrugged. "It's not really a secret anymore—or at least, it won't be soon." Because now that I was back in that city, now that I was back here, I realized something.

I didn't fucking want to leave. I didn't want to run anymore. I wasn't as scared as I thought I was. I'd already killed once; what was another? In the end, I wanted Jackie to pay for what she'd done. She didn't deserve our father's empire—not after she had killed him to get it.

Warm, masculine fingers brushed my knuckles before Hadrian's palm connected with mine. "Angel?" Bright cerulean blue eyes met mine as the man's head tilted. His hand tightened. "As in Evangeline Price?"

I met his gaze directly and took a breath. "Yes," I said. "I'm Evangeline Price."

25

ANGEL

Hadrian was a handsome man, with a wicked grin that matched Scarlett's. I could see why she'd fallen for him. He was a tall, wiry, muscled man with dark hair cut short around the back and longer at the top of his head. As my name crossed my lips and his eyes lit on me, a spark of recognition entered his eyes. The hand that gripped mine tightened—unrelenting—and it only made me want to tighten my own grasp in return.

He blinked as if realizing what he'd instinctively done before releasing me. "Sorry about that," he said with a careful laugh as he scrubbed the back of his head and took a step back. "It's good to meet a friend of Scar's, I just never anticipated that you'd be—"

"Related to the mob?" I arched a brow. "Why not? She is a world-renowned thief, isn't she?"

Scarlett laughed. "Not so much anymore," she admitted, stepping between us. I saw the look she cast Hadrian's way—it was a mixture of a question and a warning. As if she was both asking what the fuck his problem was and to not cause any issues.

If I was going to actually move forward with my current forming plan—stay in America, go after my sister, and take my life back—I'd need to get used to it. People were going to react whether I wanted them to or not, just to my name. My real name and not the one of many I'd used over the last five years. There was a power that came with truth—with my name and what it was attached to.

"Now, what did you need help with?" Scarlett asked, redirecting herself to me as she backed against one of the tables and leaned on it, crossing her arms over her chest. Hadrian's gaze snapped to the expanse of the chest that the shirt she wore allowed him—dipping down low in a V-neck above low-rise jeans.

I wondered if that was something Gaven did when we were together—and I was clothed, of course.

"I have a client outside," I said.

"Criminal Witness Protection?" Scarlett snickered. It was a name she'd dubbed my business two years ago when I'd explained what I did.

I shook my head. "You know I deal with more than criminals; I deal with people who can't rely on their governments for protection. I help them disappear when needed."

Hadrian spoke up, focusing back on me. "Is that what this client needs?"

I grimaced. "Not exactly. This one is a bit more complicated. Ronald is a scientist working for a company here in New York. He's developed a new product that medical corporations are going to want to use, but he wants to give the product out for practically free."

Hadrian frowned and scratched at the shadow of a beard forming on the underside of his jawline. "What's the product?"

"Organs," I said. "Scientifically grown to suit the needs of a specific individual."

A low whistle shot through the room. "Shit, yeah, there's no fucking way a corporation is gonna let something like that go to market without having their hand in it, and definitely not for free. Something like that will make millions."

"Think billions," I replied with another shake of my head. "They want his formula for how to do it and they want him gone."

"They're trying to kill him," Scarlett surmised.

I nodded. "Yeah, we actually just got away from a kidnapping attempt at the motel I was having him hide out at while I was…" I didn't want to mention Gaven. "…indisposed."

Scarlett's lips twitched at the last word, but she didn't press for more information. She knew a little bit about the husband I'd left behind and how we'd come together, but she couldn't know that I was indisposed because he'd found me and held me captive for several days.

"Okay, so you want to protect this guy and make him disappear with his work?" Hadrian asked.

"Yeah, that's what I'd like to do," I said. Though, if I were to ask Ron, I knew he would want to go public with what he knew. He mistakenly thought that if the public knew of his invention and what it would do for the good of mankind, he would be protected. I wish he were right, but I knew better. The media was nothing if not a tool for corporations to use at their will. They'd label him as a crazy idealist and he might be protected for as long as he was in the public eye—but eventually, the public would forget, the world would move on, and he'd be snuffed out in the shadows.

I'd seen it happen a time or two in the last few years and I hated the thought of him being yet another casualty of that corporate greed. If I were honest with myself, I knew that a part of the reason I wanted my life back was because I wanted the allies and power that came with it. If I had more than just myself, I could have protected Ron much better.

"So, a new identity then," Hadrian said as he turned away and went back to his seat in front of the wall of computer screens. "That's easy enough to do."

"More than that," I said, resisting the urge to roll my eyes. If all he needed was a new identity, I could've done that myself. "He's going to want to leave his work somewhere. He wants it out there in the world, and before I make him disappear, I want to help him get it there."

Hadrian's hands froze over the keyboard and he looked back at me incredulously. "You want to actually help him go up against the medical corporations? That's fucking insane."

Scarlett tapped one long, manicured finger against her chin. "Is it really that crazy?" she asked.

Hadrian's gaze snapped to her and he lifted a finger, pointing it her way. "No," he practically growled. "You are not considering this. She'll be a target; if you help her, so will you. I will not have you painting a big fat target on your gorgeous ass, baby. If you want red on you, I'll spank you. Otherwise, stay out of it."

I blinked at the carnal words but didn't have a chance to step in or say anything as Scarlett rounded on him. "She's my friend, Hadrian," she snapped. "She asked me for help—not you."

"The answer is still the same," he replied. "It's a flat fucking no. If you think you can fight me on this, you know you'll be outnumbered. Shall I call Wolf right now?"

Scarlett snarled at her husband. "Just because your ring is on my finger and your collar is on my neck," she said, reaching up to touch the light gold necklace encircling her throat. "Doesn't mean you can control every aspect of my life, Hadrian."

Hadrian arched one dark brow. "Want to make that a bet, baby?"

The two of them were at a stand-off, but my

ears were ringing with the words that had come out of their mouths. Collars and spankings. Were they … no, they couldn't be. I shook my head and dismissed it. Even if they were in a similar relationship to the one I shared with Gaven, it didn't mean anything to me or pertain to the matter at hand.

I moved closer to the two of them, capturing their attention as I began to speak. "I don't want anyone else to get a target painted on their backs," I said. They both swung their heads my way. Hadrian narrowed his gaze. "What I need help with is coming up with a plan—to not only protect my client but to deliver his formula to the right hands so that it can't be covered up no matter what the corporation and the media try to do."

Hadrian cursed. "That's a tall fucking order," he said, biting the words out through clenched teeth. He shut his eyes and leaned back into the chair, his hands white-knuckling the armrests. I could practically see the steam pouring from his forehead and his ears.

"But you'll help?" Scarlett asked.

Tense silence met that question. After a beat, she circled the tables and returned to his side. Her hand touched the top of his head and then she ran her fingers down into his hair, stroking the short strands back as he opened his eyes and met her gaze above his.

"Please?" she asked again. "She's my friend. You know I don't have many of those."

I waited with bated breath to see what Hadrian

would decide. If he turned me down, I'd have to think of something else, and honestly, I wasn't even quite sure if I could protect and hide Ron—not with Gaven on my heels.

Hadrian's arms lifted from the armrests and wrapped around Scarlett's slender frame, pulling her between his legs as he pushed away from the desk to give her room.

"You have me," I heard him say, his voice muffled against her stomach as he pressed his face into her. "And Wolf and our daughter."

She continued to soothe him, running her hands through his hair and somehow, I felt like this was a scene I shouldn't be privy to. This was a private moment between them, and watching it made me feel more of a pervert than anything Gaven had ever done to me. Turning away helped, but not by much because I could still hear them.

"I know," Scarlett said, "but you aren't friends— the three of you are family. Please, Hadrian. Please help me help her."

My chest clenched. It was clear just by listening to their conversation that they truly loved and cared for each other. They were what Scarlett said they were— family. I didn't have a family. Not anymore. Jackie was a problem, not a sister. She was a blackmailer and a traitor. And Gaven … well, I'd run from him too many times for him to see me as little more than a liability. He still wanted me, but likely only because he wanted answers and his shot at the Price Empire.

It made me a sucker of a woman, but once my sister was dealt with I would give it to him. I wanted what Scarlett and Hadrian obviously had. Trust. Caring. *Love*. I wasn't sure if I'd ever get it—or if Gaven could be the one to give it to me—but we were already married. So, I had to at least try.

"Fine." Hadrian's begrudging response had me spinning back to face them.

"You'll help?" I clarified.

Hadrian leaned around Scarlett and glared my way. "Yes," he replied. "But I want your fucking guy up here. He shouldn't be out in the street, waiting in the car."

"I lost the men that tried to kidnap him hours ago," I defended. "And he was tired. I just wanted to let him sleep."

Hadrian released Scarlett with a grunt of frustration. "Do you not know how many cameras are stationed around the world?" he demanded. "It's not just CCTVs that you need to look out for. Get him up here. *Now*."

I blew out a breath, and though I wanted to say something snippy in return, I pushed the urge down. He was going to help, and that was enough for now. "Fine," I said, nodding.

"I'll come with—" Just as Scarlett tried to make that offer, Hadrian's hand captured hers and he tugged her back towards his lap until she fell into it with an oomph.

"Not you," he said. "I need to make something

clear to you, Scar, while she goes to get her miracle man."

This time, I did roll my eyes. Ronald was not a miracle man—well, perhaps he would be if his discovery and formula made it out to the rest of the world—but to me, he was purely a job. One I needed to hurry up and finish so I could go after Jackie.

"I'll be right back," I said—not that the two of them could hear me. Once Hadrian dismissed me, they fell into their own little world.

With a sigh, I went back the way I'd come, striding down the rickety staircase leading into the stale air of the closed bookshop on the ground floor. Outside, it looked like the rain had let up and was only a sprinkle.

I headed for the front and quickly undid the deadbolt on the front door before stepping outside. With the rain slowing to a light drizzle, the world felt warmer than before. The nondescript sedan I'd driven here in remained parked on the curb.

Fishing my keys out of my shorts pocket, I hit the unlock button and popped the driver's side door open. I was already talking before I bent down. "Hey, Ron, it's time to wake—Ron?"

The passenger side was empty. I looked to the back, wondering if he had woken, found me missing, and decided to nap in the back, but no. The backseat was just as empty.

"What the fuck?" The inside remained untouched, and nothing had been disturbed other than the missing man. The windows were rolled up and unshattered. I stood again, and just as I turned my head, wondering if Ron had stepped out now that it wasn't raining as hard for a breath, something slammed into the side of my skull.

I stumbled away from the sedan, slamming into the open driver's side door before falling hard on the ground. My ears rang and stars danced in front of my vision. A somewhat familiar head of ginger hair appeared before me. It was one of the men from the motel and his face was crunched in anger.

"Sorry about this, Miss *Price*." The man spit the name in my face as he grabbed my hair, yanking it back and causing a sharp jolt of pain to skit down the back of my neck. I cried out and reached up to alleviate some of the pain. "For not recognizing you before, but don't worry. This time—we won't make the same mistake."

I struggled against his hold as he jerked me up from the ground, my sneakers slipping on the wet pavement. "Let go!" I yelled, flailing. I punched out at him, but he was faster than me and instead, he backhanded me—sending my skull ringing once more as my head snapped to the side. Last time had obviously been luck on my part. He was far stronger than I remembered.

"We only expected Ronald," he said, "but when Miss Jackie heard there was a woman with him, she knew exactly who you were, and we're to bring you to her."

"Jackie?" I blinked as spots of white and black

danced in front of my gaze. *Fuck. No. Shit.* Not yet, I wasn't ready. My mind reeled.

"That's right," the ginger man snapped. "Don't worry—you'll be asleep for the drive."

"Asleep? What—"

I didn't finish my question. I couldn't have even if I wanted to because the next thing I saw—the *last* thing I saw—was his fist coming straight for my face. Then it was lights fucking out.

26

GAVEN

The Price Mansion had changed much since I'd last been here. Lighter, more feminine aspects replaced the once-masculine decor. Pale curtains fluttering in the windows. Rows and rows of flowers arching up the driveway. Perfectly manicured trees. The sprawling grounds were well kept—they always had been, but now something about them set me on edge.

Perhaps it was the added security and the faceless men who were unrecognizable that led me through the gate. No one I could name. I'd heard that Jackie exchanged guards like some women exchanged boyfriends. I wouldn't expect anything less. She seemed the type to get bored easily. There was one thing, though—they were silent and unflinching and didn't speak unless spoken to. Not at all like comrades but like servants.

That was never how Raffaello ran his empire. He ran it with fierceness and an iron fist, but he respected his men and they respected him. He was different from me in that aspect—he had men to take care of and I'd only ever had myself. Things were different now. Matteo got out of the car and followed me up the front steps. After what had gone down at the club, I'd called him and he'd arrived in record time. Now, the two of us were here, ready to step into the belly of the beast. To end this and bring my wife fucking home where she belonged.

No more running, Angel, I thought to myself. *Once Jackie is gone, you're all mine.*

After the night I'd been unceremoniously booted from the place that had been meant for my reign, I hadn't returned. I didn't want to—not until I was sure it would be mine. Now, though, I saw little other choice.

As I stepped inside the double wooden doors into the foyer, I was catapulted back five years—when I married and was left by my treacherous wife the same night. When I did finally get my hands on her again, I'd tie her to me in a way she couldn't escape. I'd break her fucking legs to keep her from running, and then—just for extra measure—I'd damn well put a tracker on her. Somewhere she couldn't reach so I wouldn't risk her cutting it out herself. I knew she was resourceful. She would if she really wanted to. I had to make it impossible.

I promised myself when I took my first life that this would be my world—and that I would do whatever it took to get what I wanted. Even if it meant taking from others, and destroying their lives, I would do it. The soreness of my hollow insides reminded me too much of hunger, and it was only ever full when she was around.

"Gaven, what a pleasant surprise." I looked up to the staircase as the same stone-faced man who had let me into the mansion now gestured for me to extend my arms out to the sides. Another man stepped forward and did the same with Matteo. I raised my arms with a scowl, and Matteo followed suit. As we were patted down, my attention returned to the woman descending the stairs.

Five years had not hurt Jacquelina Price at all. In fact, it seemed that time only agreed with her. Her dark hair was tied up into a professional and elegant chignon at the back of her head, and her equally dark lashes were painted blacker and stretched up to her brows. Her lips were a bold red, curving into a smug smile as she moved down the stairs toward me. Her long black sheath dress was held tight to her curves and I was sure to any other man, she would be a feast for the eyes. In mine, it was merely like looking at a snake masquerading as a person.

"Jackie," I said, "it's been a long time."

She laughed, the sound smoky and purposefully thick with seduction. "Yes, it has. What brings you here?"

The man in front of me pulls a gun from my chest holster and sets it on the front table next to him. My scowl deepens as he moves around me and pulls the one from the small of my back and adds it to the quickly piling collection of weapons from both Matteo and myself.

"I'm sure you can anticipate what I'm here for, Jackie," I snapped.

"Have you finally come to your senses?" she asked, stopping at the end of the stairs. "Are you finally willing to admit that you want me?"

Disgust rolled through me. I level her with a bland look. "No."

She sighed. "Oh, well, then no, I have no clue what you're here for, Gaven."

"I'm here about your sister."

Jackie stepped down from the last stair and glided past Matteo and me, not even sparing the man who her father had known and respected for most of his life with a single glance. For Matteo's part, he kept his own expression unbothered.

"What about her?" Jackie asked in a bored tone. I didn't trust it. I narrowed my gaze on her. Did she truly have no clue of Angel's whereabouts? Did she even know that Angel was back in the States? It didn't matter either way. So long as Jackie lived, then Angel would still run. She would still be threatened. I had to eliminate that threat. Only then could I have everything I'd ever wanted.

"She's back."

Jackie paused in the doorway to the next room and turned back, cocking her head at me. Her eyes roved down my chest and paused at my groin before finishing at my feet and then flashing back up to my face.

"I admit," she began, "I didn't expect you to come to me if you ever found her." She stepped towards me as her man finished divesting me of my weapons. If that made her feel safer, then so be it. If she thought I needed a gun to kill, she was dead wrong. I could snap her neck easily enough with just my hands. Then again, she was dead either way—she just didn't realize it yet.

As Jackie drew closer, her long fingers came out to stroke up my chest. Thick, nauseating perfume invaded my nostrils. "I'm not going to lie," she continued. "I thought you would try to capture her and hide her from me—I thought that perhaps you would try to use her against me—my father's murderer." The lie slid off her tongue so easily. "So, for you to come to me with this information is quite … promising."

Jackie walked her fingers up the line of my chest, only stopping when I snatched her hand and held it away. I arched a brow down at her as she fluttered her long lashes up at me. I examined her face, seeking some sign of surprise—but what little there was seemed to be reserved only for me.

She knew. Deep down, in my gut, I knew it was true. I swore internally. She had already known that Angel was back in the States. And if she already knew, then Angel was in danger *now*.

My hand on Jackie's tightened as I circled her wrist, creating a manacle with my fingers. She didn't seem frightened. In fact, she leaned further into me, raising her face to mine.

"I should have you taken out back and shot for all you've done to me, Gaven," she said, her tone light despite her words.

I arched my brow. "Oh? Why is that?"

She laughed again, her eyes slanting towards Matteo and then back to me. "Well, on top of stealing some of my best men, I know that you've been keeping secrets from me. Your new drug being one of them."

"What I do with my own business isn't your concern, Jackie."

"Oh, don't be like that," she said, twisting her arm to break my hold. I let her go. "We're family. We'd be a whole lot more, too, if you'd let us." I watched her move back towards the doorway, pause, and pivot to face me. One hand found the frame as she leaned into it. "I could give you everything you ever wanted, Gaven. I've offered it to you, and you know I'm not used to being refused."

No, she wasn't. A woman like Jacquelina Price had damn near everything she wanted. She felt powerful. In charge. That made her cocky. She was a woman in a man's world, trying to take it over the same way a man did—through murder and deceit. I couldn't say I didn't at least admire that conniving piece of her, but not when it came at the expense of my own goals.

"While I usually don't mind games, Jackie. I usually get to choose the partners I play with."

Her red lips curved wider. "So *play with me*." The innuendo didn't go unnoticed.

"You tell me what I want to know, and perhaps I'll consider it." At my side, I felt Matteo tense. We were surrounded by Jackie's men. Their gazes were locked on us as they awaited a command from their Mistress. That was one thing about Jackie that I knew wouldn't suit me. She wasn't a woman who could give up control. She wanted to maintain her power over each and every person. She wanted to be the only one at the top, and she didn't care whose throat she had to slit on her way up.

Jackie tilted her head to the side as she stared back at me. She was analyzing me as much as I was her. We were locked in a silent battle of wills, and I wouldn't be able to make a move until I knew what she was going to do. Finally, after what felt like an eternity, she sighed and shook her head.

"No, I don't think I will," she said. Despite my outward appearance, which I knew from experience, didn't reveal a damn flicker of emotion, my heart hammered against my chest. She flicked her hands to the guns laid out on the table. "You'll leave those on your way out," she stated.

A low growl rumbled up my throat and I stepped forward, only to pull up short as one of her silent men stepped in front of me, halting my momentum. I glared at the man as Jackie clicked her tongue.

"So violent, Gaven," she chastised. I lifted my gaze to hers. She was smiling, amused. Of course, she was. She knew that Angel was in the States, and more than that, if she wasn't asking me any questions, that meant she knew more than that. She was already on the hunt. She likely had men searching for her. "I used to like that about you, you know," she continued. "All that volatile heat of you could have been used for so much more."

"Where is she?" I snapped. "You're not asking me anything—so that means you already fucking know."

"Angel?" She tapped her chin again and hummed in the back of her throat. "Maybe I do, and maybe I don't. Whatever the case, though, it doesn't concern you anymore. My father might have been willing to hand over his family business to someone like you, but I'm not so stupid."

Raffaello Price had known something about his eldest daughter that the rest of the world didn't. Not yet, at least. When I'd chosen Angel as my bride, he'd seemed almost … relieved. A father wasn't supposed to have favorites—or so a man like him had believed. It was clear, though, that Jackie still held some hateful grudge for the man. All her crocodile tears from his funeral five years ago were nothing but window dressing. This woman was fake, from the nails on her fingers to the smile on her face. I'd bet good fucking money that if I cut into her flesh, I'd find nothing but stuffing and plastic. Perhaps now was the time to find out.

I moved forward, causing the man in my way to put out a hand. "Don't even think about it," he warned.

"Remove your hand," I said through clenched teeth. "Or lose it." He withdrew his hand from my body but still refused to move out of the way—a pity. I would have liked to rip his hand clean from his body at this moment.

"She's mine, Jackie," I said, directing my gaze back to the woman behind him. "I will handle Angel."

"No." Jackie shook her head and then lifted a hand, flicking it towards the door. "Now, you should be on your way. I have a guest arriving soon." The way she leveled me with a look of utter self-satisfaction told me that she was pleased by this new turn of events. I needed to get closer to her if I had a chance at wrapping my hands around her throat.

"I'm warning you now, Jackie," I said, my voice dripping with venom. "If you hurt my wife, I won't let it go."

A laugh arched out from her throat as she tossed her head back. The sound echoed up to the rafters of the old mansion. A hard hand touched my shoulder, shoving me back. I didn't think. I didn't even hesitate. I reached up and gripped the man's hand, and as I looked him right in his face, I bent it straight back until a snapping sound echoed in my ears and his knuckles were pressed into the back of his wrist. For extra measure, I locked onto his fingers and snapped two of them to the side, effectively breaking them as well.

The look of shock that crossed his face was almost comical. His mouth opened on a shout, but I pulled back and punched him in the face. He went down in a heap on the floor—knocked out cold with a bone protruding from where I'd broken his hand clean from his arm. I had warned him and that was more than others would do.

Immediately, four sets of guns were trained on me. Fingers on triggers. Safeties off. I froze and glared at Jackie. She didn't even seem that concerned that I'd probably made one of her men permanently disabled—because there was no doubt in my mind that he'd struggle with that hand for the rest of his life. In fact, her eyes sparkled with delight rather than insult.

I should have snapped her neck when she'd been touching me earlier. Before anyone had been aware. I could have. I could have seduced her life from her. Run my fingers up her sides and then choked her. One small twist was all it would've taken. It would've been easier even than breaking that man's hand.

"You're a smart man, Gaven Belmonte," she said instead of commenting on my actions. "You're outnumbered here. I could have my men kill you with a snap of my fingers."

"Then why don't you?" I pressed. We were entering dangerous territory. Each of us daring the other.

"Because, Gaven, I still think we can be useful to each other. Once my little sister has been taken care of, you'll have no one else to rely on but me. I'm still unmarried and unlike a man … I don't care if you're a virgin."

Rage pounded through me. I could feel my muscles straining beneath the fabric of my suit.

"Gaven." Matteo's voice pulled me back from the edge—literally—of losing complete and utter control. "We should go."

Jackie grinned again. "Yes, Gaven. Listen to your pet. Go … before you make a mistake you can't take back."

Matteo moved forward, taking my shoulder firmly as he pulled me back. One step. Two. Three. The four guns of her guards remained on us as we backed toward the front door. Matteo opened it and grabbed the keys that had been left on the table along with the guns. "Remember, Matteo," Jackie said as he reached back for our phones as well, "leave the guns."

He was silent in his response, but he did nod as he scooped up the cells and pocketed them both. I, however, was too far into my head to do so. It wasn't until we were outside with the doors shut behind us that I felt a fresh breath of air in my lungs. It burned through my throat.

Kill. I wanted to fucking kill her. Slice open her insides, wrap her intestines around her throat, and watch the life drain from her. Murder had become a way of life long ago, but I'd never wanted to enjoy it as much as I did at that moment.

A cell phone rang, and as Matteo and I headed for the car we'd left parked in front of the mansion, he pulled it out and answered. "Yes?"

He paused, grabbed ahold of me, and shoved the phone into my hand when I turned to him. "I'll drive," he said. "It's for you."

With gritted teeth, I snatched the phone from him and put it to my ear. "This better be fucking good," I snapped into the receiver. "What?"

"You have a fucking problem."

I frowned at the voice. "Hadrian? What the fuck do you mean?"

"Your wife is here in New York, and she's in trouble."

Things just got better and fucking better.

Waking up after being knocked out with a fist was not on my list of situations I'd ever like to repeat. It was like waking up with a raging hangover without having any of the fun from the night before. A low groan echoed up my throat as I blinked my bleary eyes open and stared at the room I was in. Gray darkness invaded and it took me a moment to recognize the heat surrounding my face and seeping into my neck was a bag over my head. Not two seconds after I'd made that realization though, the bag was ripped off—the hand doing so catching a few strands of my hair and yanking them out as well.

I gritted my teeth and glared up at the man responsible. The ginger from before. Asshole.

It wasn't Gaven and it wasn't the corporation after Ron. It wasn't about Ron at all. It was about me, and Ron was just collateral damage. So much for my sparkling business record.

"Hello, baby sister." Like a true villain from some cheesy B-rated thriller, the clicking of Jackie's heels accompanying her voice—which I hadn't heard in five years—set my nerves on edge.

I clenched my jaw and settled my gaze on her as she stepped in front of me. Blood red lips, black winged eyeliner, and a perfect updo all sculpted my older sister's look. She smiled, her skin not even wrinkling the slightest bit as she looked down on me.

I stared back at her. "Jackie."

"Welcome home," she said. "Though it won't be for long, you should enjoy it while you can."

"You mean the home you stole?" I asked, lightly. "The one you slaughtered your own father for?"

Her smile tightened. "I stole nothing that I didn't deserve," she snapped. "I was built for this life, and I told you that if you wanted to survive it—then you should make sure to never show your face again. Yet..." she waved red painted nails in my direction, "here you are."

"Forgetting that you had your men drag me here?" I asked. "Always convenient that forgetfulness of yours. Are you sure you're not going senile in your old age, Jackie?"

I didn't see the slap coming, but I wasn't all that surprised by it. The painful echo of her palm hitting my cheek rang around the room and through my skull for a moment before my mind caught up with my body. Turning my face back in her direction, I licked my lip. Blood lingered on my tongue and I prodded the fresh cut on my lower lip with it before shaking my head.

"Why did you bring me here, Jackie?" I asked, continuing the conversation as if nothing had happened. I knew that would rankle her. I wanted it to. "And where is my client?"

"Ronald Wiser?" Jackie clarified. "He's here. Not to worry, though. I have no intentions of doing anything to him—my plan was simply to capture him to lure you out. I didn't know, yet that you'd gotten away from Gaven's grip. You were always good at running away."

"You should let him go," I snapped. "He has nothing to do with this—it's just you and me."

"You should worry about yourself more than your client, little sister," Jackie replied. Pivoting away from me, she strode towards the far side of the room, giving me a moment to actually analyze where I was.

The familiar walls were painted light gray, and the curtains had been changed from black to a pale lavender. If it weren't for the length and width of the room, the old Victorian windows, and the desk that sat in front of them, it might have tricked me into thinking it was a different room. But it wasn't. I recognized it, and as my eyes fell to the floor over the red carpet, I remembered the last time I'd been in here.

The same room my father had been killed in.

The doors to the office opened and I jerked my head up, shaking off the melancholic memories as a new man stepped inside. He was tall with a dark wash of scruff across a face that was almost leathery. His eyes were black—whatever color they might have actually been swallowed by his pupils.

He glanced over at me with disinterest as Jackie welcomed him inside and touched his chest. Without hesitation, the man bent down and gripped her waist. She went up on her toes, smiling as she offered her mouth to his. He took it, the wet sounds of their kiss filling the room. I grimaced and tried to look anywhere else but the two of them as they made out.

Other than the ginger at my back, at least three other men were stationed around the room. One by the windows, one at the doors, whoever the fuck she was sucking face with, and another against the wall. No sign of Ron, though she had said he was here.

My hands were tied firmly behind my back with some sort of durable tape. I adjusted my shoulder, pulling against the binding as discreetly as possible to determine how hard it would be to get out. Definitely not easy, I realized as the tape ripped and tugged at my skin. I winced. It felt like the adhesive was strong enough to rip flesh from bone. Before I could test it further, Jackie pulled her face away from the man's and turned back to me.

Somehow, her lipstick was still perfectly in place —guess the kiss had only been loud because I knew for damn sure had I been kissing Gaven like that, he would've ruined my makeup. She swiped one nail down the side of her mouth—as if removing some unseen wetness as she left him and strode back to me.

The man followed. "Is this the one you wanted me to take care of?"

"Yes." Jackie smiled at me. "This is my sister. Angel—meet Blade. He'll be your killer tonight."

Blade? I looked up at him in disbelief. *What grown fucking man wanted a cheesy fucking name like that?* As that thought spun through my mind, Jackie's words over-powered them, reminding me that there were more important things to focus on than some pathetic name of some pathetic killer.

"You think killing me will keep you safe, Jackie?" I snapped, growing angrier by the second. "You fucking killed your own father and blamed it on me. Father's old men know as much. Gaven knows as much. You're not getting away—even if you kill me."

Long black lashes lowered and then lifted as Jackie blinked at me and then, with blatant fabrica-tion, she stifled a fake yawn. "Doesn't matter to me," she replied. "In the end, you'll still be dead and only one Price will be left." Her smile returned as she leaned down in my face and reached up, grabbing me hard. Her nails dug into my cheeks as she held onto my jaw. "*Me*," she sneered.

A coldness entered my body. Almost the same kind of coldness that I'd felt after killing that man in the motel parking lot. Except this type was a little different, it felt … darker. More sinister.

Whatever thin tendril of connection I'd once

had to my sister had been severed, and as the dark snake-like eyes in her skull bore into mine, I realized something else. I *wanted* to hurt her. No normal person wanted that. No normal person contemplated killing their own family for revenge. They left justice to the authorities, but I knew without a shadow of a doubt that no police or government agency could stop Jacquelina Price.

Before I thought better of it, I reared my head back and slammed my forehead into her nose. She was so close that I could hear the crunch upon impact. A violent throb burst behind my eyes, but Jackie's shocked scream was reward enough and I looked up just in time to see her stumble back—a hand clasped over her face as blood dripped from between her fingers.

"You bitch!" she shrieked.

Sweat dripped down my back as I stared up at her. Something wet touched my forehead and slithered down between my eyes and over the bridge of my nose. A droplet of her blood? Or had I broken my own skin? It didn't matter.

"Remember what Dad always said?" I asked as I glared back at her, shaking with rage. "Whatever you do in this life, there is always a price to pay. I hope you're ready to pay it, Jackie, because it's coming for you. As soon as I get out of here, you're as good as dead."

Jackie's hands lowered, and for the first time, I saw the extent of my damage. Her nose was definitely broken—it was askew from her usually perfectly done-up face. Blood trickled from both nostrils, smearing over her lips and down her chin. She growled and turned, stomping to the man against the wall.

"Knife!" she practically screamed.

When the man didn't seem to move fast enough for her, she shrieked in frustration and slapped him before delving into his pocket and yanking out a pocket knife before kicking him right in the balls. I winced as the man crumpled to the floor. The poor bastard was little more than a punching bag for her rage. Every man in the room seemed to go rigid at Jackie's actions and tension filled the space within the four walls.

If she were aware, Jackie didn't show it. Instead, she flipped open the knife she'd stolen and stalked back to me. The blade slammed into my shoulder with shocking speed. The air in my lungs came out in a rush as I choked and hissed through the pain. Yanking it out again, Jackie went to stab me again and was stopped by the man she'd kissed.

"If you don't want her to die too soon, then I recommend you let me take care of the rest," he said.

Jackie's chest heaved, her breasts rising and falling in rapid succession. She was flushed from her face down to the tops of her tits. Blood trickled from the wound she'd given me, soaking into the faded hoodie I still wore. It felt like my shoulder was on fire. I bent my head and breathed through my nose. Tears threatened to spill over my lashes, but I sucked them back, refusing to give her even that satisfaction.

I was different than I had been five years ago. I was stronger. I was far better than she ever would be. I repeated that mantra in my head as I heard the man say something else to her. Whatever it was was lost on me as I focused on not crying. Jackie's response, however, was loud and clear.

"I want it to hurt," she cried. "Make it hurt, Blade. I want her to suffer!"

"Of course." Blade looked from Jackie to me as I lifted my head, and as I stared back at him, I realized he was not Gaven. They might have both been killers, but this man had no attachment to me and no reason not to follow Jackie's commands. He nudged Jackie towards the door. "Go get your nose fixed up," he said. "I'll take care of her."

Jackie's hand clapped over her face as if she'd forgotten her broken nose. She flinched as she accidentally bumped it. The look she cut my way would have set me on fire if it burned any hotter with hatred. "I have to go make sure Gaven doesn't show up on my doorstep again," she said, her voice slightly muffled but still every bit as resentful. "Make sure she's dead, Blade. When I return, I either want to hear screams or nothing."

"You should have taken care of the man before," Blade replied, but as he stepped forward, he reached into his suit pocket and withdrew a small pouch—it looked almost like a roll-up shaving kit.

Jackie snapped her fingers and gestured for the

remaining men to follow her out. The man on the floor, clutching his dick and balls, groaned but got to his feet and limped after the rest of them.

Blade didn't move until the door clicked shut behind him and only then did he stride across the room to the desk slightly behind me. I turned my head, gritting my teeth as the movement stretched my skin down my neck and subsequently my wounded shoulder. Setting the small satchel he'd withdrawn, I watched as he unrolled it.

Instead of shaving supplies—not that I'd really thought it'd contained something so mundane—the bag revealed several sharp-looking knives and tools. I was not so naive that I didn't know what they were for—they were instruments of torture. Fuck. I had to figure out how to get out of this and soon or else Jackie would get her wish.

"Your sister is quite the hot-tempered woman," the man said, almost casually. Selecting one particularly wicked-looking knife, the man held it up and twisted it in his grip as he admired the polished metal.

I inhaled sharply. "She's only going to drag you down with her," I cautioned him. "You should stop while you can—my husband—"

"Yes, she told me all about your husband. Mrs. Price—or should I refer to you as Belmonte?" Blade turned to me and moved around until he was standing in front of me.

I stiffened and cried out as he set the very tip of his knife into the top of my bare thigh and dragged it downward, cutting a perfect line down the center of my upper leg. Blood welled up and slid down either side. I panted, gasping for breath.

"Since your husband is much like me—or at least in the same business—you'll understand then that this isn't personal." The knife pulled away from one thigh and touched the other one. "If you tense, it'll make it hurt more," he warned right before he performed the same cut.

"Fuck!" The curse slipped out. He was right—tensing definitely made it hurt like a bitch. I shook my head, trying to rid myself of the need to cry. I'd done a lot of things in the past five years, been put into a lot of different situations, but I'd never been tortured. I wasn't confident in my ability to hold out until I figured a way out, and I was starting to wonder if I ever would get out.

In the back of my mind, Jackie's earlier words echoed back to me. Something about Gaven coming here … was he still here? If he were, there was no fucking way he'd let this happen. Even if he was pissed at me for running away again, Gaven was nothing if not possessive. He would want to punish me himself, and certainly not like this, not when I was still considered the key to his success and desires.

After the second cut, I started to realize why Blade went by that name. He was adept with them. More than adept; with each cut, he seemed to fill with life. His eyes heated as he crouched before me and watched the blood drip down my inner thighs.

My stomach cramped. My head pounded. My shoulder fucking throbbed.

"Even if you're a hitman," I said through clenched teeth, "you should understand that working for the wrong people can get you targeted. My husband's going to fucking kill you for this."

Blade blinked and looked up at me, almost annoyed by my disturbance of his entertainment. He sighed and straightened. The man towered over me, all dark shadows and furrowed brow.

"Your sister is obsessed with things that don't matter," he said. "If your husband doesn't kill her, then I will eventually."

The admission shocked me. "Wow." I huffed. "You're quite cold for a man who just had his tongue down her throat."

He shrugged. "Just because I have every intention of getting rid of the woman, doesn't mean I can't enjoy what she so easily offers in the meantime."

"Then why bother following her at all?" I snapped, leaning forward as I worked my shoulders against the chair I was strapped to. The tape around my wrists pulled, my flesh smarting at the small rips, but still … I was getting there. Closer and closer to freedom. I couldn't rely on Gaven to save me. If he even knew I was here, there was no telling if he'd make it in time. Plus, there was still my client to consider.

Blade flipped the knife in his grip up into the air and deftly caught it again. Blood stained the flat metal side. My blood. I glared at it, finding the sight more offensive than anything he'd said or done thus far. The second I got the chance, I was going to shove that knife right through his throat.

"Here's one lesson before you die," Blade said, leaning over me as he gripped the back of the chair with his free hand. He turned the knife back to my face and held it inches in front of me. "Consider it a farewell gift."

"Fuck your gift," I sneered, spitting back at him as I struggled against my bindings. The tape was getting looser with each movement. He didn't even appear concerned, the arrogant ass.

"Now, now," he said, using the sharp end of his knife to lift my chin, smearing my own blood on my skin as he did so. "Don't be like that. This is important to me."

I breathed through my nose. My anger gave me strength. It poured through my system, heating me from the inside out. I glared into Blade's face and waited.

"Victory, little girl, goes to those who will do anything to get it."

Well, that, I had to admit, was right. But if he thought he was the victor now, then he was in for a rude awakening. As he pulled his blade from my face and lifted it in the air, I felt one hand break free at my back.

"Now, scream pretty for me, sweetheart," he said. "I want your sister to hear you from all the way across this house."

I stared into his eyes and just before he slammed the sharp point of his blade into my other shoulder, I twisted and dodged. The knife lodged into the wood at the back of the chair and I turned and glared at him.

"You first, *sweetheart*," I said as I curved my now free hand around the hilt of the blade and yanked it out.

He arched a brow as I stood up, pushing him back. Yeah, he still thought he had the upper hand. He was taller. Bigger. Stronger. But I was pissed— and he was definitely underestimating the level of feminine rage contained in my much smaller body.

Anyone could be a killer if you gave them the right incentive, and right now, incentive was all I fucking had.

I took a step towards him and stopped as a loud shattering noise erupted. Glass breaking. Masculine screams echoed through the closed doors. Both Blade and I turned towards it.

Well, I thought, *looks like I was wrong. Gaven really was here.*

28

GAVEN

Jacquelina made a mistake when she booted me from the Price Estate. If she really had been smart, she would've killed me then and there. Instead, she thought herself invincible. She might have been cunning enough to betray her father, cutthroat and heartless enough to frame her sister, but she wouldn't last in this world. I would make sure of it.

In the darkness of the country road, a small light appeared in the darkness, bobbing up and down as the holder grew closer to where Matteo and I were stationed in the woods directly behind the Price Mansion. Matteo disappeared from my side and a familiar voice called out a moment later.

"Fucking hell!" Hadrian sounded irritated. "Call your man off, Belmonte, or I swear to God I'll put a bullet in his brain myself."

"Not before I do," a feminine voice replied.

I whipped around and snarled. "Who the fuck did you bring?" I demanded.

Hadrian grasped the barrel of Matteo's gun as it was aimed at his chest and shoved it to the side before side-stepping him and lifting his free hand to curl two fingers into the darkness. A moment later, a tall, slender, dark-haired woman appeared, holding her own weapon. She had it aimed at Matteo, who blinked back at her, undisturbed.

"Put it down, Scar," Hadrian said as he shut off his flashlight and stowed it in his back pocket. The lack of new light cast the rest of us in shadow once more, with only the moon hanging above us as a means of seeing. Thankfully for me, I'd been in many situations like this one, and my eyes adjusted quickly.

She glared at Matteo but followed the man's command, lowering her weapon before tossing the long rope of braided dark hair over her shoulder. Hadrian sighed and continued forward, moving until he was at my side at the mouth of two large oaks where I'd been sitting for the last hour, watching the estate.

"Scarlett's my wife," Hadrian answered my earlier question, side-eyeing me. I tamped down my surprise. I knew very few men in our positions that ever married—unless they were required to like I had been. Hearing that he was not only married but had brought his wife to such a dangerous mission shocked me. "And," he hedged, "she's your girl's friend."

"Friend?" I repeated the word and turned, looking over the new woman once more with a keener gaze. *So this was the infamous Scarlett Thief.*

"Eyes on the face, fucker," Hadrian snapped, practically snarling at me.

"I'm not interested in your woman," I replied coolly. No, the only woman I wanted was rather slippery. My attention went back to the mansion. The back door opened, and several guards poured out— one limping as he did so. They exchanged places with the men stationed on the back grounds.

"No, I suppose you aren't," Hadrian conceded. "For what it's worth, I'm sorry I wasn't able to stop your wife from being taken. We weren't exactly equipped to handle a large force ourselves."

"But we'll get her back," the woman—Scarlett, he'd called her—said. "I promised her we'd help."

"That was with her client," Hadrian reminded his wife.

"Doesn't matter." Scarlett shook her head. "A couple of years ago, Eve got me out of a pickle— whether it's her client or being kidnapped by her deranged sister, I owe her."

"Eve?" I frowned back at the woman. I hated that damnable alias of hers. "Her name is Angel."

"Right." Scarlett nodded. "Sorry, it's a habit."

I eyed her again, but then my gaze drifted back to the building. She was in there somewhere. Scared? Probably. Reliving her father's death? Most likely.

"So, what's the plan, man?" Hadrian asked.

Just as I parted my lips, a new voice rang out in the darkness. "Take the mansion, obviously."

The cavalry had arrived. Ian, Archer, and Jensen melted out of the woods like they'd always been there. Their bodies were laden with supplies—bags of weapons and ammo. As Jensen approached and tossed one at my feet, it landed with a loud thump. I didn't hesitate to bend down and unzip the contents.

After Matteo and I had lost our main weapons to Jackie, we'd only had our backups in the car to rely on. Having a rifle back in my grip felt like coming home. I checked the boxes of ammo and found that they'd delivered on their promise. Once I'd hung up with Hadrian—and found out that I'd been right in my assumption that Jackie had captured Angel—I'd called them in, and this was what we'd been waiting for.

The bag contained several handguns, a sniper rifle, and enough bullets to take down an army. I glanced up at the men. "Thank you," I said, meaning the words more than I ever had in my forty-one years on this earth.

Ian nodded. "You helped us with Perelli," he said. "No thanks necessary."

Matteo shifted closer to me and I handed him one of the guns from the bag. "How do you want to do this, boss?" he asked as he took the weapon and checked the clip.

"We hit them hard and fast," I said. "We don't

give them room to fight back. They aren't expecting more men." I loaded another gun and stuck it into the back of my pants before casting him a warning glance. "Make sure the guys at the front are ready. I want you to circle around and lead them through."

"You'll go through the back?" he confirmed.

I nodded. "Yeah."

"You're not going alone?" Matteo's meaning wasn't lost on me, especially not when he lifted a brow at the others lingering nearby.

"No, he's not going alone," Ian answered. "We'll be with him."

"They'll watch my back, Matt," I said. "Now go."

He hesitated, but without much of a reason to refuse, he was forced to give me his nod and once he was gone, I threw myself into preparing to take the Price Estate. It'd been a long damn time since I felt my blood pumping like this, and familiar sensations were spiraling through me.

The thrill of the hunt sizzled in my veins. The knowing that blood would soon be coating my hands and that I would hold bodies and lives, once more, in my command made my insides riot with excitement. Perhaps, in another life, I could have been another man—one more deserving of Angel—but this wasn't another life. This was here and now. This was our reality, and I was thankful for it because it meant that all of the darkness I held would now be used to protect what was mine. I only hoped she was still alive when I reached her because if she wasn't … I shuddered to think of what I would do.

As if he could sense my thoughts, Ian moved to my side along with Archer. "She'll be okay," Archer said. "I think your girl's stronger than you think."

"She is," Scarlett piped up.

I nodded and focused on loading another handgun. Maybe they were right. Angel was no longer the innocent eighteen-year-old who had been forced to marry me. She was older, wiser, and far more worldly now. She was intelligent. Creative. Intuitive. Resourceful. She'd escaped me not once, not twice, but three times. That was no easy feat, and yet she'd made it as simple as possible. She'd used my obsession against me, and even if it burned in my gut, I had to admire that too.

"We get in," I started, shoving the second gun into my chest holster before I lifted the rifle and slung it over my shoulder. "We move fast—before they know what hits them." I look to Archer. "You bring your field shit?"

His head lifted and fell. "Yup." He patted the bag he carried. "Got all I need." He turned to Hadrian. "Want to help me fuck up their security?"

Hadrian grinned in response. "I thought you'd never ask."

"Alright," Ian said. "Hadrian and Archer will stay behind, cut their cameras, and take down the fence's defenses so that we can scale without getting our asses fried." He reached into his own bag and pulled out several Bluetooth in-ear devices. He tossed one to each person in the vicinity before putting his own in. "We'll use these to communicate."

"I'm going too," Scarlett said, stepping forward.

Hadrian practically growled. "No, the fuck you're not," he snapped. "You're staying here with Archer and me."

Scarlett whipped around on him. "She's my fucking friend, Hadrian."

"And her husband will take care of her," he replied. "Just like Wolf or I would for you. Stay here."

"But—"

"We'll need someone to guard the hackers," I said, stopping her tirade before it could start.

Hadrian, it seemed, wasn't done yet, either. "You have an obligation to go home to our fucking daughter, Scar," he said.

Scarlett blanched but didn't refute the statement. "I want to help," she said instead.

With a sigh, Hadrian approached her and cupped her face. "You will," he said. "Archer and I need to make sure no one sneaks up on us while we work. You'll guard us and make sure we're safe while we fuck them up from the inside out. Got it?"

A moment passed, and she finally nodded in acquiescence, and not too soon either. I was ready to get a move on. We had wasted enough time as it was. It was time to lead the team into the mansion and get my fucking wife back.

"Alright, now that we've got that decided."

Jensen's voice rang throughout the clearing as he moved towards the opening of the trees. He paused and looked back before lifting a pair of dynamite sticks with a grin. "What do you say we blow both gates open and go get our target?"

29

ANGEL

Explosions rocked the grounds. The sound of them was not at all familiar, but I knew what they were—and they were just what I needed them to be. A distraction. Before he could react, I barreled into Blade and took him to the ground.

The knife in my hand turned and I slammed it into his side, enjoying the satisfying shout of pain that escaped his lips. The doors blew open and several men barged inside as I withdrew the blade and then scrambled away. Holding the knife up, I stared wide-eyed as the ginger from earlier growled and stormed forward.

A sharp pop sounded somewhere from the hallway and he froze for the briefest of moments. His eyes went down, and I followed the trail, spotting a large dark spot forming in the center of his chest. Blood.

Acting on instinct, I dove forward as he collapsed to his knees. My hands went to his side and I ripped the gun strapped there from its holster. Turning, I took aim and pulled the trigger. Once. Twice. A third time. Both men on either side of the ginger went down like piles of bricks before they could even draw their own weapons.

The recognizable sound of my sister's shrieking dragged me forward. I stepped over the bodies and stumbled into the hallway, falling into the wall as my foot slipped. Liquid slid down the front of my aching, burning legs. My earlier stab wound wasn't much better. Who the hell had killed Ginger? I looked down the hall and frowned as a man decked in all black was shooting around the corner. I dimly recognized him as the man from the sex club—Ian.

What the hell is he doing here? I wondered.

I didn't have to wonder for long. He turned and cast a look back and blinked when he spotted me. "Get over here!" he snapped.

He was here with Gaven then, I realized. Hurriedly, I scrambled after him, the sounds of screaming and more gunshots ringing throughout the house and getting louder. The smell of gunpowder permeated the hallway. I closed my eyes and leaned against the wall as I got to the man. My body ached and my head threatened to cave in on itself.

"Are you okay?"

That question had me reopening my eyes as Ian hovered over me, his brow scrunched in concern. I parted my lips to reply, but as I did, he turned away again and pressed something inserted in his ear.

"Hey, this is Marshall. I've got the target with me. She's wounded. She'll need treatment."

"I'm fine," I defended. "I can make it out of here."

He looked back at me and his expression remained concerned and doubtful. He shook his head and then grabbed my good arm, pulling me away from the wall. "Come, we've got to move. This part of the estate is under fire."

That much was for sure. I didn't argue with him as he led me around the corner and down another hallway. It'd been five years since I'd been home, and despite the obvious changes that had been made while I'd been away, I still recognized we were heading for the bottom floor towards the foyer.

I turned my head as we passed other hallways on our way down. I'd heard Jackie scream earlier, but where was she? Was she already dead? For some reason, I didn't like that. No, I didn't want Jackie to die and disappear from my view. I wanted to see it. I wanted to watch the light dim from her eyes the same way she'd watched our father's. She deserved that. To see her own failure.

"Wait!" I shouted as I pulled up short. "My client! There's another man here, his name is Ronald Wiser. We have to get him."

"Don't worry about it," Ian snapped. "One of my men already found him." He frowned back at me. "You should really worry more about yourself." His gaze panned down to my bloody legs.

"I told you I was fine," I reminded him tartly.

His lips twitched, and the frown eased slightly. "God, you remind me of my wife."

I couldn't help but smile at that. "America?" I confirmed.

He nodded and then his grip on my arm turned hard. He yanked me to a stop so fast I swore my arm was about to pop out of my socket. "Fuck!" I cursed and tugged my arm from his grip as I turned to see why he had done it. We were standing at the top of the stairs that led down into the foyer and as I scanned the area, I stopped on the figure standing before the wide open front doors.

In the time since I'd last seen her, Jackie's face had reddened considerably around her nose where I'd broken it. She had a newly patched white strip over it, however, as she stood there, her sheath dress ripped in various places and her heels missing. Her hair was half undone—one side tied to the back of her skull and the other with several strands sticking out wildly. In her hand, she clutched a handgun pointed directly at us.

"You're not getting away this time, Angel!" she shrieked. "I won't fucking have it. You won't take this from me. You've taken everything else that was supposed to be mine!"

The gun in my hand felt both heavy and light as I lifted it. Her eyes widened and then she sneered. "You don't have the fucking guts to shoot me, you fucking cunt."

"You sure about that, Jackie?" I asked plainly.

With a violent scream, her arm jerked back as

her gun discharged with each shot, but her aim was off. She shot up the staircase, bullets pelting the wood as she unloaded. I didn't wait for her to actually hit me. Even as Ian grabbed ahold of me and tried to pull me back—away from the line of fire—I couldn't let this opportunity pass me by. Not again.

I lifted my arm and pointed my own gun and pulled the trigger. The litter of bullets into wood halted immediately, and Jackie's eyes widened before she looked up at me.

"Angel!" Distantly, I heard Gaven's shout and then he was streaking through the foyer.

Jackie blinked up at me, as if she couldn't quite believe it. Ian stopped trying to move me. Gaven's much larger form barreled right into her and I watched in almost slow motion as she went down beneath him.

The gun in her hand went flying, skittering across the hardwood floor as her head bounced once, twice on the floor, and then stopped. "Gaven, don't!" Ian shouted. Gaven's fist was pulled back, his own gun aimed downward, but at Ian's call, he stopped.

All at once, he seemed to realize what I'd done.

Jackie's eyes were open—staring up at the ceiling frame of her childhood home's front doorway. I gently pulled away from Ian and, this time, he released me. I descended the staircase, holding onto the railing as I moved around the bullet holes, not stopping until I reached Gaven and Jackie.

She wheezed as blood trailed up through her

breasts to rest in the hollow of her throat. Gaven looked from her to me and then frowned, confusion filling his expression.

"You … shot her?"

I nodded. "Yeah," I said. I dropped the gun to the floor and leaned down, going to my knees next to them. The open cuts on my thighs screamed in agony, but I ignored them. "You wanted to know the truth, Gaven?" My sister's eyes moved to me and her lips parted, but no words escaped. "She was the one who killed Raffaello Price—Jackie killed our father. Not me. After we were married, I never planned to leave you like that, but I found them, and … she threatened to frame you if I didn't run."

"Angel…"

Jackie coughed and a smattering of blood left her lips, dotting her cheeks and chin. I leaned over her and Gaven backed up. Pressing my hand into the center of her chest, right where I'd shot her, I dug my nails into my sister's body, wanting to see her feel the pain—even if it wasn't the same kind of pain I'd experienced when she'd killed our father and took my life from me.

She bore her teeth at me and wheezed out an agonized breath. "Does it hurt?" I asked her.

"F-fuck you … you b-bitch."

"No, Jackie." I reached for Gaven's gun, feeling like it was only perfect justice. She took from him, too, after all. Five years gone. Five years that I could've been at his side, forming his empire as his Queen. Five years I'd had to run, hoping to protect him from her when I should've done this all along. Five years without my father … all because of her.

Everything that had been taken from me for the last half a decade was because of her. So much could have been different, but worst of all, I knew that if I let her go, if I let her live and I gave into the small piece of me that just wanted to go back in time before everything had blown up in my face, this anxiety I felt would never end. She would always be there. If she lived, even if she was locked away somewhere, I'd always wonder when she'd escape. When she would come for me.

I was tired of that. Exhausted by all of the running and hiding. I wasn't willing to do it anymore. So, this was it. This was the end of her and our relationship. My finger slid over his on the trigger and we lifted the barrel together until it was aimed at her face.

"Fuck you, Jackie." The trigger compressed and the pop of the gun echoed in my head. Her face caved inward, right in the center of her forehead—a circular burn forming right where the bullet entered, and suddenly, the light that had been dying moments before was no more.

Jacquelina Price was no more, and now, I was the last living Price Heir.

"Angel." My hand fell away from Gaven's gun and I gasped for breath.

All at once, the pain in my body slammed into me. From my shoulder to my legs, I felt it. The adrenaline was draining quickly and my vision went blurry. "Shit." Gaven's curse reached my ears a split-second before his strong arms closed around me.

I felt myself being lifted against his broad chest. "I-I'm sorry," I said. "S-so sorry, Gaven. I didn't—"

"Shhhh." Warm lips touched my forehead. "Quiet, Angel. Just let me take care of you now."

"I-I never said it," I told him. "But I think I … I love you."

The body against mine seemed to freeze. "What did you say?"

My eyes closed as the world around me threatened to spiral into darkness. "Love you," I murmured. "It's over now … I won't … I won't leave again. Promise."

The chest against my side expanded with a shuddering breath. Gaven's low voice rumbled against my ear. "No, you won't," he said. "I've got you now, Angel, and you're going nowhere ever again."

I wanted to respond. I really did. But the surge of adrenaline was already gone, fleeing my system like ants from a burning pile. The world was becoming hazier. Sounds fading. The only thing I knew was that the last thing I felt was the heat of my husband's body against my own.

If this is how it ends, I thought to myself before losing consciousness entirely. *Then becoming a killer wasn't so bad.*

30

ANGEL

It had been so long since I slept next to another person. Hell, it wasn't like Gaven and I had done it even once—but somehow, after my wedding night, I'd gotten used to the idea of him near me, especially at night. Sleeping alone for the last five years hadn't made it go away.

So, when I woke sometime later, surrounded by darkness, the naked heat against my back didn't startle me. In fact, as if it was the most natural thing in the world, my body sank back against Gaven's chest. His arm encircled my waist, and he pulled me against him, the crinkle of gauze and padding sounding against silken sheets. I opened my eyes and looked down to see that though my body was devoid of clothes, my wounds had been dressed and wrapped.

Gaven's lips touched my throat, the stubble on the lower half of his face scraping against the sensitive flesh. Instinctively, I lifted my chin, giving him access. My lips parted as he set his teeth to my flesh and bit down. "Ah!" I arched against him but found myself unable to move as his hand slid up from my middle to my chest and he anchored me to him.

"If you weren't wounded, I'd tie you up and spank the absolute shit out of you," he said darkly. The pain of his bite slid through my insides, wetting my pussy and pebbling my nipples.

"If it makes it any better, just know that I'm sorry," I whispered back.

It felt like an eternity passed before he released me and I collapsed onto him and the bed, shuddering as my heart beat an uneven rhythm in my chest. "I had a doctor insert a tracking chip beneath your skin while you were being treated," he said.

Somehow, that didn't bother me. "Okay."

"Okay?" I felt him stiffen against my back.

"Yeah," I said. "It's okay. Track me, Gaven. Claim me. Hell, break my legs if it'll make you feel better. I'm yours, and now that Jackie is gone, I'm done fucking running. I want my life back."

The world turned, and suddenly, I found myself with my spine against the mattress and a massive hunk of angry male flesh hovering above me. "After all the shit you've put me through, you're going to stop fighting me? Just like that?"

"Yeah," I said with a solid nod. "Just like that. I meant it when I said I was done. I'll be whatever you want, Gaven—Master." I reached up and brushed my fingers along his jaw. My shoulder twinged, but not much.

Midnight blue eyes narrowed on my face. "And if I say I want you pregnant and carrying my heir?" he prompted.

I shrugged lightly. "That was always something you wanted," I reminded him. "If it weren't for Jackie, then you would've gotten me pregnant years ago."

"You resisted it before," he said. "You wanted to go to college."

"I think what I really wanted was freedom," I admitted. "I think I've had enough freedom in the last five years to last me a lifetime. Now, I just want you." I inhaled. "Oh, but if you want a baby, you should know that we probably need to bring the doctor back. I wasn't planning on having sex with anyone while I was away from you, but I got an implant a while back."

Gaven's gaze bore into mine. I waited for his reaction, sure he'd be angry, but after several beats, he did nothing but sigh and lower himself against me. Shockingly careful, he spread my legs and settled against my chest, turning his cheek so that his head was right between my breasts.

"I knew about the implant," he said a moment later.

I blinked in confusion. "You did?" Why hadn't he said anything?

"Yes." He nodded against my skin, and I shivered at the feel of his beard growth scraping me. My insides were growing hotter. He had to know what he was doing to my body—even as beat up as it was. "It was removed when I first captured you."

It took a few seconds for his words to fully make sense. "You ... had it removed?" I repeated. A mixture of shock and confusion swarmed me.

He looked up at me. "I told you, love," he said. "When I fuck you, there's nothing between us."

I knew he was telling the truth. He had no reason to lie. Regardless, I reached across to my arm where the implant should have been. I felt around the area and found it empty. *How the fuck hadn't I noticed?* I shook my head. Sneaky fucking man.

Another thought occurred to me. "Oh my God," I pushed him back and felt my stomach. "Was I—"

"No." Gaven sat up and shook his head. "No, the doctor said you're not pregnant. I thought I'd managed to do it back at the club, but it appears not."

Relief flooded me, and I relaxed back into the bed. My arms arched up around him, pulling him back into my embrace as well. "That's okay," I said. "It's fine now. We can practice as much as possible until it happens."

"Oh, we will," Gaven said, his voice darkening. His eyes met mine and I saw the same hunger rising within me reflected in his irises. He gritted his teeth and turned away. "Later," he said, "when you're better."

"No!" Grabbing a hold of his shoulders, I tugged him closer, back down over me. "I don't want to wait," I said. "I want it now. Please … Master. Please fuck me?"

"Angel…" Gaven's voice was tight with barely repressed restraint, "You're hurt."

"I'll heal," I assured him. "And don't act like you don't like seeing me in pain anyway—it turns you on."

One finger trailed down the front of my thigh, where a long patch had been placed over the cut there. "I like seeing you writhe under the pain I give you, Angel," he said. "Seeing my marks on your skin is different from seeing someone else's." His expression turned murderous.

"Did he get away?" I asked.

"I'll find him," was Gaven's response.

I nodded. "I know you will." Another thought occurred. "And Ron? Is he safe?"

Gaven's mouth pulled down. "Your client was placed into a safe house. I'm having my men look after him until he decides his next course of action. He's been taken care of, so you're not to worry about him. You just focus on healing."

My lips twitched. "Yes, Master." I loved the way his body responded to that word. His shoulders tightened. His stomach muscles sucked in, and even if he tried to turn his lower body away, I saw the way his cock thickened and grew erect.

"You don't know what that means, do you?" he asked.

"What? Calling you Master?" I smiled. "I know I want to find out—really find out." I touched his hand and then pulled it up my body over my stomach. "I want you to give me what you need, Gaven. I want to be everything to you. Your wife and your submissive."

"We've been playing at it thus far, Angel," he said. "What we had isn't real BDSM. It's a facade."

"I know." I touched his finger to my lips, parted them, and sucked it inside. His cock twitched. "I want the real thing," I confessed.

"That requires trust," he said.

I nodded, curling my tongue around the digit in my mouth.

"Do you trust me, Angel?" he asked.

I popped his finger from my lips. "More than anyone else in the world, Gaven. No more lies. No more running. I want to be what you need. Your wife. Your Queen. The mother of your children. Please…" I shifted my hips, lifting them. "I need you."

A beat passed. Tense silence cut through the space around us as I waited for his response. Hope bloomed in my chest and then swelled, growing larger and larger until I feared it would burst inside me and send pieces of my body flying around the room.

"Open for me," he commanded. That single order deflated the balloon in my chest and made butterflies take flight.

Gaven turned me onto my side and took the spot

he'd occupied earlier at my back. His hand slid around me and down as my legs parted. His cock, already hard and ready, prodded against my asscheeks before slipping between my thighs and moving for my entrance. "So wet already…" he murmured as his finger flicked at my clit, making me cry out again before he delved further down. "Are you hungry for my cock, Angel? Do you want me to take you?"

I hissed as his fingers touched my opening. "*Yessss…*" I couldn't deny it. It was right there, and I wanted it.

Gaven's low growl of approval rumbled against my spine. *Please*, I begged silently, hoping he would hurry up and slide inside of me. My insides coiled with need. Every awful thing he'd ever said to me— about me—was right. I was a deviant woman, cock-hungry, and such a fucking whore for him. Only him, though.

"Spread your legs," he said. "Hold yourself open for my cock."

I did as he ordered, reaching down and lifting my leg up with one hand under my knee as it bent and he shifted closer to my back. Gaven slid it over his hip gently, careful of my wound. He pulled back and adjusted his cock, pressing the head of his shaft against my pussy, slipping it inside the barest of inches. I whimpered in the back of my throat, needing more.

"Shhhh." He hushed me. "Don't be so impatient, love." But I *was* impatient. I couldn't help it. I arched my ass back against him, trying to take him in further, only to be met with a sharp slap to my cunt with the hand that was still playing between my folds.

I nearly let my leg slip from my grasp as I cried out. "Needy little sluts don't get what they want, Angel," Gaven warned me. "Be good for your Master; good girls get all that they deserve."

As much as it pained me, I knew he was right. If I was a good girl, he'd reward me, and oh, how I wanted that reward. I wanted his cock in my pussy. I wanted his hand wrapped around my throat. So, as hard as it was, I remained still as he slid the barest of inches further into my channel. It was painful to keep myself in place when with one shift, I could have him impaled in my cunt in an instant.

Gaven didn't seem that concerned with my tortured thoughts, though. Even if he could hear their silent pleas, he moved slowly. Damn him, but I knew it was because he was worried about hurting me. I wanted the pain, though. I wanted every sensation he caused, even if it was discomfort.

Easing through his passage until he was balls deep in my cunt and I swore I could see stars dancing behind my eyes as they slid shut. My inner walls tightened, clamping around him, begging him to stay when he withdrew. Thankfully, though, his cock didn't listen because in the next instant, when he thrust back into me, my body was lit on fire.

My nails scratched at the sheets as my fingers pressed harder beneath my knee. It was all too slow. I wanted it hard, rough. I wanted … pain.

My eyes opened with the surprise of my realization. I craved the agony Gaven gave me; I wanted him to hurt me because, with the hurt, I knew pleasure would soon follow.

"You're so tight, love," Gaven groaned against my ear. "Your cunt is clamping down on me, sucking me in. You want my seed, don't you? Are you ready to have my baby?"

A soft gasp escaped me as he drove into me the barest bit harder. "Yes," I moaned. "Please, Master. Please come inside me. Fill me up."

As if my confession spurred him on, soon, each sharp jerking movement of his hips as they slapped into my asscheeks caused fresh sounds to echo up from my throat. After several moments of the onslaught, Gaven shoved my hand and leg down and urged me over onto my front. My chest pressed into the mattress and I turned my cheek against the sheets as I sucked in breath after breath.

His grip tugged my backside upward until I was ass up and face down in the bed as he drove into me, wrecking my insides with his cock. The wet, slick sounds of my pussy, as it ate up his dick, was humiliating as much as it was arousing.

One firm hand left my hip and came down hard across my ass. "More," he growled. "Push back against me, Angel. Show me how much you want me."

It didn't take any more encouragement from him. My forearms were shoved into the mattress a moment later as I arched back against him, shoving my ass against him with each thrust he made. "Master…" I groaned, whimpering as I felt my lower belly heat up. "Master … oh fuck, please."

I didn't even hear the words as they escaped my lips, but Gaven did. Because each word made him pulsate inside of me. His cock swelled inside my pussy. His hands slid across my asscheeks, one side pulling me open as I imagined him staring down at where we met—his cock in my core. The other, though, had a different goal. Fingers prodded at my pussy, stretched as it already was around his shaft. A fresh moan rumbled up my chest as he pressed in alongside his already thick cock.

"What a hungry little hole," he panted above me. "Is my cock not enough for you, Angel?"

I was drooling against the sheets, moaning and delirious with the promise of relief. My insides were a rioting mess as I shoved my pussy back against him. I didn't even care as he inserted another finger, two hooked just inside the rim of my cunt as he powered into me. He pulled, and the sharpest hint of pain hit me, but all it did was make the pleasure that much more intense.

"Master … please, may I come?" I needed it. The release was right there. So close, and yet … I craved his permission.

"All by yourself?" Gaven's low voice was like

ambrosia to my ears. "How selfish … no, you may not."

I whimpered in sorrow. "Please," I begged, hoping if I just gave him something more—my submission—he would cave and give it to me. "Please, Master. I'm so close…" Dangerously close. Sparks were already dancing in front of my eyes. My belly cramped as I tried to hold myself back.

"Don't you fucking dare come before I give you permission," Gaven growled. "If you do, Angel, I promise you'll regret it."

Gripping the sheets, I leveraged up and gasped for relief as I tried to think of something else—anything to keep myself from coming undone around his cock. "I-I…" I couldn't speak, couldn't tell him that I needed him to stop if he wanted me to follow his command. Tears dripped down my cheeks, sliding from my lashes over my face and falling from my chin to hit the sheets below us.

His fingers stretched my hole as he thrust into me sharply and I cried out as pain assaulted me. "Master!" My back bowed. My orgasm faded slightly, just enough for me to catch my breath.

"That's right, love, I'm your Master," Gaven said, his words filled with satisfaction. "Master of your body and your soul."

"Yes…" I mumbled. "Yes. Yes. Yes." I thrust my hips back against him as he continued to fuck me. Whatever he wanted, I would give him. If he wanted a delirious sex slave who would crawl at his feet and suck his cock at all hours, I would do it. I would present myself naked to him in front of whoever he wanted. I wouldn't care who watched as I let him fuck my pussy and drown me in his cum. I was lost to the masterful technique of his cock and fingers as he continued his ministrations.

It was easier this way, to let him have control. My whole body was relaxed—as if it'd given up the fight. I couldn't remember why he had thought to be gentle with me in the first place. The pain of my wounds was nothing compared to the pleasure he was giving me. All I knew was that I'd lose my mind if he didn't allow me to come soon.

As if he sensed that, too, Gaven pulled out of me—both his fingers and his cock—causing me to cry out in hopelessness. *No! I wasn't there yet!*

I felt him get off the bed and a moment later, his hand landed in my hair, gripping tight. More tears continued to leak down my face as he used his hold on my hair to direct me off the bed as well. My knees hit the floor as he stood over me. I tipped my head back, and though I couldn't see myself, I was sure my face was a mess of tears and blotchy skin.

"Open your mouth," he snapped.

My lips parted automatically and with his free hand, Gaven grabbed ahold of the base of his cock and pushed the head into my mouth. I choked, eyes widened as he didn't ease it into me. He thrust over my tongue and past my gag reflex, holding me tight as he shoved his cock down my throat.

Looking up through wet, fused lashes, I watched as his head craned back and he sawed back and forth. His cock forced its way between my lips, filling my mouth with the taste of him and my own juices. It was sharp and tangy. I closed my eyes and relished in it as my pussy dripped between my legs, drenching my thighs.

"You suck me so good, love," Gaven's gruff voice filtered through my head. The praise lit me up from the inside and made my cunt throb. I kept my hands on my thighs as I let him use me. He gripped my hair tight and used his hold to fuck my face just the way he intended. "Good girl ... you're doing so well. What a pretty little whore you make for your husband, Angel."

My eyes opened, and I looked up at him, blinking as I realized he was staring down at me. I could only imagine what I must have looked like with my cheeks hollowed out as he thrust his cock into me. He bared his teeth, the veins in his neck standing out as he groaned. A shudder worked through him and his hips stuttered against my face until he pulled my face sharply into his crotch. Squeezing my eyes shut again as his cock pressed impossibly deep, I swallowed around the hardness in my throat, coughing as he choked me on his shaft.

"No, shit!" his cock disappeared from my lips. He panted, straining above me as he held himself back. His eyes glittered dangerously down at me. "That's not where my cum should go if we want an heir to our empire, is it, sweetheart?"

I whimpered in need.

I wanted to feel it—the pulse of his throbbing

dick as he unloaded himself in my throat. I wanted it so deep that not a single droplet even touched my tongue. He was right, though. That's not where it needed to be. I looked up at him through my lashes and over the hard ridges of his shredded abdomen.

"Beg me," he ordered.

I licked my cracked lips, wincing as the cut I'd forgotten from the slap Jackie had given me reopened. I tasted the tinge of blood, but that didn't lower the heat inside of me.

"Please," I croaked. "Please fuck me, Master. Fuck your wife and fill me with your cum."

A moment later, his arms came around me, hefting me back up. I stumbled slightly, listing to the side, but Gaven didn't let me fall. Instead, he lifted me again and deposited me back onto the bed with my head back and my legs dangling over the side. My hands hit the mattress as I sucked in breath after breath as he rose up and flipped me over onto my knees. Hands reached beneath me. Fingers plucked at my clit—reigniting the fire in my stomach. I cried out and moaned, circling my hips as he tortured me. A harsh slap rained against my ass.

"Good girl," he said, his voice thick with something I had never heard from him before. I wasn't quite sure what it meant, but I did know that it meant something wonderful as he gently urged me over onto my back again.

My cheeks heated as he pressed my legs up against my chest, the plastic crinkling of my bandages the only sound other than our harsh breathing. I didn't care. All I cared about was the fact that he would be inside me soon. His hands pushed me further, slow and sure, practically bending me in half.

"Hold your legs for me, love," he commanded, "and I'll send my filthy little girl to heaven."

He didn't need to ask me twice. My hands latched onto my legs, arms wrapping around them as I felt air wash over my soaked pussy. Hunger and need warred within me.

Gaven's fingers prodded at my opening, smearing the wetness already there around and around before they slid up to my clit. Taking the delicate little bundle of nerves between his thumb and forefinger, I held my breath as the anticipation built. He pinched my clit and I cried out, shuddering as I was sent barreling toward my orgasm from earlier.

"Not yet," he whispered, his fingers easing off of my clit.

I could feel my thighs shaking. I cried, sobbing against my knees as the need became too much. Tears slipped over my temples and down into my hair as his breath hovered over me. Almost … so close.

"You're so pretty down here, baby," I heard Gaven say, the puffs of air from his words sliding across my wet flesh. "So red and swollen from my cock." His fingers speared into my throbbing cunt and my head craned back against the mattress.

"You're torturing me!" I sobbed.

"Yes," he answered. "And you love it, but I suppose enough is enough, isn't it?"

"Please..." I practically begged. "Please, I need it so much."

"What do you need?" Gaven asked as I felt his fingers open me. They pressed along either side of my hole, spreading my lips as I clenched my inner muscles. "Tell me, and perhaps I'll give it to you."

"You ... Master," I said. "I need you."

A beat passed between us. Silence, and then I heard his response. The softness of his voice is as unfamiliar as the hoarse note it carries. "Right answer," he said. A split second later, his lips covered my pussy and his tongue pushed inside.

I cried out as he licked at my hole, driving his tongue into my cunt over and over again as he devoured me. No other man had ever made me feel this way. No other man had ever even come close.

As I held myself open for my Master, I felt myself fade. Gaven ate my pussy like a man starved. He nipped at the bud of my clit with his teeth every once in a while, likely to hear my voice because it was the only time I cried out. I was too over-whelmed, otherwise, by the pleasure of his lips and tongue as he sucked my hole and sent me exactly where he promised—Heaven.

"Come, baby," I heard Gaven groan into my cunt. "Come all over my face like the hungry slut that you are. I want you to soak me in your juices before I give you a baby."

That was all it took. His permission rolled

through me and in the next instant, I felt my orgasm slam into me. My insides collided and cramped with the power of it. Sobs broke free from my throat as I arched my back. Sweat coated my skin, making the soft baby strands at the edges of my face stick to my skin.

It wasn't enough for Gaven, though. As I came, I felt his arm come under me, lifting me against him as he pressed his face between my legs. The scrape of his bearded scruff moved against my inner thighs, heightening the pleasure and pain as—after so long —I was allowed my release.

It was dangerously long, clouding all of my thoughts until I couldn't feel anything but what his mouth was doing to me. Finally, after what felt like an eternity among the clouds, he eased himself away, and I found myself drifting back to reality.

"Not yet, love."

I moaned at Gaven's words as he anchored himself between my legs. As he filled me, sliding into my cunt with sure strokes, I felt my thighs trembling. That same feeling of euphoria rolled through me again.

Tears filled my eyes and dripped down my temples. Reaching up, Gaven's fingers latched onto my nipples. He twisted and tortured the needy little buds. "Soon, your tits are going to be filled," he said. "You'll be even more sensitive than you are now."

His fingers disappeared and a moment later, his mouth landed on them. All the while, his cock still thrust into my insides, spearing through my pussy with sharp, forceful movements. A cramping in my lower belly assaulted me.

I cried out. "Oh, God!"

Gaven lifted his head from my chest and fucked into me again. "My name's not God, Angel," he hissed out. "It's Master. Call for me if you want release. Go on, I want to hear you say it."

"Please!" I screamed. "Oh, Master. Master, please. I'm gonna come!"

Fingers flicked over my clit and just like that, fireworks exploded inside of me yet again. I screamed through my next orgasm and felt Gaven's hips piston against my body, stopping and holding as he bottomed out inside me. The hot wash of his cum filled me up. I shook and trembled and keened as I felt him unload inside of me just like I'd begged him to.

Once it was over, exhaustion clung to my limbs, and Gaven had to be the one to unlock my arms from my legs. I was too delirious to manage it myself. Once he did, I felt his arms slide under me and he lifted and pushed me further into place on the mattress. My eyes closed and after several moments, I felt the sheets being pulled away and tucked around my body as he moved under the covers against my naked skin.

The wetness between my legs now held new meaning. I closed my fingers over my lower stomach beneath my belly button. Soon, there would be new life inside me. A new beginning for both Gaven and me. I closed my eyes and snuggled deeper against him.

"Thank you, Master," I whispered into the darkness.

Gaven's lips touched the back of my head. "You're welcome, *wife*."

And just like that … I knew I was home.

EPILOGUE
GAVEN

7 months later...

I found the man I sought in a little apartment on the Lower East Side. Not a single one of his neighbors even suspected his vocation. No one ever did. I knew better than most that monsters like me looked like everyone else. This man, in particular, lived in a small but expensive two-bedroom unit with added security both at the front and back entrances of the building. His biggest mistake, however, was the living room windows. Wide, tall, overlooking the street.

On one hand, they could have been used as an added escape route—likely his own thoughts—but in this instance, they would be used for his death. It was just too pathetic. Too many killers got complacent in their work. The more they killed and got away with it, the more comfortable they became.

After all, it took a certain amount of ego to take a life and go back to theirs like nothing had happened.

Snow fell across the expanse of the city, ice decorating the overhangs in long strips that would be knocked off come morning. For now, though, it made the world feel as if it were cloaked in a frost spell. My breath fogged in front of my face with each exhale.

Across the street, I huddled down on the balcony of an empty model apartment of a similarly expensive residence such as the one my target was currently enjoying himself. A grin widened my lips. He thought he was safe. It'd been months, after all, since he'd gotten away from nearly taking everything from me. Months since he'd accepted the contract that would ultimately lead to his demise.

I knew the game. It hadn't been personal. It had been just a job.

But not this time, not to me.

Evangeline Price wasn't a job and she was no longer just a tool. She was mine. Everything about her was mine to own, mine to control, and mine to worship. This man had nearly stolen that all from me and the reminder of her fear was burned forever into my head.

It didn't matter to me that, for him, she *had* been just a job. He had nearly stolen something from me and that was an act that I could not forgive. I waited for the man to pass in front of the window of his living room, pressing my foot against the steel bars of the balcony railing as I balanced the rifle on the ledge and aimed it.

It'd been decades since I'd first done this—years since my last contract kill and the only contract I now intended to honor was signed in my own hand and that of my wife's. The final contract a man like me had never expected to have. A marriage contract.

A smile tugged my lips up as the man on the other side of the glass poured himself a glass of alcohol, not knowing it would be his last. Overhead, the moon hung full—a white eye scanning the vast expanse of a city that never slept. Nestled in the comforter of stars, I used the light it gave along with the lights of the rest of the city—the yellow glow from other apartments and headlights down below.

A car honked in the street. The man's shadow moved away from his kitchen and finally towards his living room. I adjusted my rifle and lifted it away from the balcony's edge instead of putting it on the lower stand by my feet. Once it was on its stand, adjusted, and prepped, I got down on my stomach on the cold, hard granite balcony floor.

My stomach was covered in a thick cashmere sweater—one that my sweet Angel had picked for me. No doubt if I dirtied it too much, I'd have to listen to her vent to me about expensive clothes and trying to keep them nice so that they would last. Honestly, I found that even her angry domestic ranting didn't rankle me anymore. It was cute. She was cute. At eighteen, I'd never even considered how nice it would be to not only wear expensive and warm clothes but to have them picked out by someone who actually cared what they did for me. If they tucked me away from the chill in the air or if they fit right.

Angel cared, and that was why I had to do this.

I lined up my shot and sucked in a mouthful of frosty air, letting it burn into my lungs the same way it had decades before on that first night I'd taken a life. The man's head dipped. A button was pressed, and the curtains drew down—shielding him from my view. That wouldn't stop me.

Reaching up, I lowered the goggles I'd pushed onto my head and left there when I'd first gotten here. Flipping down the outer lens and pressing a button on the side, the image of the man's heat signal was outlined in my view. In my pocket, my phone buzzed.

With a silent curse, I retrieved it and looked down at the screen. Through the infrared lens, the phone glowed. I flipped the lens back up and read the latest text.

Angel: *Can you pick up ice cream on your way home?*

I typed back a quick reply before sliding the phone back into my pocket and readjusting my hold on the rifle's handle. Hunger curled deep in my gut as I lined up my shot. Bloodlust. Rage. Pain. Everything my Angel had felt when this man had tried to take her life—take her from me—I knew it well.

Now, he would know nothing more.

I pulled the trigger.

Despite the silencer on the end of the rifle, there was a quick pop next to my ear as the bullet rang out from the barrel. The window cracked—a single fissure running in two directions towards the top and bottom from a singular hole that the bullet made. The man's head jerked in my infrared view, and his body collapsed.

That was it. It was done.

I packed up my gear, sliding my infrared goggles off and stowed them in the nondescript gym bag I'd brought. After I'd taken apart the rifle and slid it inside, I quickly slipped into the empty apartment and changed—swapping my jeans and sweater for a pair of long-running pants and a tightly fitted black t-shirt with a hoodie. Anyone who noticed me as I made my way out of the building would only see what I wanted them to see—a man on his way to the gym.

Several blocks down, I unlocked the SUV I'd driven into the city for this mission, tossed my bag into the trunk, and then left the area. Turning the radio on and leaving it on low volume, I half listened to the two hosts discussing the new miracle formula now making waves in the medical world. The black market of organs and organ transplant lists was about to be rocked with a young scientist's revolutionary growth method for creating organs grown in labs to replace those used in surgeries and transplants.

Halfway home, I remembered Angel's text and swerved into a 24-hour grocery store I'd damn near bypassed. Shit. If I forgot ice cream again, she'd flay me alive.

Who knew pregnant women could be ten times scarier than any mob boss or hitman? Ten minutes later and two large cartons of mint chocolate chip ice cream heavier, I got back on the road. Once I hit the outskirts of the city, I gunned the engine and let the speedometer race upward.

The Price Mansion came into view—new iron gates to replace the ones we'd blown open months before and sprawling grounds set before the golden hue of the illuminated windows. My chest ached as I pressed a series of buttons on the comm unit next to the gate and one of the guards opened the entryway. Rocks flew beneath my wheels as I sped toward the front of the manor.

A new kind of hunger was spreading within me. One that had little to do with bloodlust and more to do with the warm, waiting female body within the walls of my home. Jerking the SUV to a stop, I parked it in front of the double doors of the mansion, shut off the engine, and hopped out— snagging the ice cream as I went.

I didn't make it halfway up the steps before the doors opened and I heard a very gruff Matteo call out. "Please, Ma'am, come back inside. He'll be here soon. It's too cold for you to be out there!"

"I'm pregnant, Matt," my wife replied. "Not an invalid."

Her head was turned as she stormed through the doors, so she hadn't seen me yet. I took the last steps two at a time. As fast and silent as I could so that when she finally turned around, she was faced with nothing save for me.

Angel jumped and crashed into my chest as she came to an abrupt halt. My lips twitched and then spread into a smile as she tilted her face upward. A telltale bump pressed against my groin. Switching one of the bags in my hands to my other hand, I reached out and cupped the back of her head. My fingers slid through the bun she'd tied her longer, dirty blonde hair up into as I settled my mouth firmly on hers.

Without hesitation, her lips parted for me. They opened under my advance, and she even rose onto her toes for more as her tongue tangled with mine. I could have stood there kissing her for hours—days—years. But a blast of cold air whipped past me, reminding me that while I was cloaked in a hoodie and not nearly as affected by the elements, Angel was soft and petite and very fucking pregnant.

Nudging her back inside, I lifted my gaze and noted that Matteo was already shaking his head and disappearing into another room—leaving the two of us alone. I redirected my attention downward.

My thumb touched Angel's wet bottom lip. "What were you doing?" I demanded.

"I was going to wait outside for you," she replied.

My smile dipped. "It's freezing outside," I reminded her before dropping my free hand to her belly. "And you're not allowed outside without me."

"Allowed?" She blinked up at me and scowled. "Don't start that again, Gaven. I thought we talked about this. Just because I let you do whatever the hell you want in the bedroom doesn't mean you can control me outside of it."

"Sexually," I said.

Her lashes lifted and she gaped at me. "What?"

I leaned down so that our faces were barely inches from each other. Her warm breath touched my chin, my throat, and made me want to see her on her back, head over the end of our bed—pussy, tits, and belly on display for me—while I thrust my cock into the back of her throat.

"You let me do whatever the hell I want to you … sexually, sweetheart," I elaborated. "Not just in the bedroom."

She grumbled but didn't deny it. Instead, she conveniently switched topics. "Did you bring my ice cream?" she demanded.

I grinned and held up both bags. "Yes, I did."

She grabbed the bags from me and opened them. A soft moan left her lips and I felt my running pants grow tighter as my gaze flashed to hers. "You got mint chocolate chip," she said. "I fucking love mint chocolate chip."

I shook my head and wrapped one arm around her shoulders, leading her out of the foyer and further into the mansion towards the kitchen. "I know," I said. "And so does Raff."

Angel cast an annoyed glance my way. I was getting used to those, too. "You're so sure it's a boy," she said. "What if it's a girl? Are you gonna call her Rafaella?"

I shrugged. "That sounds good to me."

With a sigh, as soon as we hit the kitchen, she left my embrace to hurry across the tile and unload the ice cream. She filled a bowl for herself and then stowed the remaining containers away. I watched and waited, my shoulder against the doorframe as she bustled around the open area normally filled with employees during the day. I liked it like this—with just her and me. Her face was bright with excitement as she dove into her bowl of ice cream. She moaned again and licked the spoon clean.

Unable to help myself—not with those intensely carnal sounds she kept making—I shoved away from the wall and circled the island to put both hands on the countertop on either side of her. "Are you done with your snack now, love?" I asked, nuzzling the side of her throat.

The quick inhale before she spoke made my insides heat. "Maybe I am, and maybe I want another bowl," she said, her tone strained as she forced casualness that I knew she didn't feel.

No, she didn't feel at all casual right now. I lifted my hands from the countertop and gripped her tits, relishing in the weight of them. They'd gotten heavier in the past few months as she'd gotten rounder and rounder. Her nipples hardened into tight little buds and I pinched them between my thumb and forefinger, gently rolling them back and forth. Another thing I hadn't anticipated was just how attracted I would be to my pregnant wife. Seeing her like this, soft and full with the evidence that I'd marked her—made her mine—made me want to see her like this always.

"Gaven…"

"That's not what you call me when we play, is it, sweetheart?" I prompted her, tightening my hold on her nipples until she cried out and clamped both of her own hands on the ledge of the counter.

"Master!" she gasped out the word. "Master … please…"

"Please, what?" I kissed her throat. "Good girls ask for what they want, Angel."

"I want to come," she pleaded.

"Do you?"

She nodded and tipped her head back to look up at me with glassy eyes. The gaze of a perfect sub—and almost perfectly satisfied.

"How?" I asked. "Do you want to come on my hands?" I moved away from her nipples, stroking down her sides. "Do you want my mouth?" I kissed her throat again, setting my teeth to her flesh and biting down until she undulated against the stool she sat on and let out a keening wail. "Or perhaps you want my cock?"

In a flash, Angel shoved away from the counter and spun to look up at me. She hooked her hands at the back of my neck and went to her toes just as I leaned down and wrapped one arm under her knees and another around her back. As I lifted her against my chest, her lips met mine—harder than before. She kissed me like a woman in need of sustenance.

I began walking—keeping my eyes open as I wove through the doorways and up the stairs toward our bedroom. She didn't stop kissing me, even when I pulled my lips away. Instead, her sharp little teeth bit down on the column of my throat.

I jerked as we stopped in front of our bedroom. "You're going to pay for that, Angel," I warned her.

She licked the spot before gazing up at me with a smile. "You'll make me like it," she replied.

"Oh, will I?"

Angel reached out with a very knowing grin, grasped the knob, and opened the door for me. I strode inside and kicked it shut before letting her lower body go, slipping down the front of my pants so that she could feel my erection straining against the fabric.

"Yes," Angel replied. "Because that's just the type of cruel master that you are."

She was right. I was a cruel master, and she was the most wicked of angels. We were a match made in Hell, and even in death, I doubted we would ever part.

ABOUT LUCY SMOKE

Lucy Smoke, also known as Lucinda Dark for her fantasy works, has a master's degree in English and is a self-proclaimed creative chihuahua. She enjoys feeding her wanderlust, cover addiction, as well as her face, and truly hopes people will stop giving her bath bombs as gifts. Bath's get cold too fast and it's just not as wonderful as the commercials make it out to be when the tub isn't a jacuzzi.

When she's not on a never-ending quest to find the perfect milkshake, she lives and works in the southern United States with her beloved fur-baby, Hiro, and her family and friends.

Want to be kept up to date? Think about joining the author's group or signing up for their newsletter below.

Newsletter

ALSO BY LUCY SMOKE

Contemporary Series:

Gods of Hazelwood: Icarus Duet (completed)

Burn With Me

Fall With Me

Sick Boys Series (completed)

Forbidden Deviant Games (prequel)

Pretty Little Savage

Stone Cold Queen

Natural Born Killers

Wicked Dark Heathens

Bloody Cruel Psycho

Bloody Cruel Monster

Vengeful Rotten Casualties

Iris Boys Series (completed)

Now or Never

Power & Choice

Leap of Faith

Cross my Heart

Forever & Always

Iris Boys Series Boxset

The *Break* Series (completed)

Break Volume 1

Break Volume 2

Break Series Collection

Contemporary Standalones:

Poisoned Paradise

Expressionate

Wildest Dreams

Criminal Underground Series (Shared Universe Standalones)

Sweet Possession

Scarlett Thief

Fantasy Series:

Twisted Fae Series (completed)

Court of Crimson

Court of Frost

Court of Midnight

Twisted Fae: Completed Series Boxset

Barbie: The Vampire Hunter Series (completed)

Rest in Pieces

Dead Girl Walking

ABOUT A.J. MACEY

A.J. Macey has a B.S. in Criminology and Criminal Justice, and coursework in Forensic Science, Behavioral Psychology, and Cybersecurity. Before becoming an author, A.J. worked as a Correctional Officer in a jail and is now married with a daughter and two cats named Thor and Loki.

A.J. has two pen names in the works:

A.J. Macey - romance stories
Aria Rose - epic/high fantasy

Stay Connected

Join the Reader's Group for exclusive content, teasers and sneaks, giveaways, and more:
A.J. Macey's Minions
Join the newsletter for weekly sneaks, sales, and the ongoing NL story:
Sign-Up Here

ALSO BY A.J. MACEY

BEST WISHES SERIES (A.J. MACEY):

Book 1: Smoke and Wishes

Book 2: Smoke and Survival

Book 3: Smoke and Mistletoe

Book 4: Smoke and Betrayal

Book 5: Smoke and Death (coming summer 2021)

FSID AGENTS SERIES (A.J. MACEY):

Book 1: Whisper of Spirits

Book 2: Whisper of Pasts

Book 3: Whisper of Blood (coming summer 2021)

HIGH SCHOOL CLOWNS & COFFEE GROUNDS (A.J. MACEY):

Book 1: Lads & Lattes

Book 2: Misters & Mochas

Book 3: Chaps & Cappuccinos

Book 4: Fellas & Frappés (coming spring 2021)

Post-Series Novella: Getting Lei'd & Iced Lemonade

(coming summer 2021)

THE ACES SERIES (A.J. MACEY):

Book 1: Rival

Book 2: Adversary

Book 3: Enemy

THE CAT'S CREW SERIES (A.J. MACEY):

Book 1: Rumors (coming late 2021)

CUT THROAT LOVE SERIES:

Book 1: Feral Sins (coming late 2021)

VEGA CITY VIGILANTES SERIES (A.J. MACEY):

Book 1: Masked by Vengeance

Book 2: Cloaked in Conspiracy (coming Halloween 2021)

Book 3: Revealed through Redemption (coming Halloween 2021)

NOT YOUR BASIC WITCH CO-WRITE SERIES WITH JARICA JAMES (A.J. MACEY):

Book 1: Witch, Please

Book 2: Resting Witch Face

Book 3: Witches Be Crazy

Epilogue Novella: Born to be Witchy

CRIMINAL UNDERGROUND CO-WRITE BOOK COLLECTION WITH LUCY SMOKE (A.J. MACEY/MACEY ROSE):

Sweet Possession

Scarlett Thief

Sinister Engagement (coming spring 2021)

Sinister Obsession (coming summer 2021)

THE SENTINEL TRIUNE (ARIA ROSE):

Book 1: Heart of Gold (coming 2021)

Printed in the USA
CPSIA information can be obtained
at www.ICGtesting.com
LVHW061314071023
760211LV00001B/78